Ul

∞ ∞ ∞ ∞ ∞

M.K. Eidem

The Imperial Series

Cassandra's Challenge

Victoria's Challenge

Jacinda's Challenge

Stephanie's Challenge

Tornians

Grim

A Grim Holiday

Wray

Oryon

Ynyr

A Grim Pet

Kaliszians

Nikhil

Treyvon

Kiss

Kirall's Kiss

Autumn's Kiss

Foreign Language (Italian)

Grim: Tornians Book 1

Una Grim Vacanza: Tornians Book 2

Wray: Tornians Book 3

Published by Turtle Point Publishing

Cover Design by Judy Bullard

Edited by: azedit@southslope.net

Chapter One

Ull's knuckles whitened when he gripped the edges of the viewport as he stared down at the small blue planet. It had taken him longer to get here than it should have, and it was all the Emperor's fault. Ull should have been sent directly to Earth, but Wray had ordered him to take the Searcher and follow General Rayner, not only to Luda but then on to Pontus before heading here.

They'd wasted nearly a week on Luda, meeting with King Grim and his female, who, as far as Ull was concerned, should never have been included in the discussions. But King Grim, like his brother, Emperor Wray, had become weak since they'd joined with their Earth females. They seemed to have forgotten that *males* were the ones in charge, not the females. That *males* made the decisions, and that *females* were supposed to obey them.

General Rayner was no different, even though Ull had heard he was the strongest, most feared warrior in the Kaliszian Empire. He, too, listened to the female he claimed as his True Mate and even deferred to her at times.

What weak males they all were. Ull knew he would never allow himself to be like that.

When they'd finally left Luda, it took them eight days to reach Pontus, the small planet just on the other side of the Tornian-Kaliszian border. It had once been a beautiful, productive planet full of animal and plant life. It had been able to feed nearly the entire population of the Kaliszian Empire, but that was before the Great Infection had turned it into a barren wasteland.

If he'd had his way, they would have only been on Pontus long enough to collect the Earth males and females the

Kaliszians claimed to have, then taken off again. But General Rayner's female had refused to allow that. She demanded time to 'explain' to them what was happening first. So, two days later, they'd eventually been able to leave on the two-week journey to Earth.

Now they were finally here, and it was time for him to secure females for his brothers-in-arms, proving to all that he indeed was a fit and worthy male. But he wouldn't be doing it the way the Empress and the Queen of Luda demanded. No, they were females, and he was a highly trained warrior, a first male, and would one day be the Lord of Betelgeuse, and a Lord didn't follow instructions given by *females*.

Turning away from the viewport, he looked to Captain Veron, who stood behind the navigation console. While the Emperor had entrusted Ull with this vital mission, he hadn't trusted him with Earth's actual location. No, that the Emperor had given to his most trusted Captain who had met them en route to Pontus.

"Notify the Emperor we have arrived," Ull ordered. They'd set up several transmission relay satellites on their way to Earth. They gave them the ability to send and receive verbal and text messages as far as Luda, but with several hours of delay. The Tornians were building a more advanced series of relay satellites, but it would take some time before it was complete. When it was, the Emperor would be able to communicate directly with Earth the same way he did with the Kaliszian Emperor. "I'm going down to the planet to scout the area."

"We need to determine the date first." Veron pressed several buttons on the console stabilizing their orbit. "Queen Lisa told us when her friend would be at the location."

"When she *thought* she would be there. She couldn't be certain," Ull stated while striding toward the door.

"This wasn't the plan." Veron moved to block Ull's way to the door.

"*I* am in charge of this mission, Captain," Ull growled nearly nose-to-nose with Veron. "Not you. Your only responsibility was to get us here. You've done that. Now stand aside."

Veron hesitated for a moment but knew Ull spoke truth. He was only in charge of getting them to Earth. Wray had given Ull complete control in accomplishing the rest of the mission, so Veron stepped aside.

Watching the younger Warrior pass, Veron hoped the Emperor's trust wasn't misplaced.

∞ ∞ ∞ ∞ ∞

Ull's shuttle silently landed in a secluded area near the location the Queen of Luda had directed them. The shielding of the ship made it undetectable, except for the leaves and loose dirt it blew around. Not that there was anyone there to notice. The Queen had sent him to what she called a cemetery, a place where her people buried their ancestors.

On the flight down, Veron had notified him that he had been able to establish the date, and they were within the time frame the Queen had given them. Now all Ull needed to do was find the location the Queen had mentioned and wait for the female.

∞ ∞ ∞ ∞ ∞

For the second time, from his perch in a tree, Ull watched this planet's sun begin its daily ascent. It was beautiful the way it gradually lightened the sky and chased away the darkness. He couldn't remember the last time he'd watched the start of a new day. Maybe when he was a youngster and his manno would take him on hunting trips. They'd stay up late, and his manno would point out important stars, telling Ull stories of the ancestors. Then he'd rouse him to watch the beginning of a new day.

'It is a chance to begin again,' his father had said during those trips. *'A chance to right the wrongs you made the day before, learning from them.'*

Since then, Ull had always been on the training fields, sparring instead of watching the start of a new day. As the rising sun burned away tentacles of fog that clung to the ground, it felt as if it was doing the same thing to the anger and murkiness that had filled his mind for so long. How long? He wasn't sure, definitely since the Joining Ceremony.

He remembered walking into that Assembly feeling so proud, strong, and self-assured. He'd known who he was, where he belonged, and his place in their society. By the end of that day, he would have a female, assuring the continuation of his bloodline. Then it had all gone wrong.

By the end of that day, he *hadn't* had a female. None of the twelve males presented, including Ull, had been. Also, by the end of the same day, two Houses were decimated, their Lords killed, and a princess was born.

Ull had no problem coming to his Emperor's aid, along with the rest of his House, for what Bertos and Reeve had done, and attempted, was pure evil. He had even agreed with the naming of Callen as the new Lord of Vesta. It was only when his younger brother, Ynyr, was named a Lord that things had begun to get hazy.

He'd been as shocked as the rest of the Assembly, but then he'd felt so much pride. The pride that now everyone knew just how fit and worthy his younger brother was. He and his manno had smiled at each other as tears ran down his mother's face.

But then one of the Earth females had chosen Ynyr as her male. A rage began to build in him, unlike anything he'd ever felt before.

It clouded his judgment.

It had him thinking things he'd never considered before.

It had him saying hurtful things.

It had him doing things he *knew* were unworthy of a future Lord, like what he planned on doing here.

∞ ∞ ∞ ∞ ∞

"Hi, Mamá. Daddy." Trisha sat down on the bench her tío had placed beside their graves. She still found it hard to believe it had been two years since her mamá had died. There were days it seemed like a lifetime ago, and then others when she found herself picking up the phone to talk to her before Trisha remembered she was gone. Her mamá had been Trisha's rock growing up. She'd always been there, supporting her, loving her, telling her by word and example that she could be anything she wanted to be. Do anything she wanted to do.

Patricia Garcia had married the love of her life, Martin Burke, at eighteen. She'd told her daughter the story many times about how she'd rounded a corner and run into an unmovable wall. A pair of muscular arms wrapped around her before Patricia could fall. When her eyes looked up, she realized the wall was actually a broad chest. That broad chest had belonged to Trisha's father, in his uniform, straight out of basic training. That had been it for Patricia, for both of them.

For two years, they'd dated, despite her family's protests. Not only was Martin two years older than Patricia, but he was seriously Caucasian. During that time, the only family member who supported their relationship was Patricia's older brother,

Aaron. Aaron hadn't judged Martin on the color of his skin or his ethnicity, but on who he was and how he treated his little sister.

It had been Aaron who had shown up at the courthouse when she'd married Martin on her eighteenth birthday.

It had been Aaron she had called, asking him to be the godfather of their child, when she'd found out she was pregnant.

And it had been Aaron who stood beside them holding her and her daughter's hand when they lowered Patricia's husband into the ground.

"Tío Aaron would be here if he could, but you know how it is with the Secret Service and reporters. There's rarely a private moment when you're the President of the United States. Heck, he couldn't even visit you in the hospital without it being a major production." She lifted her face to gaze up at the turning leaves. "I miss you, Mamá, so much. But I'm glad you aren't struggling anymore, aren't in any more pain, and I know you're glad to be back with Dad."

She looked at her father's tombstone. He'd been so young when he died. The same age she was now, but he had accomplished so much in that short time.

He'd protected his country, married the love of his life, and had a child. All in just twenty-four years.

"You always kept him alive for me, Mamá. Telling me how much I look like him, even though we both know I look more like you. How he would be so proud of me, but I know it's you he would have been most proud. You're the one who never gave up, who never quit. You put not only me but yourself through law school. Then went on to become a professor, all as a single mamá."

"God, if I could do half the things you did, Mamá, have half the impact... I'd consider it a life well-lived, but I doubt that will ever happen. Not now." Tricia wiped away the tear from her cheek then gave her head a sharp shake. There was no time for that now. "I screwed up, Mamá. I shouldn't have left the girls. Not with Peter. But I didn't know what else to do. I let Carly and Miki watch videos on my phone until it died and forgot the charger. When it got late, and Peter came over, I couldn't call Lisa to verify that she'd sent him. I should have known better, should have known Lisa would never let *that* man watch her babies. But by the time I did, it was too late. Lisa and the girls were gone, and Peter was spouting nonsense about a growling seven-foot giant. I've spent the last four months trying to find them, Mamá. I even asked Tío for help, but it's like they disappeared off the face of the Earth."

The snapping of a twig had her spinning around, but before she could process what she was seeing, her world went black.

∞ ∞ ∞ ∞ ∞

Veron's eyes widened as Ull entered the ship carrying an unconscious female in his arms. They hadn't planned it this way.

"What, in the name of the ancestors, do you think you are doing?!" Veron demanded. "Queen Lisa gave specific orders that this female was to be *approached*, not *taken*!"

"I don't take *orders* from a female," Ull growled back even as he carefully laid the female down on the couch in his quarters. "What the Queen wanted was never going to be possible, especially when it was too 'inconvenient' for her to accompany us."

"Inconvenient?" Veron all but shouted. "She is with *offspring*! There was no way Grim would allow her to travel without him, and *he* couldn't leave Luanda, not when he now has so many females to protect."

"Then she should not have been involved in the discussion," Ull argued back.

"She's the one that had all the information we needed," he reminded Ull. "The one that knew who we needed to contact." He gestured to the female on the couch. "Her."

"And now we have," Ull told him.

"Not in an honorable way." Veron ran a frustrated hand through his hair. "We came here to return those that were taken, not take more."

"We came here to make a treaty with Earth to protect it from the Ganglians and Zaludians. In return, they would give us access to their females," Ull told him the most simplistic aspect of the plan.

"You know Wray wants to do more than that," Veron fired back. "He wants to end the Great Infection. For all species."

"The Great Infection never reached here," Ull spat out, angry with that for some reason. "They aren't going to care about helping us end it. Give me the educator."

"No," Veron told him, gripping the box that contained the device tighter. "The Emperor ordered that she must voluntarily put it on."

Ull opened his mouth to argue that the Emperor wasn't here when a low moan stopped him. They both looked to the couch.

∞ ∞ ∞ ∞ ∞

Trisha lifted a hand to rub the back of her neck and groaned. Why was it throbbing? Had she slept wrong on her pillow again? And from where was that growling sound coming? She didn't have a dog. Opening her eyes, every muscle in her body tensed. A man was standing over her. A huge man who was staring down at her. A man she didn't know. She tried not to panic.

She'd always known this was possible, but never believed it would happen. That she'd be kidnapped because of who her *tío* was. While it wasn't a secret, she also stayed mostly out of the public eye. First, because of her age, then because her mamá had gotten sick. Tío Aaron had tried to make her accept a protective detail, but she'd refused. She wanted to live as normal a life as possible. Now she realized she'd been stupid.

She let her gaze travel over the man's features so she could identify him when she was rescued and found her mind fighting to reconcile what her eyes were seeing.

His features weren't right.

His skin wasn't just white. It had a pearly luminescence and rosy tint to it. His hair was long and pulled back from his face, but a few dark strands had come loose, and they brushed along a nose that was broader and flatter than usual. His cheekbones appeared chiseled from stone while his gray eyes stared down intently.

"Who are you?" she demanded, trying to keep the quiver out of her voice. She wouldn't show how scared she was. "What do you want?"

She thought she was going to be able to keep it together, then his full lips pulled back, revealing teeth longer than any she'd ever seen as he *growled* at her. Screaming, she shot up off the couch, plowed the heel of her palm into his strange face, and ran.

Veron just stood there for a moment, shocked. He couldn't believe this female had not only attacked a male but had injured him if the way Ull was holding his nose was any indication. Veron wouldn't have believed it was possible if he hadn't seen it with his own eyes. He was beginning to find he liked these Earth females, but that didn't mean he was going to let this one get by him. Taking a step to the side, he blocked her path to the door and braced for attack.

Trisha ran for what she hoped was a door only to skid to a halt when another huge *green* man stepped in front of her. Seriously? A little green man? Okay, not so small, more like the Jolly Green Giant, who wasn't so jolly. Crouching down slightly, with her hands away from her body so she could protect herself if she needed to, she slowly began to back away from him.

"You will pay for that!" Ull growled, spinning around to face her. He felt a moment of remorse when he saw her defensive position until he realized it wasn't because of him. It was because of Veron, who was standing there, blocking the door. She found the Captain more menacing than him.

Trisha changed the angle of her retreat when the rose-colored guy turned and growled at her.

"What… what are you?" She stuttered, backing away from both of them until a wall stopped her. Damn it! She knew better than to back herself into a corner.

Veron bumped Ull's arm with something, and when he glanced down, Ull saw it was the tablet containing the memory crystal with the Queen's message. Knowing they would get nowhere until they could communicate with her, Ull powered it up then turned the tablet to face the female, as the Queen's face filled the screen.

"Trisha? Trisha, it's me, Lisa," she said in English.

Ull stopped the recording. The Queen had instructed him to replay this part again and again until Trisha was listening, then to let it run. He replayed it and watched her facial expressions.

She went from being terrified and trying to hide it, to shocked, disbelieving, hopeful, and then suspicious. When she finally looked up from the tablet to him meeting his gaze, he knew it was time to continue the recording.

"Trisha? Trisha, it's me, Lisa." Lisa's image gave her a shaky smile. "God, I wish I was with you right now so I could explain this face-to-face, but as you can see..." The video that had just shown Lisa from the chest up zoomed out, indicating she was obviously pregnant. "Traveling isn't an option for me right now. I know this is a shock. It surprised me too, but never doubt I'm thrilled about this pregnancy." She ran a gentle hand over her distended belly as she continued. "So are the girls. We are all safe and happy. Happier than we've been in a very long time. If we weren't, I'd give you our code word. Girls, say hi to Trisha."

Trisha's breath caught as Miki and Carly's smiling faces came into the screen and the heavy weight she'd been carrying, that her friend and children had been harmed because of her, fell away.

"Hi, Trisha," the girls chorused.

"We miss you," Carly said.

"When are you going to come to Luda and visit us?" Miki demanded. "We miss you."

"That's enough, girls," Lisa smiled down at them. "Now, tell Trisha goodbye. Cook is waiting for you to help him bake cookies."

"Yea! Bye, Trisha," they said together.

There was a pause in the recording, and Trisha watched as Lisa's eyes followed the girls out of the room before turning back to the screen, her eyes turning serious.

"While we are safe and happy, there are those that aren't, and even more that are going to be in danger if you don't help us. I know that statement raises more questions than it answers, so

I'll try to answer them, but first I need to make introductions. If everything went as planned, two males are standing before you. The green one is Captain Veron, and the rosy white one is Warrior Ull. They are both fit and worthy males."

Trisha's eyes went to each male as Lisa described him.

"They are called Tornians, and as I'm sure you've guessed by now, they're aliens." Lisa gave her a small smile. "Yes, there really are aliens. They are the ones that took the girls and me from Earth. Not these two specific ones, but it was the Tornians. The most simplistic version of all this is that the Tornian race is dying out because they have so few females, and as you can see," she gently rubbed her baby bump again, "Earth females are compatible with them. So, when the Tornians found this out, they came to Earth to get some." Lisa shot an angry gaze off-screen. "It's something I don't approve of but haven't been able to put a stop to." Lisa's gaze returned to her. "But you can."

"What? Me? How?" Trisha questioned then remembered she and Lisa weren't actually having a conversation.

"I know you're sitting there asking questions, Trisha, and I'm trying to anticipate them. But in all honesty, that would take days, and there is a faster way. I was knocked out and woke up with something over my eyes. God, I'm glad you don't have to go through any of that. It was terrifying."

Trisha's gaze shot to the one holding the tablet. Ull, Lisa had said his name was Ull.

"The thing over my eyes was called an educator. They developed it, so non-Tornians could quickly learn the Tornian language, culture, history, and laws. I'm asking you to trust me, Trisha. I need you to put on the educator I sent to Earth with Veron. It's perfectly safe. My male, man," Lisa's gaze went to someone Trisha couldn't see, "Grim, personally programmed it. I also had him add how the girls and I got here and what we need from you and why. It's sealed in this box." She reached out and took something that was handed to her by a muscular bronze-colored arm. She showed it to Trisha then tapped the black emblem of some bird on the front. "This is the royal seal of House Luanda. Make sure it's intact when Veron gives it to you. I'm asking, no, I'm begging, Trisha. Let Ull put the educator on you."

Chapter Two

As the recording ended, Trisha looked to the green male Lisa called Veron and saw that he was now holding a closed wooden box with a large black seal on the front, just like Lisa had shown her. Lifting a hand, she rubbed her throbbing temple and tried to take it all in. Could this really be happening? Maybe she was having some strange reaction to the medication her doctor had prescribed. A bizarre reaction. Was this her subconscious trying to absolve her of her guilt for what happened to Lisa and her girls?

There weren't aliens standing in front of her. Were there?

They weren't actually kidnapping women so they could breed with them. Were they?

But the two standing in front of her seemed so real.

Not sure if she wanted him to be real or not, she slowly reached out to touch the one closest to her. Ull.

If he wasn't real, then she could relax and enjoy the fact that he was a prime specimen of a male. After all, he was a great deal taller than her five foot eleven inches, and that was a rare thing for her. Oh, there were guys taller than her, but not by this much. Ull had to be at least six foot six. He was wearing black pants that clung to his thickly muscled legs, with his calves encased in knee-high black boots.

But if he was real. Trisha's eyes widened when she found warmth as she flattened her hand against the massive chest the vest he wore had no chance of covering.

"Oh my God," she whispered. "You're real."

Ull didn't move when she spun away from him. He couldn't. She'd touched him. Voluntarily. Outside of Joining. Why? Why would she do that? It had only been for a moment, but that soft touch had his heart pounding as if he'd just finished an extensive round of sparring. It had affected her, too, if the way her eyes widened was any indication. Was she interested in him? When she turned back to him and reached out, he thought she was going to touch him again. Instead, she slowly ran a finger along the Queen's face still displayed on the tablet he held. He found himself jealous of the emotion he saw on her face for the other female. When she glanced up at him, he watched that soft emotion become determination before she stepped around him and moved toward Veron.

Veron watched the female approach him, unsure of what she was going to do. Lisa had told him what she would be asking of her friend and had made him vow he wouldn't force the educator on her. They needed an alliance with Earth, a friendly one, one that benefited everyone. Based on earned trust and mutual respect, especially as the Tornians had already stolen females that they wouldn't be returning.

He remained utterly still when she reached out and gently traced the raptor on the seal. He wasn't sure if Lisa had explained how to break it.

Trisha was amazed by the detail on the seal. It was a beautiful bird. It was a shame she had to break it. Slipping a nail under the edge of the seal, she braced her thumb in its center and pulled up, breaking it in half. Opening the hinged top, she found the device inside that Lisa called an 'educator.' It was a curved band made from some black material she couldn't identify. Lifting it out, she could see how it would curve around her head. The narrower ends would rest behind her ears while the wider center covered her eyes.

Lisa had said she needed to let Ull put it on her. Lisa was her friend, and Trisha trusted her. Lisa wouldn't ask her to do anything that might harm her. Turning back to Ull, she extended the educator out to him.

Ull couldn't believe the courage of this little female. She didn't know either of them, hadn't even known they existed until a few minutes ago. Yet here she was, willingly handing him the educator. Trusting him, all because another female had asked her. No Tornian female would do such a thing. He was beginning to believe these Earth females indeed were different.

For the first time, he let himself look at her. She was a great deal shorter than him but taller than any other Earth female he had encountered, with the top of her head coming up to his shoulders. Her hair was short, only coming down to just below her jawline. While the length displeased him, the varying shades of brown fascinated him. While she'd been watching the recording, he'd been closely watching her. Her facial expression had relaxed slightly, revealing the fullness of the lips that were now in a thin straight line beneath a tipped-up nose and prominent cheekbones. Her skin was a great deal darker than his, but not nearly as dark as Grim's or Wray's. It made her blue eyes that much more startling.

Slowly, so not to frighten her, Ull reached out and took the educator from her then gestured to the couch, and realized this female wasn't only brave, but she was smart. She understood what he wanted without understanding his language. By the time he handed the tablet to Veron and turned back to her, she was lying on her back.

Moving to the couch, he sat down near her waist, then reaching out, let the tips of his fingers rest along her eyebrows before he brushed them down along her nose, closing her eyes. Once they were closed, he carefully slipped the educator over her eyes, then activated it and forced himself to rise and step away.

∞ ∞ ∞ ∞ ∞

"I can't believe she allowed you to do that," Veron said quietly as Ull stepped to his side.

"She's a truly courageous female," Ull couldn't help but admit.

Veron's eyebrows shot up in surprise. It was an unusual thing for a Tornian male to express, especially Ull, who had yet to accept the changes that were happening within their Empire. Changes that allowed a female to choose *any* male she wanted, regardless of whether he had accumulated the credits necessary to provide for her or not, as previously demanded. That decree by the Emperor had rocked the Empire and completely changed the landscape of Tornian society.

"I have yet to encounter an Earth female that wasn't," Veron finally replied. "They all seem to have the capacity to care about more than just themselves and are willing to reach out and help others, even if it puts them at risk. I know of no females, from any species, that do that."

"It's a miracle their species has survived," Ull said gruffly.

"But they have," Veron reminded him quietly. "Even flourished, if truth be told."

Sometime later, movement from the couch had Veron glancing at it, but Ull was already there. He carefully sat down, and after checking the educator, he found it had nearly completed the program. Ull couldn't explain the eagerness that filled him waiting for it to finish. *He* wanted to be able to talk to Trisha and to be able to understand what she was saying. *He* wanted to explain to her what was happening. Not Grim's female.

He heard the low beep that indicated the educator had shut down. Reaching out, he carefully removed the device, then set it aside and waited. This educator had contained a great deal more information than a normal one, so it was natural for it to take her longer to wake. Still, as the minutes passed, he began to feel the slightest hint of anxiety. Had something gone wrong? Had she been harmed? None of the other Earth females had experienced any problems using the educator. Not even the ones the Kaliszians had discovered.

Ull was about to call the Healer when her eyelashes began to flutter, and her startling blue eyes stared directly up into his. They seemed cloudy and unfocused at first, then they cleared and sharpened.

"Do you know my name?" he asked her quietly.

"Of course, Lisa told me. It's Ull," she immediately responded as if it were obvious.

He just waited and saw her eyes widen when she realized she hadn't responded in English.

"How," she paused, then shook her head slightly as if to get everything back where it belonged. "Okay, so the educator worked."

"So it would seem," Veron said, moving to the side of the couch, picking up the educator and returning it to its box.

"And you are Veron, Emperor Wray Vasteri's Captain and trusted friend."

"Yes," he acknowledged, and when she moved to sit up, both males stepped back.

Trisha swung her legs over the edge of the couch, resting her elbows on her knees as she rubbed her temples.

"Are you alright?" Ull couldn't stop himself from asking. He'd never been concerned about a female's condition before. He'd never had reason to be. If a female felt the need, she contacted a Healer. It was something Tornian females regularly did. If the Healer found a severe problem, *he* then contacted the female's male. But with Trisha, he found he needed to know from her.

"I'm fine," she said as she continued to try and rub away the faint headache she felt starting. "Just trying to process all the new information rattling around in my head."

"Rattling around?" Ull's concern deepened.

She smiled slightly then looked to where both of them stood. "It's just slang. It just means I need a minute." And she did. There had been so much in that educator, more than language, more than history. Lisa had included the basics of what was currently happening along with the complexity of it.

One. A species called Ganglians, whose large hairy size resembled the legendary Big Foot, were coming to Earth and kidnapping women, correction females, and either raping them or selling them as sex slaves.

Two. A species called Zaludians, who were a smaller scavenger species, were coming to Earth and stealing food to sell to the Kaliszians.

Three. A species called the Kaliszians, who resembled humans except they were a great deal taller, had hair only down the middle of their heads, and their eyes glowed. They were slowly starving to death because they could no longer produce the food necessary to feed their people.

Four. A species called Tornians, who also resembled humans, except that their skin tones were more metal- and jewel-toned. They were also slowly dying, but for them, it was because they were producing fewer and fewer females.

And *that* was the basics.

The complicated part was that entirely by accident, the Tornians had discovered they were compatible with human females when they'd saved one from the Ganglians. Because of this, the Tornians had sought out Earth, then done as the

Ganglians had and kidnapped some. One being Lisa along with her daughters.

The Kaliszians also learned that they were compatible with human females when they discovered Mac and Jen on one of their planets. They later found more humans on Ganglian ships. The Kaliszians didn't need the males or the females, but as they hadn't known Earth's location, they couldn't return them. Only when they discovered a ship full of food from Earth did they reach out to the Tornians for Earth's location.

Both species hoped to gain something by contacting Earth. Kaliszians wanted food. Tornians wanted access to females. In return, they were both offering to protect Earth from the Ganglians and Zaludians.

God, what a cluster fuck! Why had Lisa thought *she* could help with this? Sure, she had a master's degree in Law, but it was international, not interplanetary. Yes, her tío was the President of the United States, but that didn't mean Trisha could get them in to see him. Hell, there were days when even *she* couldn't get in to see him. And that didn't even cover the fact that the Tornians *weren't* going to be returning the females they'd kidnapped.

Oh yeah, that was going to go over really well.

"You guys couldn't have fucked this up more if you'd tried, could you?" she muttered, pushing herself up to her feet.

"What do you mean?" Veron asked.

"You kidnap women. Force them to Join with one of you. Then come to Earth and expect us to let you have more?" She gave them both a disbelieving look. "Seriously? Are you out of your mind? You'll be lucky if you don't get lynched."

"They are being taken whether you like it or not," Ull growled, "By the Ganglians. We chose only unprotected females that carried no male's scent."

"Right. Like that's going to win you any points," Trisha snapped back. "People are going to be pissed. The only ones that have a chance of coming out of this clean are the Kalisziansbecause they are returning all the people they've found."

"Not *all* of them are returning," Ull reminded her, and that dark anger began to grow again at the thought she could believe the Kaliszians were more honorable, more worthy than the Tornians.

"Yes, the two that wished to stay behind with their True Mates. Lisa included that in the educator," she told Ull at his disbelieving look. "But that was *their* choice. A choice you aren't giving the women *you* kidnapped."

"Our males need them," Veron said quietly, and while he knew this was still truth, he no longer supported it as strongly as he had when they'd first taken the females. Grim had been right. They hadn't been given a choice and gone willingly. "One has already willingly chosen a male and is extremely happy. She is already with offspring."

"Lucky her," Trisha muttered.

"I believe Lady Abby does consider herself lucky. As does Lord Ynyr," Veron told her.

She saw the look that crossed Ull's face at Veron's last comment. "What? You don't believe Abby is happy?"

"It is not for me to say," Ull growled.

"Ull! That is unworthy of you. You must let it go. He is your brother."

Trisha's eyes went from one male to the other. "Okay, what am I missing here? Is Abby *not* happy?" Both males just continued to glare at each other until she demanded. "Ull?"

At her demand, Ull finally looked down at her. "Lady Abby is happy with Lord Ynyr."

He didn't sound happy about that to her, and she didn't understand why. "He's your brother?"

"Yes."

She waited, and when he didn't say more, she asked, "What's wrong with him?"

"Nothing!" Ull immediately denied and felt the rage that always filled him when he thought of Ynyr and Abby's Joining start to fade away. To maintain it, he would have to tell Trisha an untruth, and for some reason, he couldn't do that. It was because of that he realized just how unworthy his dark thoughts about his brother were. He'd never understood where those thoughts came from. He'd always been incredibly proud of his brother, and all Ynyr had accomplished.

"Ynyr is a fit and worthy male. Perhaps the best I have ever known. It is why the Emperor chose him to be a Lord. It is why Abby chose him to Join with and not me. They are extremely happy together, and Veron is correct." Ull looked to the other male. "She is happy and has conceived their first offspring. Which is another reason that we need Earth's assistance."

Trisha was shocked at the sudden change in Ull's attitude. He'd gone from pissed off and non-supportive to praising and fully supporting the couple. All with the same intensity. Was he bipolar? Or was something else going on? Wait, what had he said about Abby?

"Wait. Abby was going to Join with *you* then changed her mind?"

"No," Ull told her gruffly. "Although it was a possibility had the original Joining Ceremony gone as planned."

"You were one of the Warriors on the floor," she whispered, not knowing why that upset her so. Lisa had included everything that had happened during that Assembly, but she hadn't named the warriors.

"Yes," Ull told her shortly.

"So, it's not that he has *Abby,* and you don't. It's that he has a *female* and you don't. You're jealous."

Ull opened his mouth then snapped it shut again, not wanting to speak an untruth. He hadn't considered it could be that before. After all, he was first male of a Lord. Was he that petty, that selfish, so like one of their females? Goddess, he prayed not.

Seeing he wasn't going to answer her, Trisha turned her attention to Veron. "I want to meet the abductees."

∞ ∞ ∞ ∞ ∞

After meeting the abductees, Trisha realized she'd heard about both groups. The most recent was the incident at a lodge deep in the Alaskan wilderness. It had made international news. A group of high-level executives from a global petroleum company had been on a team-building retreat when it had happened. All the women, including those from the lodge staff, had gone missing. Several men died, and rumors had run rampant. They ran the spectrum from a pack of bears attacking, to environmental terrorists, and even to aliens.

The consensus leaned toward environmental terrorists who wanted to publicize their cause and ransom the women to fund it. Except no group had come forward, and no ransom ever demanded. The women had just disappeared.

Now Trisha knew that what had been considered the off-the-wall theories were the right ones. The lodge had been attacked by aliens, the Ganglians. That had been nearly three months ago, and while not harmed, the women were traumatized and scared.

The same couldn't be said for the second group. This group contained only men who, though recovered, had a horrific tale to tell. Kidnapped while out in the woods playing weekend warrior, they'd been enslaved, beaten, and starved. One of them had died, and the two women who decided to remain with the Kaliszians were part of their group.

Her mouth had dropped open when she realized this was the group that had gone missing over eighteen months ago. The National Guard had been called out to help search for the group and found nothing but one cell phone. It was believed, in the end, that they had all gone into one of the caves riddling the area and hadn't been able to find their way out.

Well, they had been in a cave. It was just on an alien planet.

Both groups were grateful to the Kaliszians for rescuing them and couldn't say enough good things about them. She'd also met the Kaliszian representative, Minister Jakob Ruskin, who had been watching over them. He seemed to be an older man, but she wasn't sure how to judge the age of an alien and didn't seem that different than a Tornian to her. Except he only had hair down the center of his head, braided with beads, and his eyes glowed. He seemed knowledgeable, and the men vouched for him, saying Minister Ruskin was in charge of the planet they stayed on and treated them well.

They had very little to say about the Tornians, or just weren't comfortable saying it in front of Ull and Veron. She didn't miss the way their eyes would look to them then away. They would only say they had been treated well on the trip from Pontus to Earth, but none of them had met a Tornian before the Tornians had arrived on Pontus to take them to Earth.

Both groups wanted to know how much longer it would be before being reunited with their families. *She* was the one that would be making that happen, or so they were told.

Thank you very much, Lisa. Now she just needed to figure out how to do it.

Chapter Three

"Trisha?" The deep voice echoed throughout the house.

"In the kitchen," Trisha called back, trying to keep the nerves out of her voice. This man helped raise her, was her tío. He had always loved and supported her and would forgive her for the deception she used to get him here.

She'd called a family meeting. It was something her mamá had started, and it meant there was no excuse. Everyone had to be there, President or not. They hadn't been called often, only for significant events, like…

When her mamá had gotten tenure.

When Trisha had gotten early acceptance into Yale.

And when her tío had decided to run for President.

Those were happy times, but a family meeting was also called when her mamá found out she had cancer, ovarian and uterine. Patricia Garcia-Burke had faced it the way she'd faced all the hardships life had thrown at her. With grace, strength, and being more concerned about how it would affect her loved ones than herself.

She'd called the last family meeting to tell them she had decided to end her treatments. She'd completed all the treatments her doctor had recommended. It was during those treatments that Trisha had met Lisa and her girls. When the cancer had returned, Patricia agreed to be part of an experimental drug program. She'd had no expectations of being cured but hoped whatever discovered in the trial, would one day help someone else. Those treatments had been brutal, and by the time it was over, her mamá weighed less than one hundred pounds. That was when she called the meeting announcing she wanted to enjoy whatever time she had left at home with her family.

It had been a heartbreaking yet beautiful time, those last few weeks with her mamá. They'd talked when her mamá had the strength, and Trisha learned things she'd never known. About her mamá, her father, and herself. It had made Trisha realize just how precious life and your loved ones were.

"What's wrong?" Aaron Garcia demanded as he strode into the room, finding his niece already sitting at the table.

Trisha let her gaze travel over her tío. She'd always thought he was the most handsome man she'd ever met. His tawny skin tone, expressive brown eyes, and brilliant white smile always put everyone at ease. He was slow to anger even in the most stressful of situations, and he patiently listened to all sides, then weighed his options to find the best solution. But when he did get angry, you'd better duck and cover. He was passionate about what he believed in and loyal to his core. It's what made him a good President and an even better man. Everything she wanted in a man she.

So why did she find herself comparing him to the ill-tempered Ull?

"Trisha?" The concern in her tío's voice pulled her attention back to him.

"Sorry," she told him, "just lost in thought."

"What's wrong?" he asked. "Are you hurt? Ill?"

Guilt ate at her. She'd refused to say what was going on over the phone, knowing he wouldn't believe what she was telling him, unless he saw Ull for himself. Still, she was a terrible liar.

"No, this isn't about me, but there are some people that need your help."

"Trishy," Aaron ran a shaky hand through his hair. He'd been terrified on the way over. Terrified, she was going to tell him she was sick. That she was dying as his sister had. He wasn't sure he could go through that again, to helplessly watch another woman he loved suffer and not be able to do a damn thing about it. He was the god damn President of the United States, and what good did it do him if he couldn't help those he loved?

"I'm sorry, I didn't mean to worry you like that. But I needed to talk to you face-to-face and outside of the White House. This was the only way I could think of to get you alone and not be disturbed."

Aaron knew she was right because he'd left specific instructions that they weren't to be interrupted unless the country was under attack.

"Okay," he said, sitting down. Reaching over, he gripped Trisha's hand, silently giving her his support. "So, what did you need to talk to me about?"

"Lisa and her girls."

"Trishy…" He knew how much the disappearance of her friend and children bothered her, and how she blamed herself. Peter Miller was a deranged man, and there was no telling what could have happened to his niece if she had stayed in that house. "It wasn't your fault. You've done everything you could to try and find them."

"And I have," she quietly told him.

"Have what?" he asked, leaning forward to catch her words.

"Found them." Her gaze remained steady as she held his.

"What?!" He didn't try to hide his shock.

"Lisa contacted me." Trisha gave him a shaky smile. "She and the girls are safe and happy."

"She did? When? Where is she?" He couldn't believe it. When the family had first gone missing, he'd used every resource at his disposal to try and find them and had come up with nothing.

"That's what I needed to talk to you about in person and alone. You see…" she trailed off, knowing this was going to sound crazy.

"Trisha Joy!" His fist slammed down on the table. "Tell me what the hell is going on!"

Before she could answer, the door leading to the garage burst open, and Ull stormed into the kitchen, his sword drawn.

"No!" Trisha jumped to her feet, putting herself between Ull and her tío, who had risen as she faced Ull. "Ull, stop!"

"He was threatening you," Ull growled.

"No, he wasn't," she denied. "He was just being… adamant about knowing why I wanted him here." Looking over her shoulder, she saw her tío's eyes had gone wide, and his mouth was hanging open. "Now, put that sword away before you hurt someone."

Ull lowered his sword, but he didn't sheath it. Knowing that was the best she was going to get for the moment, she spun around to face her tío, placing her hands on his chest.

"Tío Aaron," she began.

"Who the hell is that, and what did he do to you?" he asked, looking at her in dismay.

"Do to me?" She wondered what he was talking about then realized she was speaking Tornian. Taking a deep breath, she consciously made herself speak English. "Can you understand me now?"

Her tío gave her a jerky nod.

"I'm sorry. I didn't mean for you to find out this way." She turned to give Ull an exasperated look. "This is Ull, and he was supposed to wait until I told him to come in, but he thought you were going to hurt me." She switched back to Tornian. "My tío would never hurt me."

"What are you saying?" Aaron demanded. "Speaking?"

"I told him you would never hurt me, and I'm speaking Tornian," she said, looking back to her tío. "It's Ull's native language. He can't yet speak or understand Earth's languages."

"Earth languages?" Aaron questioned.

She took a deep breath. "Ull isn't from Earth, Tío. He's from a planet called Tornian."

"A *planet* called *Tornian,*" Aaron stressed the two words.

"Yes. I know it's hard to believe, but Ull's an alien," she decided just to put it all out there. "He's come to Earth because his people need our help, and we need theirs."

∞ ∞ ∞ ∞ ∞

Trisha watched as her tío carefully set the tablet back down on the table they were all sitting around. She'd replayed the recording Lisa had sent her and was now waiting for his reaction.

"You actually put that thing on?" His voice was gravelly with concern as his eyes locked onto hers.

"Yes," she told him quietly.

"Why in the name of God would you do that?!" he demanded.

"Because Lisa asked me to," she told him. "She's my friend, and she needed my help. How could I refuse after what I did?"

"Trisha..."

"I know what you're going to say, and maybe it was foolish of me, but I know Lisa better than you do. She helped me so much when Mamá was sick, even though she was struggling too with Mark. I know she would never have reached out to me this way, never would have asked me to do this, if it wasn't incredibly important. And, Tío Aaron, it is."

“It didn’t harm you?” Aaron asked quietly, his eyes searching hers, trying to see for himself that this was still his niece.

"No." Reaching out, she squeezed his hand. "It felt a little strange, but it didn't hurt, and I feel fine."

“A doctor still needs to check you out to make sure.”

"If that's what it takes to reassure you, then I will." Although she knew she'd put it off for as long as she could. "But none of the others experienced any side effects, so I'm sure I won't either."

“Others?" He frowned at her. "What others?”

Trisha leaned back in her chair, running a frustrated hand through her hair. This was taking way too long. She loved her tío. Loved that he was cautious and caring, that he always made sure he had all the information before making a decision. But right now, it was irritating.

"There were others taken besides Lisa and her girls, Tío. Not by the Tornians, but by a species called Ganglians." She looked to Ull, who had been surprisingly silent while she and her tío conversed. "You brought the educator?" she asked in Tornian.

Instead of answering, he reached into his vest and pulled out the box with its broken seal and handed it to her.

Taking it, she turned back to her tío. "I need you to trust me, Tío Aaron. There is so much you need to know and understand, and if you let Ull put this on you, you will. You'll be able to communicate with him. Ull's the one the Tornians sent to negotiate with Earth."

"You trust him?" Aaron asked, eyeing the rose-colored male suspiciously.

Trisha let her gaze travel over Ull as she carefully chose her next words.

"I don't really know him," she began, "And don't agree with some of the things he's said and done in the short time I have. But he's the one the Tornian Emperor sent, and Lisa stressed that they are an honorable species. And we could trust them."

"What did he do to you?" Aaron demanded.

"Let's just say Ull is used to being in charge and having his orders followed without question." She gave her tío a teasing smile. "We both know how good I am at doing that."

Aaron started to chuckle. He knew his niece, and if there was one thing she didn't tolerate, it was arrogant men who thought they ruled the world just because they *were* men. "I'm sure you explained it to him."

"Most definitely, which is why the two of you need to communicate directly, and you can't do that unless you use the educator."

"Why can't it be programmed, so *he* understands English?" Aaron asked.

"I'm sure it can be, but first someone who *knows* English has to understand Tornian technology so it can be uploaded properly. Right now, there isn't anyone like that. So, until there is, we have to learn *their* language."

Aaron stood running his hands roughly over his face as he thought about what she was asking of him. If he'd been just her tío, he would have done this, trusting her without hesitation. He wasn't; he was the President of the United States of America. His life wasn't his own, and his decisions affected millions of people.

"I know what you're thinking, Tío Aaron, and if you're not willing to take this risk, they can approach someone else. They just won't be as considerate as they have been with us. There's too much at stake for everyone."

"What are you saying?" he demanded. "What will they do?"

"Honestly?" She gave him a concerned look.

"Always," he said.

"I think they'll kidnap another world leader, force the educator on them, then go from there. Sometimes it's easier to beg for forgiveness than it is to ask for permission. You've said that on more than one occasion, and it seems to be a universal thing."

"Shit, if they take the wrong one..." he began to pace, a sure sign he was agitated.

"One that doesn't have the world's best interests at heart..." she continued for him. "Only their own..."

"It could be disastrous," he finished.

"Which is why Lisa thought of you," she told him quietly, rising to stand in front of him, halting his pacing and putting a hand over his heart. "You are the most honorable man I know, Tío. You truly want to help people, not because it benefits you but because you care what happens to them. This is going to affect and change the entire world. If not done in the right way..."

"It will destroy it." He knew Trisha was right. When this news got out, their world would be changed forever. He could either be a part of making sure it was changed for the better or sit back and hope for the best. He had never been very good at the latter. "I need to contact my detail and let them know I'm going to be here longer than planned."

∞ ∞ ∞ ∞ ∞

Even as a young child, Aaron Garcia had always known he was meant to be more than just the first-born son of Juan and Marie Garcia. More than just the older brother to his six younger siblings. He'd worked hard, studied harder, and made sure he stayed out of trouble to set a good example for his younger brothers and sisters. He'd also always looked up to and respected his parents. He'd seen how they'd struggled and the sacrifices they'd made so their children could have a better life than they had.

They'd raised him to believe that a person should be judged by their actions and deeds, not by where they came from or the color of their skin. That's why he was shocked when they forbid his baby sister from dating a man who clearly loved and cared for her. All because of the color of his skin.

As the oldest, Aaron had taken it upon himself not only to meet but investigate the man that his baby sister claimed to love. And while Martin Burke had grown up rough, he had no criminal record and was doing everything he could to better himself. He also put Patricia first, stressing to Aaron how he expected her to finish high school and go on to college. All Martin was asking was to be a part of that. He'd even gone as far as swearing to Aaron that he wouldn't have sex with her until they were married.

Aaron had scoffed at that. After all, he'd once been an eighteen years old boy, and he knew how quickly things could get out of control. But Martin had kept that promise, much to Patricia's annoyance. It was why they had married the day she turned eighteen because *Patricia* was the one done waiting. His baby sister was unstoppable when she went after what she wanted. Especially when she was in the right. That was why he'd stood up for them at their ceremony even though no one else in the family had shown up. He knew how badly that had hurt Patricia, but she didn't let it stop her. Martin had also kept his other promise and made sure Patricia had gone to college.

She'd graduated early, even though she'd given birth to Trisha during that time. She'd just completed her first year of law school when Martin died. That would have destroyed most people but not his sister. While devastated, she'd taken no time off from school, stating Martin wouldn't have wanted her to. He could still remember how strong she'd been standing there at Martin's grave holding the flag presented to her in one hand and her two-year-old daughter's in the other, all while tears streamed down her face. That was the day he saw what real strength and courage were. It wasn't the one that was the biggest or most powerful, but the one who got back up after getting knocked down who had the most strength and courage. That person tried to make the world a better place, not just for the ones they loved but for everyone.

Now, thanks to the educator, Aaron realized the '*everyone*' his sister had fought so hard for included more than just the people of Earth. God, she would have loved to have been a part of this. To have helped make a difference for billions upon billions of beings, not across the world, but the universe.

Lying down on the couch, he gave his niece a small smile, then looked to the alien called Ull, and nodded.

∞ ∞ ∞ ∞ ∞

Ull let his gaze travel over the smaller male that lay on the couch as he removed the educator from its box. The male's dusky skin tone was darker than Trisha's, and his eyes were brown, not the striking blue of Trisha's, but still, there was no doubt they were related. It was there in their distinctive features, in the way they spoke to each other, and in the way they interacted. The love and respect they had for each other were palpable, just as it was between Ull and his manno. Or as it had been before the Joining Ceremony. Now Ull wasn't sure how his manno felt about him, and he had no one to blame but himself. He wasn't sure why it was easier to see that now. Was it because he was so far away from home and everything he knew? Or was it the female standing silently beside him?

Movement on the couch had his attention returning to the task at hand.

Chapter Four

Trisha stood beside the couch, anxiously chewing on her thumbnail as she watched the educator run on her tío. Was she doing the right thing? What if it harmed him? He was the only family she had left. She didn't count her abuelo or abuela, who were both still alive, as were her many other tías, tíos, and primos because she had rarely seen them. There were still too many hard feelings on both sides. Oh, they'd attended her mamá's funeral, but Trisha knew it was only because of Tío Aaron. It would have looked bad in the press for them not to attend, and appearances were everything to them. They took too much pride in their son being the first Hispanic President of the United States to let anyone know how they'd disowned their daughter because of who she loved. Not when Tío Aaron had run on a platform that everyone deserved equal treatment, no matter their skin tone.

Now she was putting him at risk.

She was just about to demand Ull take the educator off when it beeped and shut down. As soon as Ull removed it, she was sitting beside her tío, holding his hand.

Ull was surprised how much that bothered him, Trisha's holding another male's hand, even if he was related to her. He also hadn't liked how worried she'd been when the educator had been on the other male. Females were supposed to be cared for and protected, so they never worried about anything.

"Tío?" she asked quietly, squeezing his hand as his eyes started to flutter.

"It will take a few minutes," Ull told her, finding himself moving closer in the hope it would comfort her.

"Did it take me this long to wake up?" she asked, looking up to Ull.

"Yes. King Grim's female had him include a great deal of information."

"You mean Lisa," she corrected.

"What?" he asked, frowning at her.

"Her name is Lisa," she reminded him. "Why do you demean her that way?"

"How am I doing that?" Ull asked his confusion easily seen.

"By calling her King Grim's female, as if she were one of his possessions instead of a living breathing person."

"She is both."

"You're saying she's his possession?" Trisha demanded.

"No. I'm saying she is female, and as you say, a living breathing person." Ull didn't understand why she was pushing this.

"But you look down on her." Trisha wasn't going to let this go.

"I don't," he denied. "She holds an important place in our society, but shouldn't be interfering. Warriors should be handling it."

"Oh really," Trisha felt her ire begin to grow.

"Now you've gone and done it," Aaron murmured in Tornian as he opened his eyes. "Nothing gets my Trisha fired up more than blatant male chauvinism. You'd better dial it back if you expect her to help you."

"Tío Aaron," Trisha immediately forgot about Ull, but not what he'd said, as she turned her attention back to her tío. "Are you alright?"

Aaron sat up, swung his feet to the floor, and with his elbows resting on his knees, rubbed his temples just as Trisha had done. "I feel like I've just had a data dump into my head."

"It's a little overwhelming at first, but give it a minute," she told him, understanding what he was feeling. "It will settle down."

After a moment, Aaron stood and growled aggressively at Ull. "You steal women from Earth, refuse to return them, then come here thinking you can barter for more?" He gave Ull a disbelieving look. "Women aren't things that are given away and passed around."

"Yet that's what's been happening," Ull growled back. "And not only did you not know about it but have no way of preventing it from continuing." He refused to back down from this smaller male, no matter who he was. Ull was a first male, after all. But he could also see this other male believed what he was saying. Could females really be treated so differently on this planet?

While his temper was flaring, Aaron kept it in check because of what this man, male, Ull, said was true. Aaron was the President of the United States, and he'd had no clue this was happening. No one had. "What a fucking mess."

"I said something along those same lines," Trisha said, moving to stand next to her tío as she glared at Ull. "Except I assigned blame."

"I just bet you did," Aaron looked down at her and found himself chuckling for the first time since he'd arrived. "You're fearless when you're fighting for what you believe is right."

"Just like you and Mamá taught me," she smiled back at him.

At that moment, Ull suddenly felt alone even though he was still in the room. The connection between these two was one of the strongest he'd ever seen, even though this male wasn't Trisha's manno. There was trust, understanding, and respect. It was something you didn't see between males and females in his world.

'What about between King Grim and Queen Lisa?' his honor reminded him.

'Or Lord Ynyr and Lady Abby?' it continued.

'General Rayner and his Ashe, Jennifer?'

'Emperor Wray and Empress Kim?'

'Then there's your own parents who refused to leave one another as tradition demanded?'

It was something he'd refused to see or believe. Instead, he'd told himself those males were going soft so they could have offspring. But it wasn't truth, and it didn't seem to be truth on Earth either. Could he have had it wrong all this time?

"Ull?"

Trisha's voice pulled him from his thoughts. "What?" he growled.

Trisha jolted, her eyes widening at how deadly Ull sounded, then removed all emotion from her face. "Tío Aaron asked you a question."

"What was it?" Ull demanded, his gaze going to the other male as he forced himself to not apologize for alarming her, even though he wanted to.

"First," Aaron growled back as he stood, even though he knew it wouldn't bring him eye-to-eye with Ull. He refused to give the male anymore advantage over him than he already had. "You will never speak to my niece in that tone again, not if you want our help."

"I could always approach someone else," Ull growled back even though he couldn't help but be impressed with the courage of this smaller male. It took guts to stand up to someone you *knew* could harm you.

"Then, you'll have to explain not only to your Emperor but Queen Lisa, why you expressly disobeyed her orders on who to contact." Aaron had been in enough political power struggles in his time to recognize that in this, he had the upper hand. Ull seemed to realize that too, and he gave Aaron a slight nod.

"I asked," Aaron finally returned to his original query. "How soon would you be returning our people to us?"

"That would depend on what we can work out for my people gaining access to your females," Ull replied.

"That's not how this is going to work, Ull," Trisha said, interjecting herself into the conversation, not liking how Ull and her tío were glaring at each other. "Your people committed the first offense. You *stole* women from Earth, women you aren't planning on returning. So, what you're going to do to *start* making amends is get everyone I met on the Searcher down here where they can get a medical checkup. Once we're sure they're okay, only *then* will we discuss your proposal."

"What's the Searcher?" Aaron demanded.

"The name of their ship that's orbiting Earth," Trisha told him.

"Wait! You're telling me he," he jerked his thumb toward Ull, "took you into space? With your permission?"

"Yes and no. Basically, Ull kidnapped me," she told her tío.

"You son of a bitch!" Aaron took a threatening step toward Ull.

"No, Tío Aaron," Trisha immediately stepped between them. "That doesn't matter right now."

"The hell it doesn't!" Aaron growled. "You're my *niece*!"

"I know. And trust me, Ull will pay for that. But right now, we need to focus on the bigger picture. We need the President of the United States here right now, not my tío."

Aaron sucked in a deep breath and forced himself to calm down, because she was right, even as his gaze remained locked with Ull's. "Don't think I'll forget this," he growled at Ull.

"Understood," Ull growled back.

∞ ∞ ∞ ∞ ∞

Trisha silently watched as Tío contacted his security detail and ordered one of them to come inside with a secure phone. She recognized the man that entered. His name was Brock, and he was the head of the President's detail. Trisha found him friendly enough, on previous occasions. Given the circumstances, there was none of that now. As he handed the President the phone he'd requested, his gaze searched every visible inch of her home for threats. She was glad she'd had Ull return to the garage.

"Thank you, Brock, that will be all," Aaron told him.

"Are you sure, sir?" he asked, his gaze fixed on the door in the kitchen that led to the garage.

"Yes, I'll contact you again if I need anything else." This time there was no missing the dismissal in Tío's voice. With a curt nod, Brock turned to leave, but not before he gave Trisha a look that told her he knew something was going on. Trisha waited until the door closed before releasing the breath, she hadn't realized she'd been holding and looked to her tío.

"He knows something is going on," she told him.

"I'd be more surprised if he didn't," Aaron told her as he entered a number into the phone. "Brock is very good at his job."

As the call connected, Trisha went to the garage door to let Ull back in.

"Who was the male?" Ull immediately demanded.

"It was the head of my tío's security," she told him. "The educator said your Emperor and Lords all have their own special guards."

"Yes, it is a high honor to be picked as one," Ull informed her.

"Well, the President of the United States has them too. They're called the Secret Service."

"Why are they secret?" Ull asked.

"I guess because while they are there to protect the President, they're also supposed to blend in, so people don't know who they are. I'm sure there's more to it than that, but that's a general understanding."

"Alright, I've set things in motion," Aaron said, disconnecting the phone.

"What things?" Trisha asked.

"We're going to a facility in North Dakota," he told her.

"North Dakota?" Trisha frowned at him. She thought he would have suggested something closer, like Camp David.

"Why does this location surprise you?" Ull demanded suspiciously, his gaze moving between Trisha and her tío.

"Because while North Dakota is a large state in our country, it's sparsely populated. It's close to the Canadian border, and while it has mineral resources, it's primarily an agricultural area. There's no reason for a large government facility to be there."

"There is now," Aaron told her without expanding, and Trisha's eyes widened.

While Earth still wasn't a perfect place, it had come a long way in the last twenty years, with more and more countries coming together and putting aside their differences. It had started in Europe with the forming of the European Council. Each country elected one representative to sit on it, and they, in turn, selected who would be their Chancellor, or Council leader, who would be their delegate to the newly formed World Council. Africa and mainland Asia soon developed their Councils with many of the nations in the Indian and Pacific

Oceans joining with Australia. Only the North and South Americas hadn't 'realigned,' but there were rumors about it.

"So, the rumors are true," she murmured.

"Rumors?" Ull demanded.

"That the individual countries on the North American continent are putting aside their differences for the betterment of their people and coming together as one, just like the other parts of the world have."

"Yes," Aaron told her, "but there are a great many things we still have to finalize, but one already decided is where the Council will meet."

"And you decided on *North Dakota*?" Trisha couldn't hide her disbelief.

"The chosen area favors no one as it is the center of the continent," Aaron told her. "Facilities have been built for the influx of people and to deal with the fluctuations in climate."

"Fluctuations?" Ull frowned at this.

"North Dakota can be very hot and dry in the summer months and extremely cold with large accumulations of snow in the winter ones," Aaron told Ull. "No one has moved in yet, but there is a medical staff there, so we will be able to quarantine the abductees until cleared." Aaron looked to Ull. "I'm assuming this ship of yours, the Searcher, is undetectable to our defense systems."

"Yes," Ull told him.

"And to the visible eye?" Aaron pressed.

"My shuttle is currently sitting shielded behind Trisha's home," he told her. "Have any of your Secret Service males noticed it?"

Aaron grimaced at that because he knew they hadn't. If they had, they would be storming inside to pull him out. "So, you'll be able to land the Searcher at NACB without being seen."

"NACB?" Trisha questioned.

"North American Council Base," Aaron expanded, giving her a slightly sheepish look. "It's the best we could come up with so far. I'm sure it will change."

"No," Ull told him shortly.

"No?" Aaron frowned at Ull. "No, what?"

"The Searcher isn't built for atmospheric travel. Your people will be transported down in small groups in the shuttle."

"Oh." Aaron began to tap his lip absently. "Well, that will probably be better anyway. It will cut down on the medical staff needed and won't draw as much attention."

"What is this 'medical' you keep referring to?" Ull asked, frowning.

"They're what you would call Healers," Trisha told him. "They're going to need to examine those returning so they can treat any injuries. They'll also need to make sure they aren't carrying any diseases that aren't common on Earth."

"Already done," Ull told her. "They each spent time in the deep repair unit when the Kaliszians discovered them, healing any injuries they had at that time. Our Healer also saw them on the Searcher. They have no injuries and carry no diseases."

"What's a deep repair unit?" Aaron demanded.

"Was that not included in the educator?" That surprised Ull. After all, it had healed the Earth female, Rebecca, after Risa attacked her.

"No, it wasn't," Aaron and Trisha said together.

Ull shook his head. This is what happened when a female interfered. "The deep repair unit is what every species in the Known Universe uses to repair injuries. The only thing it can't completely repair are injuries caused by a Tornian blade."

"Tornian blade?" Aaron asked. Ull withdrew his sword from the sheath on his back, and Aaron found he had to lean back as Ull pointed it at him.

"This is the weapon of choice for a Tornian warrior," Ull told them, raising his sword to admire it. "It is made from Tornian steel, the finest and strongest metal in the Known Universes. It can cut through anything and even deflect blaster fire."

"But this deep repair unit can't heal injuries caused by it?" Aaron asked, realizing Ull hadn't been threatening him.

"Can't completely," Ull corrected. "It takes the unit more time, and a scar will always remain. It is why King Grim is scarred."

"And why he was declared unfit by your Assembly of Lords." Aaron had learned that from the educator.

"Yes," Ull acknowledged.

"So, you're saying physically our people are fine." Aaron wanted Ull to confirm that.

"Yes."

"Well, our 'Healers' will have to verify that before we can reunite them with their families," Aaron told him.

"You question my word?!" Ull growled as he tightened his grip on the hilt of his sword, but it didn't faze Aaron. He'd been standing up to bullies his entire life. He wasn't going to stop just because this one happened to be an alien.

"Of course, I do," Aaron told him. "I don't know you, and you've given me no reason to trust you." His gaze dropped to the sword that was still between them before it returned to Ull's angry eyes. "Especially when you kidnapped my niece to get to me. It's not something a fit and worthy male would do." Aaron used the words he'd learned that mattered to the Tornians.

Trisha watched Ull flinch as if he'd been struck, and slowly he sheathed his sword. "Do as you wish," he told Aaron. "They are your people."

"They are," Aaron told him, "and trust me, I will. Now, how do we contact you when we're ready for you to start transporting our people home?"

Ull reached into his vest and pulled out a small rectangular black device. "This is a comm unit," he told the President then pointed to a button. "Press this, and it will connect with me on the Searcher, and we will start the transport process."

"Alright." Aaron turned his attention to Trisha. "Go pack a bag. You'll be staying with me in the White House."

"Trisha will remain with me!" Ull all but bellowed. He wasn't going to let Trisha separate from him. He wasn't sure why it mattered so much, but it did.

Trisha was shocked at Ull's reaction and how fast he could move. One moment she was beside her tío, and the next, she was pinned to Ull's side, her wrists cuffed by one of his much larger hands. While it wasn't painful, Trisha knew there was no way to break free unless Ull allowed it. Looking to her tío, she saw how ruddy his complexion had become and knew he was moments away from losing his temper, and that wasn't going to solve anything.

"There's no way..." Aaron began.

"It's alright, Tío," she quickly cut him off. "I'll go with him."

"Trisha, no!" he argued.

"It'll give me time to talk to the abductees, explain to them what's happening and why, and speak to Minister Ruskin, the representative the Kaliszians sent to negotiate a trade deal for food."

"You can do that at NACB," Aaron argued.

"True, but this will give us a head start." She tried to appeal to his practical side, knowing he always liked to do things as efficiently as possible. "That is if you trust me to do this. I know I'm not part of your staff..."

"Of course, I trust you, Trisha!" He gave her a disbelieving look. "Do you think I'd be making you my Representative if I didn't?"

"Representative?" Her eyes widened in shock. "Me?"

"Who else?" Aaron demanded. "Not only are you the one Lisa requested, but you are also the only other one besides me that will even understand him." He gestured to Ull.

"Besides the abductees," she reminded him, knowing she'd gotten him to calm down and think. "The Kaliszians made sure they were able to use a proper educator."

"Proper?" Aaron frowned at that. "What are you talking about?"

"The first group, the one enslaved," she reminded him. "The Ganglians only programmed their educator so they could understand Ganglian and Zaludian, the languages of their masters."

"And the second group?" he asked quietly.

"Had all the languages but no history," she told him. "The Kaliszians corrected that."

"So, once they return, they're going to start talking about everything they've learned and experienced," Aaron sighed heavily.

"Wouldn't you?" she argued. She knew her tío fully supported the First Amendment, which stated that an individual has the right to express their opinions and ideas without fear of retaliation, and these people were going to have a lot of opinions.

"Yes, and they will be allowed to," he reassured his niece. "It's just something else we'll have to deal with if we decide to negotiate with both the Kaliszians and Tornians."

"If?" Ull growled.

"If," Aaron stressed back.

Ull

Chapter Five

Closing her eyes, Trisha sighed tiredly and leaned back in her seat as Ull took off from behind her home. Her tío had left a short time ago, but not before giving her a hug and a kiss and whispering for her to be careful. She'd reassured him she'd be fine and hoped she wasn't lying to him. She didn't understand Ull's sudden mood swings. Was it a Tornian thing? Or was he struggling to deal with the changes happening in his world the same way Trisha was with hers? One of the things Lisa put in the educator was, even though raised as protectors, some Tornian males weren't happy that they weren't just conquering Earth and taking what they needed. The situation was getting that dire in their Empire.

Was Ull one of those males? If so, why would the Emperor send him on such a critical mission?

She wanted to sit back and enjoy this amazing thing she was experiencing. She was about to fly into space for the first time, at least consciously. Few people on Earth had ever gotten the chance to do this, but she couldn't. Not with what was going on. People, women especially, were being abducted, stolen, and enslaved, and it seemed to be up to her to put a stop to it.

Ull glanced over at the female sitting next to him as he piloted the shuttle back to the Searcher. Goddess, she was the most beautiful female he'd ever seen. He hadn't initially liked the short length of her hair. Females should have long hair. Yet now, watching how it brushed along her jaw, he was filled with the desire to do the same. Would her skin be as soft as it looked? Would she allow him to touch her that intimately? She had already touched *him* voluntarily, and she hadn't fought him when he pulled her away from the male, she called Tío. Did that mean she was willing?

Goddess, he had more questions than answers.

'Just take her,' that dark voice whispered in his mind. *'She's unprotected. It's within your right as a first male and future Lord to claim her.'*

But if he did that, it could prevent his brothers-in-arms from acquiring the females *they* needed.

'So?' the whispering continued. *'What do they matter? Your needs come first.'*

"Were you successful?" Ull saw Trisha jerk, her eyes flying open when Veron's voice filled the shuttle.

"I will speak of it once we arrive," he responded to Veron.

"We?" Veron questioned.

"Trisha is returning with me," he informed Veron.

"Willingly?" Veron growled back.

"Yes, Captain Veron," Trisha spoke when she saw Ull's face darken at the unspoken accusation from the other male.

"I see," he replied quietly.

"We'll speak once we land, Captain." With that, Ull disconnected the transmission.

Trisha said nothing and just watched Ull land the shuttle. Once done, she rose and went to where Ull had stored the bag she'd packed.

"What are you doing?" Ull demanded, following her.

"What's it look like?" she asked. "I'm getting my bag."

"Females don't carry their bags," he told her, taking it from her.

"Why?" she asked, and he gave her a confused look as the ramp lowered.

"What do you mean, why?" he demanded.

"Just that," she retorted. "For while I appreciate you are carrying my bag, why can't a female carry her own?"

"Because it isn't her place," he told her as if it were obvious.

"Her *place*?" Trisha couldn't believe he'd just said that.

"Yes, females are cared for and protected so that they can produce and carry our offspring, not baggage. That is their place."

"Seriously?! You did not just say that!" Trisha couldn't believe how angry that made her. Here was a civilization that had conquered space travel, and yet they still thought a woman's place was to be barefoot and pregnant.

"I did say that," Ull reassured her then took in the angry splashes of color filling in her cheeks. "Why does that upset you so?"

"Lady Trisha?" Veron's gaze traveled from Ull to the female that Queen Lisa had put her faith in to save their people. If the look on her face said anything, whatever Ull had said greatly disturbed her.

"What?" Trisha snapped as her gaze locked onto his. When she saw his eyes widen in surprise, she forced herself to take a deep calming breath. "I'm sorry, Captain, that was uncalled for."

"That's alright, Lady Trisha," he told her. "I know you've had an eventful day."

"That would be an understatement," she said, giving Vernon a small smile as she walked toward him.

Ull found he didn't like the way Trisha smiled at Veron. Didn't like the way the Captain smiled back at her. What did that male think he was doing? Veron couldn't smile at his female that way. That thought brought Ull to an abrupt halt. *His* female? Trisha wasn't his.

"Why are you calling me 'Lady' Trisha?" she asked, not noticing how Ull wasn't following.

"It is the title given to important Tornian females," Veron told her.

"But I'm not Tornian," she reminded him.

"Truth, but you may be the most important female in all of Tornian history, besides the Goddess, of course."

Trisha had to swallow hard at that. God, she'd always wanted to make a difference, to do something meaningful and memorable, the way her tío and mamá had, but this. If she failed at this; it would affect billions upon billions of people.

Starvation.

Extinction.

And that was only for the Kaliszian and Tornian people.

The Earth would be attacked and possibly destroyed.

How was she supposed to prevent that when she had such a short amount of time?

"Lady Trisha?" Veron asked.

Veron's voice pulled her from her thoughts. "Please, it's Trisha, or if we're formal, Miss Burke."

"Representative," Ull corrected, having moved to her side.

"What?" she looked up at him.

"The President made you his Representative."

"Oh, right. I forgot that."

"So, he's willing to negotiate?" Veron didn't try to hide his surprise or hope. He'd thought Ull had ruined any chance of that kidnapping Trisha.

"He's willing to discuss it *after* all the people on the Searcher are back on Earth," Trisha told him.

"That's…" Veron gave her a wary look.

"Not going to happen," Ull told her.

"Yes, it is." Trisha turned, so she faced both males. Her face and tone just as hard as it was when she was negotiating a major deal. "Because while this is a Tornian ship, those people are under *Kaliszian* protection, which means *you* have no say over them. So, if your attitude doesn't change, I'll be forced to advise the President that we can only deal with the Kaliszians as they are the only ones acting in good faith."

"That would be greatly appreciated, Representative Burke," Ruskin said, walking across the landing bay toward them. He'd heard what was being said and decided now would be an excellent time to make his presence known. "And I must say I look forward to working with you."

"Thank you, Minister Ruskin," Trisha said, turning to him. "I'm hopeful we can come to an agreement that is beneficial for everyone."

"As do I. The actions and decisions we all make will affect not just us, but all the Known Universes for millennia to come." Ruskin let his gaze travel over Veron and Ull, reminding them what was at stake.

"Then let's make sure we make the right ones," Trisha said then looked to Veron. "It's been a long day. I want to know where I'll be staying."

"I'll show you," Ull spoke before Veron could then turning began to walk away.

"I will see you at first meal," Ruskin said, giving her a slight bow. "Rest well, Representative Burke."

"You as well, Minister Ruskin. Captain Veron." Trisha nodded to both males before moving toward Ull, who had stopped at the hangar door when he'd realized she hadn't immediately followed him. He opened his mouth as if to say something, then snapped it shut and began walking again.

Ull moved quickly through the empty corridors of the Searcher. He wanted to get Trisha away from the other males. He didn't like them talking to or looking at her. He especially didn't like it when the Kaliszian did. The Kaliszians were starving, dependent on the Tornians for their survival, and

Minister or not, Ruskin wouldn't be able to provide for Trisha adequately.

He could, though. One day, he would be a Lord, and if Trisha chose him, he'd make sure she never wanted for anything.

"I'm not going to run to keep up with you," she told him in an exasperated voice.

Looking over his shoulder, Ull found her a significant distance behind him. "I'm..."

"In a hurry to get rid of me because I pissed you off. Yeah, I know, but that doesn't mean I'm going to let you treat me like this. You're nearly a foot taller than me, and most of it seems to be leg. If you didn't want to show me to my room, you should have let Captain Veron do it."

"That wasn't what I was going to say," he growled. "I was going to apologize. I'm not used to putting others' needs before my own."

"Yeah, I got that. Must be nice to be a first male and never have anyone tell you when you're an asshole."

That word had his thoughts flying back to the conversation he and Queen Lisa had.

'Trisha has had to survive a great deal. She's strong and independent. She isn't going to put up with your bullshit attitude toward females. She's dealt with enough assholes in her life.'

Even General Rayner's Ashe had agreed he was an asshole. Which he learned was an unworthy and unfit male that used females for his own gain.

He didn't see Trisha that way or didn't mean to.

"I... I have only recently discovered that," he finally admitted.

"Discovered what?" she asked.

"That I was never confronted about many of my actions because I was the first male of a Lord."

"Seriously? It took you, how old are you?" she demanded.

"I am twenty-five."

"Really?" She was surprised he was just a year older than her. "So, it took you twenty-five years to figure out you were privileged?"

"I always knew I was," he admitted, "but I never realized it had that great of an effect until…"

"Until?"

"Until I learned, my two youngest brothers were mistreated and ridiculed." He still couldn't believe he hadn't known what had been happening.

"Wait. What? I thought you only had one brother. Ynyr."

"I have three brothers," he informed her.

"But I thought…"

"I would prefer not to discuss it here." Turning, he started down the corridor but at a much slower pace. After one more turn, he stopped in front of a grey door, pressed his hand against a small panel, and the door slid open. "These will be your quarters."

Trisha walked inside and let her gaze travel over the room. Its walls were the same dull gray of the door as was the couch, table, chairs, and desk. The room had no softness, color, or warmth. Did Tornians live this way? Lisa had to hate it.

"If you would place your hand on the panel." He gestured to the one identical to the one on the outside of the door. Once she did, he entered a code, and the panel began to glow beneath her hand.

"What are we doing?" While Trisha didn't feel anything, with everything that had happened that day, she wasn't taking any chances.

"Securing your quarters. Now only you will be able to enter this room." Turning, he moved to a door she hadn't noticed as it blended into the rest of the wall. This one also opened as he approached. Following him, she looked inside and watched him put her bag on what would be a queen-sized bed on Earth. Comparing Ull's size to it, she realized it was probably a single for a Tornian male.

"The other door leads to your cleansing area," he told her as he walked toward her.

"Cleansing area?" Taking a step back so he could pass, she looked around the room and finally spotted the door he was talking about. Walking over, it automatically opened. In it, she saw a basin, toilet, and what appeared to be a walk-in shower. "It's motion-activated?" she asked, looking at him.

"Yes," he told her, surprised she'd been able to figure that out so quickly.

"Alright." Turning, she walked over to the couch and sat down on one end. "So, tell me how it is you have three brothers when what I learned from the educator is that a Tornian male is lucky to have one child… offspring," she corrected.

Ull didn't understand why Trisha wanted to pursue this subject. No Tornian female cared about what a male had to say or his life unless it directly affected her. Could Earth females be that different? He truly hadn't believed it, but maybe he was wrong. Slowly he moved across the room and sat down on the opposite end of the couch from Trisha.

"That is truth," Ull confirmed. "A Tornian male must save most of his life just for the chance of attracting the attention of a female."

"Attract her attention?" Trisha frowned at that. "I don't understand."

"A male must be able to show a female that he can properly protect and provide for her before she even considers Joining with him," Ull explained. "If she does choose to Join with him, then the male must continue to appease her, so she doesn't leave him for another offering more before she is with offspring."

"Wait, you mean if one of your females agrees to Join with a male, she can just leave him anytime she wants for another male?"

"Yes, she can move on for any reason, taking all the first male has given her, as long as she hasn't conceived his offspring. If she has conceived, then the female must remain with the male until the offspring presents. She can then either move on or stay. If the offspring is male, then the male's position is cemented, and his bloodline will continue. If she presents a female, his position is elevated, and the female's value goes up."

"Her *value*?" Trisha couldn't believe Ull had said that.

"A female who has already presented a female is highly sought after by other males. Because of it, she can demand whatever she wants for her gift."

"And the child… offspring," Trisha corrected. "What happens to it if she chooses another male?"

"It remains with its manno, of course," he said, giving her an 'it should be obvious' look.

"Your females just *leave* their offspring behind?" She was finding it hard to believe that Tornian females routinely abandoned their children.

"Yes," he told her. "Tornian females rarely have contact with their offspring once they are presented."

Trisha knew, without a doubt, Lisa would never do that. "But Lisa…"

"By accepting the title of Queen, she has accepted King Grim as her one and only male. The offspring she carries is female, and he has accepted her other two young females as his own."

"Carly and Miki," Trisha supplied.

"Who?" he asked, frowning at her.

"The names of Lisa's two young females are *Carly* and *Miki,*" she stressed their names.

"I believe that is truth," Ull acknowledged. "So, King Grim will have three young females, and no male would dare offend him now for fear he would withhold his females from them."

Some of this sounded familiar to Trisha, so she knew Lisa must have included it in the educator, but still, it wasn't something she'd readily known. Hopefully, she wasn't missing other relevant information.

"So your father, manno," she corrected, "Because he's a Lord, was able to attract *four* females, and was able to keep them long enough to have offspring with each of them?" she asked, returning to the subject of Ull. It would help in negotiations if she knew him better, not because she was personally interested in him, at least that was what she was telling herself.

"No," Ull told her shortly.

"But you have brothers," she pointed out, frowning at him.

"We were all presented by the same female," he grudgingly admitted. "Our mother refused to leave our manno even though many tried to lure her away... and still do."

Trisha didn't understand why Ull seemed embarrassed by that. "Your mother sounds like an amazingly strong woman. Your manno too."

"They were both selfish," he bit out.

Trisha sat back into the corner of the couch, unable to believe Ull had just said that. "How can you say that?!"

"Because it's truth," he growled. "There are other males that need her gift, especially after she presented my father with a second male. There was no reason for her to remain. She should have done her duty and allowed other males to have offspring. Instead, she has yet conceived again."

The disgust in Ull's voice was so shocking that Trisha didn't know how to respond. His mother had stood up against convention, had stood up for what she wanted, and who. That took an incredible amount of strength and fortitude. Trisha knew because her own mother had done the same thing, and Trisha was grateful for it, but Ull apparently wasn't.

"Good for her. And for the record," Trisha leaned forward to growl. "Abby did the right thing in not choosing you."

"What?" Ull frowned at her, not understanding what she was saying.

"I said, Abby did the right thing choosing your brother over you. You are one of the most unworthy, unfit males I've ever had the misfortune of meeting." Her voice grew louder and stronger with every word she spoke. "I have no idea why your Emperor would send one such as *you* here to negotiate for females because I can tell you right now that no Earth female would ever agree to 'Join' with you if that's how you think of your own *mother*! Now get the fuck out of my room!"

∞ ∞ ∞ ∞ ∞

Taking one look at Ull's expression when he entered the control room, Veron demanded, "What's happened?"

"I don't understand females," Ull growled, dropping into one of the chairs.

Veron sighed, and after pushing a few buttons so the Searcher would fly itself, he moved to sit next to Ull. There were very few Tornians on the Searcher, as Wray hadn't wanted to take the chance that a Warrior might try to claim an Earth female without her consent. It made it easier for Veron to talk to Ull in a room that was usually full of Warriors.

"I'm not sure any male ever completely understands one, whether she's Tornian, Kaliszian, or Earthian."

"They make no sense," Ull muttered.

"In what way?" Veron asked, honestly curious about the other male's thoughts.

"She asks about my family, my brothers, Joinings, and when I tell her truth, she becomes upset. With *me*!"

"Well, as the representative from Earth, I'm sure she's just trying to understand the differences between our cultures, so she knows what Earth females will be facing if they agree to Join with us. You informed her of how things are changing, correct? That we are no longer forcing our females to leave a male, they are happy with?"

"No," Ull grunted.

"What? Why?" Veron demanded.

"We never got off the subject of my family and why I had so many brothers."

"And *that* upset her?" That surprised Veron because from what he'd seen, every other Earth female had supported Lady Isis's decision to stay with Lord Oryon, even though many Tornians had shunned them for it over the years. Even the Emperor announced, before the Assembly of Lords, his support of the couple.

"Yes, and I don't understand why, especially when I told her truth. It shouldn't have been allowed, and my mother should have been forced to accept another male."

Veron's eyes widened at that. "*That's* the truth you told her?! That we *force* our females to leave a male? That it is what we will expect of Earth females?"

"No. I told Trisha how *they* choose who will be their next male."

Veron surged out of his chair, clenching his fists. "Tell me truth, Ull! Are you purposely trying to sabotage this meeting, so our Warriors have reason to attack and conquer Earth?"

"What?" Ull looked at the Emperor's Captain in shock and denied. "No! Of course not!"

Veron's eyes narrowed as he tried to judge Ull's truth. He knew about this male, had heard impressive things about him, but then that was to be expected for the first male of a Lord. He'd also heard some rumbling that Ull hadn't been pleased when Lady Abby had chosen his brother and made it clear that Ynyr would be her only male. Yet Ull had gone and assisted Ynyr in getting what was now House Jamison in order and done an outstanding job by all accounts. So why did he seem to be doing everything in his power to enrage this Earth representative?

Was it because she was female?

Was it because it had been Queen Lisa's idea? Another female.

Veron knew many Warriors were struggling with all the changes taking place in their Empire, but most saw it as a good thing.

"Do you truly believe that your mother was wrong to stay with your manno? That he should have *forced* her to Join with another?"

"Other males needed and still need her gift," Ull told him, which revealed nothing.

"Her last presentation was over seventeen years ago," Veron reminded him.

"You haven't heard?" Ull looked to him in surprise.

"Heard what?"

"My mother has conceived again," Ull told him quietly.

"Really?" Veron's pleasure was apparent. "That's wonderful news!"

"Is it?" Ull countered. "When so many males have bloodlines that are ending?"

Veron sat back down and wondered what he could say, because while Ull wasn't wrong, neither was Lady Isis. It wasn't until the Earth females had arrived that Veron had realized just how courageous Lady Isis had to have been to withstand the outside pressures that wanted her to leave the male she loved. Now, it seemed there had been some internal pressure as well.

"Have you spent any real-time with a female from Earth?" Veron asked.

"Alone?" Ull gave him a shocked look. "Of course not! That would break Tornian Law!" Just as Ynyr had done, he thought.

"Of course, not alone, but I know you met with the Emperor in the Royal Garden and that the Empress was there. You also met with Queen Lisa and General Rayner's Ashe, Jennifer, the Empress' sister before coming here. You had to have spent time with your brother's Lady during your time in House Jamison. Did you not notice how strong and independent they all are?"

"They can be that way because they have strong males backing them up."

"Did the Empress when she was captured and abused by the Ganglians?" Veron demanded. "Did her sister when she was forced to work in a Zaludian mine for nearly eight months? Or Queen Lisa and Lady Abby when our own Warriors attacked them?" Veron answered for Ull. "No! They found a way to fight back and survive on their own. It is what our females once did before we caused them to believe their only value to us was as breeders because of the Great Infection. Your mother, Lady Isis, was the only one who refused to allow herself to be used that way. It cost her, your manno, and your House, but if you asked either of them, I believe they'd tell you it was worth it. It seems to me you are the only one who has a problem with it."

"Ynyr and Zev have suffered because of it," Ull argued quietly.

"Ynyr is now a powerful Lord, and Zev, from what I've heard, will be an outstanding warrior once fully trained. So, I don't think you'll hear complaints from either of them. *You* are the only one doing that. Why is that?"

"Things are not as they were," Ull finally admitted. "As I expected them to continue."

"You mean, with our civilization dying? That our once fit and worthy Warriors now treat females the way the Ganglians do? Is that how you wish things to continue, Ull?"

"No!" Ull immediately denied. "But there are barely enough females as it is, and if they are allowed to stay with just one male…"

"Then, even as a Lord, you might not attract one, ending your bloodline on Betelgeuse." Veron finally understood what was driving the younger Warrior.

"Yes," Ull admitted quietly.

"That has a high probability of happening… for all our bloodlines," Veron told him. "If *you* are unable to reach an agreement with the representative Earth has sent us, just because she is a *female*."

"I can't seem to get her to understand what I'm *saying*," Ull grumbled.

"Then try to understand what *she's* saying," Veron told him. "I'm not saying it's going to be easy. If I've learned anything since we discovered we're compatible with Earth females, it's that they are complicated creatures. They are full of contradictions. They appear so soft, but I vow there are times when they are stronger than any Tornian blade. They love fiercely and protect what's theirs, even if it means sacrificing themselves. In many ways, they are like Tornian Warriors. Speak to and treat her with the same respect you would one of them, and perhaps you can find common ground."

Ull remained in his chair, gazing at the blue planet filling the viewport, as Veron rose to check on the autopilot. Was that his problem? That he wasn't giving Trisha the respect she deserved? He could admit, to himself, just how much he was struggling to understand these Earth females. Especially Trisha. Didn't they know how precious they were? That they needed protection from all the horrors that were in the Known Universes? Yet so many of them lived alone on their planet. Even Trisha's only male relative, the one that should have been protecting her, allowed her to travel to the Searcher with him. Alone. When she told him it was her choice, he should have denied her. He should have attacked Ull to try and prevent it, even though he would have died in the attempt. Is that why he allowed it? Or was it because of something else? The same something Veron said Ull should be giving Trisha. Respect. Trisha's tío had *respected* her, and more than that, he'd *trusted* her.

Maybe it was time Ull did too.

Rising, he looked to Veron. "Thank you, Captain, for your counsel. I see why the Emperor considers you such a trusted advisor and friend." Crossing an arm over his chest, Ull gave Veron a deep bow then left the room. He needed to speak to Trisha if she would allow him.

Chapter Six

Ull let out a heavy sigh a few minutes later when Trisha didn't open her door after he knocked. Perhaps it was for the best. Tomorrow he would try again. Moving through the corridors, he came to an abrupt halt when he heard laughter, female laughter. Entering the common eating area, he found Trisha sitting across from the Kaliszian Minister laughing. Ruskin was the first to see him frozen in the doorway.

"Warrior Ull, is there something we can do for you?" Ruskin inquired politely.

When Trisha turned to face him, Ull saw all the delight and ease that had been in her expression moments earlier disappear. "I was looking for Representative Burke," he forced himself to use her title, just as he would if she were male, but couldn't help but add. "She wasn't in her room."

"No, I wasn't," Trisha told him coolly. "Minister Ruskin was kind enough to stop by and ask if I'd had," she paused only for a moment before she found the right word, "Last meal. As I hadn't, he graciously showed me where I could eat." She looked back to Ruskin. "Thank you again for that, by the way. I had planned on eating after visiting my parents' graves this morning, but things happened."

"I'm glad I could have been of assistance to you," Ruskin beamed. "I always hate it when my Ashe or offspring miss a meal."

Ull opened his mouth to say that was because Ruskin couldn't adequately provide for them when he realized what the other male was saying. Ruskin already had a female and offspring, so he wasn't looking to make Trisha his.

Reaching out, Trisha covered Ruskin's hand with one of her own. "Well, hopefully, we can make it so no Kaliszian will ever have to go without a meal again."

"From your lips to the Goddess' ears," Ruskin quietly prayed, then asked. "Would you like me to escort you back to your quarters?"

"I'll do that," Ull finally spoke, and Trisha stiffened even more.

"I was asking Trisha," Ruskin growled, glaring at Ull. He knew the Tornian had upset her earlier, and it had taken him nearly the entire meal to get her to smile, let alone laugh. He wasn't going to allow this arrogant Warrior to ruin all his hard work. They needed her.

"Thank you, Jakob," Trisha used the Kaliszian's given name and squeezed his hand one more time before pulling her hand back to rise. "But I believe Warrior Ull and I still have a few things to discuss."

"You are sure?" Jakob asked, rising and moved toward Ull with her. "You've had an eventful day."

"Yes, but thank you for your concern," she reassured him. "I'll see you in the morning for first meal. Hopefully, by then, we'll hear from the President and can start shuttling people down."

"As you wish. Until first meal." Giving a stiff nod to Ull, Jakob left the room.

"Why were you looking for me?" she demanded as she began walking toward her quarters.

"I wished to speak to you," he said quickly following her.

"I thought we'd already done that." She moved through the corridors, pleased that she remembered the way.

"I don't believe I explained myself well before, and as it is in the best interest of both our people that we get along, I thought I should try again."

Trisha thought about that, and while she didn't believe there was anyway Ull could justify his attitude toward his mother, he was right. They needed to figure out how to work together, besides their differences, for the benefit of both their people. It was something most politicians didn't seem to understand.

Placing her hand against the panel outside her door, she stepped inside then gestured with her arm. "Please, come in."

Nodding, Ull stepped inside, and the door slid closed.

Trisha didn't speak as they both moved to their former positions on the couch and faced each other. Since Ull was the one that wanted this meeting, she'd let him be the one to start it.

Ull's gaze traveled over Trisha's guarded expression and found he didn't like it. He preferred it when her blue eyes were sparking at him, like a fully charged energy crystal. They were that way when she argued with him, and he wondered if they would when she was happy with him. Goddess, he wanted to find out.

"I feel I owe you an apology," he began.

"Feel or do?" she demanded, refusing to make it easy for him.

Ull was surprised at her challenge then realized he shouldn't be. She was a strong female.

"Do," he admitted. "I didn't respect you the way I should have. Queen Lisa was most adamant that you voluntarily agree to help us."

"Which I did," she reminded him.

"Only after I kidnapped you," he told her gruffly, his cheeks darkening. "Queen Lisa will be most upset when she learns I went against her orders. As will King Grim and the Emperor."

"Which is why you are apologizing to me." She now understood.

"No!" he immediately denied. "I decided that the most expedient way to gain your assistance was to give you no choice. It will be reported to the Emperor, and I will accept whatever punishment he deems suitable."

"You'll be punished?" She frowned at that. While what Ull had done had been wrong, he had also been right. It *had* been the most effective way for her to understand the importance of what was going on.

"Of course, I disobeyed orders." He looked at her as if that should be obvious.

She cocked her head slightly to the side and asked. "Do you often do that? Disobey direct orders?"

"Of course not," he immediately replied. "I am not only a fit and worthy Warrior but a first male."

"Then why disobey this one?" she questioned.

"As I said, I didn't think I'd be able to convince you the way Queen Lisa demanded."

"So, it's because the order came from a female, and you believe, because you are male, that you know better."

"When it comes to something like this, that is truth," he admitted.

"Why?" Trisha demanded.

"What do you mean, why?" he asked, frowning at her.

"Why do you think a *Tornian male,* would know how to approach an Earth female *better* than an *Earth female*?"

"I...," he paused, realizing he didn't have an answer to that.

"You don't," she told him. "You just dismissed the one that knew more than you because that person happened to be *female*."

Ull frowned at that. Is that what he had done? He searched his mind and realized it was truth.

Trisha watched as Ull frowned and was surprised when he didn't immediately deny her accusation. He actually seemed to be considering it. Was that something a real chauvinist would do?

"Has a female never told you what to do before?" she asked.

"No," he admitted.

"Not even your mother?" Trisha found that hard to believe. Her mamá had told her what to do all the time when she'd been growing up.

"No, because I rarely see her, although I have recently learned she kept me with her for as long as possible before turning me over to my manno."

"How old were you when that happened?"

"It was just before my second presentation day. She presented Vali, my brother, several days later."

"And after that, you rarely saw her?" Trisha found that hard to believe. After all, Ull's mother hadn't left as she'd been told other Tornian females did.

"It is the Tornian way." But he now knew that his mother did very few things the 'Tornian way. She'd been more involved in his life than he'd ever realized and she'd watched him, watched all her males, from her windows in the female level.

"Well, it's the wrong way," Trisha told him, "And you'll find very few Earth females willing to agree to such a thing."

"So, I've been told," he acknowledged.

Trisha could see Ull was struggling with all the changes that were happening in his world. It was something many on Earth would soon be experiencing for themselves. If she was going to be able to help anyone, she needed to start with Ull. She needed to fully understand the differences between their cultures, or this wasn't going to work for anyone.

"So, what are you struggling with the most?" she asked quietly.

For a moment, she didn't think Ull was going to answer, then he growled. "That you may be right, and I'm not the fit and worthy Warrior I always believed myself to be."

Trisha felt her mouth drop open. Of all the things Ull could have said, *that* wasn't even close to what she had expected. "What would make you think that?"

"A fit and worthy Warrior would never challenge his Lord. A fit and worthy Warrior would never envy a brother that the Goddess has chosen to bless with a female that loves and will never leave him. A fit and worthy Warrior would never speak to his mother as if she were beneath him."

Trisha found her throat tightening at the list of sins Ull seemed to think he'd committed. It showed a vulnerable side of him; she honestly hadn't thought existed. Was it because Tornian Warriors weren't allowed to show it? Or was it something else?

"All children, especially sons, argue with their fathers," she began.

"Not Tornian ones," Ull argued. "Especially not when their manno is also their Lord."

"I can understand that." At Ull's puzzled look, she chuckled. "I'm the niece of the President of the United States, Ull. It's not unlike being the first male of a Tornian Lord as Tío Aaron considers me his daughter. Because of that, I'm followed and photographed. I have to watch what I say and where I go, so it doesn't reflect badly on him."

"I see."

"Do you?" she demanded. "Do you realize how lucky you were that no one saw you take me? If someone had, it would be all over the news that 'aliens' were kidnapping women, and there would be no chance of a treaty."

"But that is what's happening," Ull reminded her.

"But not by the Tornians." She gave him a pointed look. "Right? You have only taken females the one time?"

"That would be truth," he told her.

"Then we can work with that, as the Ganglians are the ones who took everyone you are helping the Kaliszians return."

Ull thought about that and realized she was right. If it were discovered that the Tornians had females that they weren't returning, it would only cause problems. "The Goddess must have been watching over me," he murmured.

"Goddess?" Trisha asked.

"She is the deity we worship," he told her.

"You worship a Goddess, but treat your females as little more than breeders? How is that possible?" It was a massive contradiction in her mind.

"A female should always be cared for, protected, and cherished until she leaves a Warrior," he told her.

"And if she doesn't? Leave that is?" Trisha asked.

"Females always leave since the Goddess caused the Great Infection," Ull bit out.

"Your mother didn't leave," she reminded him, "And it's my understanding from the educator that the Great Infection happened because one of your Emperors, Emperor Berto, raped his two young females while a Ganglian watched, and a Kaliszian looked the other way, in exchange for a better trade agreement."

"That is truth," Ull agreed. "They were punished for their crimes. The Goddess had no reason to punish the rest of us with the Great Infection."

"Would you have been that forgiving?" Trisha asked quietly. "If *your* young females were raped? Or your mother?"

"No," he reluctantly growled.

"So why should your Goddess, especially when you don't treat your females differently than your Emperor did."

"How can you say that!" Ull demanded. "We don't abuse our females!"

"There are all kinds of abuse, Ull," she told him. "Physical. Emotional. You've convinced your females their only value is in the number and type of offspring they can provide. That who they are and what they want isn't important. Maybe what the Goddess wants you to realize is that each one of your females is a gift and is important, not for what she can *give* you but for *who* she is."

After a moment, Ull quietly admitted, "That is something I never considered."

"Well, maybe you should, starting with your mother."

"My mother is an anomaly," he told her.

"I don't think so," she disagreed. "I think she's what your Tornian females once were. Strong. Fierce. Willing to fight for what they believe in, even if no one else supports them." Trisha found herself thinking of her own mother and what she'd gone through and knew Patricia Garcia-Burke and Ull's mother would have been kindred spirits. "I would very much like to meet your mother one day."

Ull gave her a shocked look. "You would? Why?"

Trisha just shrugged. "She sounds a lot like my mamá."

"Your… mamá?" he said the word carefully.

"Mother," Trisha corrected.

"You are close to her?" Besides Queen Lisa, Ull knew of no mothers that remained in contact with their offspring.

"I was until she died two years ago." Trisha found it hard to believe it had been that long. There were days it still felt like yesterday. "She was an amazing woman."

"She remained in contact with you after she presented you?" Ull asked.

"It wasn't *contact,*" Trisha corrected. "She raised me, mostly alone."

Ull's eyes widened in shock. He hadn't been informed of this, hadn't known it was possible. "But your manno…"

"Died," she told him quietly, "When I was two. He was a soldier," she looked to Ull. "A Warrior. My mamá's family wouldn't accept him because of the color of his skin. So, Mamá was on her own when he died, well except for Tío Aaron."

"What was wrong with his skin?" Ull asked, looking at the caramel beauty of hers. "Was it diseased?"

"No!" Trisha found herself chuckling at that. "He was white, Caucasian, similar to you only without the rose or pearl effect. My mamá's skin color was like my tío's."

"I see, so skin color on Earth indicates status?"

"Not really, but there are some who discriminate against those who don't look like them. Isn't it that way in the Tornian Empire? You have different skin tones."

"Our skin tone only represents the original line from which we descend," he told her.

"So, you're all related?" Trisha frowned at that.

"Only to a point," he told her. "It's why it is so important for a male to be a fit and worthy Warrior because if one is disgraced, it affects everyone in his direct bloodline."

"Doesn't that get confusing?"

"No, especially not as our numbers continue to decrease. For example, Bertos Guttuso, whose House my brother is now Lord of, was disgraced when he and his Warriors attempted to overthrow the Emperor. They were killed in battle along with Bertos' female, Risa, when she attempted to kill the Empress and her newly presented princess."

"So, they're dead."

"Yes, as is Bertos' first male, Luuken, who fought alongside his manno. But Bertos had a second son, Brice. He now carries the burden of his unfit and unworthy parents and will be shunned for the rest of his life because of it."

"He refused to fight with his manno and brother?" she asked.

"As he's only three, he was not there."

"You would blame a three-year-old for what his parents did?" She didn't try to hide her shock or disbelief.

Ull shrugged. "It is the Tornian way."

"Well, that needs to change. Where's this Brice now?" Trisha demanded.

"Lady Abby has claimed him, and while my brother supports this, they are making a mistake."

"How can you say that?" Every time she thinks she's starting to understand Ull, he goes and says something like that.

"Because it is truth," he told her without a hint of remorse. "His parentage is known throughout the Empire, and no matter what he does, he will carry that burden."

"That's not fair!" she exclaimed.

"Few things in life are," he told her.

While Trisha didn't like it, she realized Ull was right. Her mamá's family had never really accepted her, and now Brice would be experiencing the same, only from his entire world. Her heart went out to that little boy, and she prayed that Abby and Ull's brother would be able to make up for it.

"Unfortunately, that's true," she murmured. "Perhaps I need to meet Brice too."

"Why!" Ull demanded in disbelief. Why would she want to meet someone from such an unfit bloodline?

"Because I understand what it's like to be shunned for something you had no control over," she told him.

"What?" he looked at her in confusion. "I have seen how your tío looks at you. He does not shun you."

"No, Tío Aaron would never do that, he loves me. But the rest of his family, my mamá's family, does. My father *was* a fit and worthy Warrior, Ull." She used the terms Ull seemed to feel were so important. "He loved my mamá, loved me, but he wasn't someone Mamá's family was ever going to approve. Not because of something *he* did but because of something he had no control over, the color of his skin. Just like Brice has no control over who his parents are or what they did. He needs to know some *won't* judge him for that. He can still grow up to be a fit and worthy male. If not in the Tornian Empire, then perhaps on Earth."

"Your people would be willing to accept him?" Ull couldn't believe it.

"They might. If *we*," Trisha gestured to the two of them, "can figure out a way for Earth and Tornians to get along."

"You don't feel you'll have a problem with the Kaliszians?" Ull didn't like the thought of that.

"Not since all they're asking for is a trade agreement, and then there's the fact they are *returning* all the abductees they've found."

"While we are not," Ull said quietly.

The room was silent for several moments before Ull quietly said. "I still find it hard to believe anyone would shun you. You are the most beautiful female I've ever seen."

Trisha's eyes widened at that, and she felt her breath catch at Ull's lowly murmured admission. "Thank you," she said when she was finally able to speak.

"You should never thank someone for truth," he told her.

"Well, beauty is in the eye of the beholder." She gave him a gentle smile.

"I don't understand what that means."

"It means that different people have different ideas about what is beautiful," she told him.

"That can't be truth. Beauty is beauty," he said.

"Do you believe your brother finds Abby beautiful?" she asked.

"Yes," Ull replied, but he seemed to have to force the words from his mouth.

"Do you?" Trisha asked because she wanted to make a point but found she wanted to know his answer. She had no idea what Abby looked like, but he'd said how he envied his brother for having her, and for some reason, that bothered her. When Ull didn't immediately answer, she wondered if her question had backfired.

"No, but that isn't why I find myself envious," he finally admitted.

"It's because she truly *loves* him and refuses to leave him." Finally, she thought she understood what was behind Ull's words and actions. He wanted to be loved for himself, just as his brother was, and even though his mother hadn't left him, he felt abandoned by her.

"Yes," he admitted quietly.

"Just as Lisa loves King Grim, as the Empress loves the Emperor, and from what Jakob has told me, the way Mac and Jen love their Kaliszian Warriors." She paused for a moment, then added. "Just as your mother loves your manno and refuses to leave him."

"I… that is truth."

"Everyone wants to be loved, Ull." She put a gentle hand on his arm. "It doesn't make you unfit or unworthy to want it for yourself, and I'm sorry that I said you were." Sometime during their conversation, they had moved closer to one another.

"It should," he said, looking down to the soft hand that contrasted so sharply with the rosy pale skin of his hard bicep. It soothed him even as it revealed their many differences.

Male. Female.

Tornian. Earthian.

Warrior… Warrior.

It surprised him to realize that because she *was* a warrior. She was fighting for her people just like he was. *This* was what Veron had been trying to get him to see.

"If it does, then I'm unfit and unworthy too," she told him quietly, unaware of where his thoughts had gone.

"What?!" Ull's eyes shot to hers full of disbelief.

"Did Lisa ever tell you how we met?" she asked.

"No," he admitted, "and I never asked." He regretted that now. He found there were many things he was beginning to regret.

"Because she's female." Trisha nodded as she gave him a small, understanding smile. While she didn't agree with Ull's attitude toward women, she'd been taught by her mamá that when you dealt with people, you had to be able to put your own beliefs aside and see the world through theirs. It was the only way to understand them, and she was beginning to understand not just Ull but all Tornian males.

"Lisa and I met in the hospital," she began.

"Hospital?" he asked.

Trisha thought about how to explain it. "It's a place where people who are either hurt or sick go to get treatment."

"Treatment?"

"To get better." She tried again. Lisa hadn't included any of that in the educator, but surely Tornians got sick. "Heal. You don't have such a place?"

"No, we have Healers and repair units."

"Those things that heal without leaving scars?" She suddenly remembered him talking about them. "Unless it is from Tornian steel."

"Yes."

"Well, Earth doesn't have those, so when we get really hurt or sick, we go to the hospital."

"And you met Queen Lisa there," he said, now understanding what she was saying.

"Yes, my mamá was sick, and so was Trisha's husband, Mark. They both had cancer but different kinds."

"What is cancer?" Now he was confused again.

Trisha felt her throat tighten up but forced herself to explain. "Cancer is a disease that can affect anyone at any age. Different kinds attack different parts of the body. Sometimes it's curable. Sometimes it's not."

"By not, you mean people die from this 'cancer'?" He'd never heard of such a thing. Yes, warriors died, but it was either in battle or from old age. It was the same for their females except instead of battle it was during presentation that they were most at risk.

"Yes," she told him quietly.

"And it is what your mother died from." Seeing the sadness in her eyes, he saw he was right.

"Yes, she fought it for nearly five years, but finally, she succumbed to it. Lisa and I met during Mamá's last two years. Lisa had just had Miki, and my mamá loved to hold that little bundle of joy while she was getting her treatment. She said it filled her with hope to see how life went on."

"Miki. She is the smaller one, correct?" he asked.

"Yes, but don't let her size fool you. She's precocious and not afraid to say what she thinks."

Ull remembered how the little one had spoken to him before he'd left Luda. *"Beware the darkness that speaks to you."* she had said. *"It knows where you are most vulnerable, and when you are at your weakest. It then lies to you with the truth, making you believe and do things you never otherwise would. Terrible things. Beware the darkness, Warrior Ull."* He had ignored her at the time, but now he wondered.

"Ull?" Trisha's voice jarred him back to the present.

"I believe you are right. King Grim will have his hands full with her in the future."

"Of that, I have no doubt," Trisha chuckled in agreement. "So, back to my story. Lisa and I bonded during those treatments." At his confused look, she explained further. "Became very close. If one of us was having a bad day or needed something, we knew we could call the other one, could rely on them, and that they would understand."

"As brothers-in-arms do after a battle." He nodded his understanding.

"Yes, and that's what it was, a battle, for both of us. Watching someone you love suffer, and know there's nothing you can do to stop it, rips your heart out." She had to pause as tears clogged her throat. "Mamá died nearly a year before Mark, and even though Lisa was juggling two little kids, a sick husband, and knew soon it would be Mark passing, she still came to Mamá's funeral."

"That was an honorable thing to do." Ull wanted to say more, wanted to ease the pain he saw this still caused her but knew he couldn't. Suddenly he began to understand what she and Queen Lisa had gone through. Goddess, these females were stronger than any Warrior he'd ever met, including him.

"After that, Lisa and I didn't see each other quite as often, but we'd still talk on the phone, and I'd come over and either watch the girls when she took Mark in for treatment or take them to the park so Mark and Lisa could have some time alone."

"You were a good friend." That shouldn't surprise him even though Tornian females weren't that way. He'd seen how the Earth females interacted, and how they supported and defended one another.

"Was I?" she asked, giving him a guilty look. "I was the one that left the girls alone with Mark's brother the night Grim took them."

"You couldn't have prevented that, Trisha," he told her. "Queen Lisa willingly gave herself to King Grim in exchange for him retrieving her offspring. It was recorded."

"Still, there might have been something..."

"No, the only thing that would have happened is King Grim would have taken you too." Ull couldn't believe how much that bothered him. Trisha didn't belong in a Joining Ceremony. She belonged right where she was, sitting on the Searcher, next to *him*.

"And then I wouldn't be here in a position to help you and your fellow Tornians."

"Yes," he agreed. "It is as the Goddess wished."

"Well, I'm not so sure about that. Anyway, the reason I brought all this up was with all the pain and suffering going on at the time, and even knowing that Lisa was going to be heartbroken when she lost the man she loved, I was jealous of her." She let him see all the pain and guilt she carried because of that. "How unfit and unworthy of a friend does that make me?"

"Why would you feel that way?" Ull asked, staring down into her sad eyes. "As you said, the male she loved was dying."

"Because even though Mark was in constant pain and knew he was dying, he was always giving Lisa gentle touches and kisses. He was always telling her how much he loved her and the girls. How even after he was gone, he would make sure they were taken care of. He even pulled me aside once and made me promise that I wouldn't let Lisa grieve for too long, that I'd make her get out and meet other men."

Ull's head jerked back in disbelief. What male would demand such a thing? While Tornian males never expected a female to be with only them, Earth males did. "Why would he ask you to do that?"

"Because Mark truly loved Lisa and didn't want her to spend the rest of her life alone," she told him. "He loved her enough to put her happiness ahead of his."

"Something, only a truly fit and worthy male, would do," Ull growled lowly, doubting he would ever be able to do such an honorable thing.

"Agreed," she murmured.

"And you want that for yourself?" He looked down to where she still touched him.

"What female wouldn't want to be loved that way," she immediately told him. "Without the dying, of course," she quickly added with a small, sad smile.

"Of course," he immediately agreed.

"So you see, Ull, wanting what your brother has with Abby doesn't make you unfit or unworthy. It just makes you human."

"I'm not human," he growled indignantly, and Trisha couldn't help but laugh.

"No, you're definitely not."

Chapter Seven

"Is that a bad thing? That I'm not human?" Ull asked, and Trisha was surprised at the vulnerability she saw in his eyes.

"No, it's not a bad thing," she told him softly. "A person should never have to change who they are to be loved."

"Which is why I was not chosen." He now understood.

"No one chose you, Ull, because you kidnapped those females and were forcing them to choose one of you, instead of giving them a choice," she corrected. "No female would find a male attractive that way."

"Queen Lisa did," he countered. "So did Lady Abby."

"I can't explain that except to say that I know Lisa would do anything, endure anything if it kept her girls safe. But from what she put in the educator and the way she looked in the video, I know she truly loves this King Grim. As for Abby, from what you've told me, I can only guess it was love at first sight. It's a very rare thing."

"They never saw each other," Ull found himself muttering.

"What?" she asked, leaning closer to hear.

Ull couldn't believe he'd just revealed that, but now that he had, he wouldn't lie, not to Trisha. "It seems that while the females were waiting for the Joining Ceremony, Ynyr walked by a hedge and heard Abby crying on the other side."

"She was scared and upset." Trisha nodded her understanding.

"Yes," Ull admitted, ashamed that he'd refused to accept that before. "So Ynyr spoke with her, tried to comfort her, *through the hedge*. He never saw her or knew her name."

"Why are you stressing that?" she asked, frowning.

"Because Ynyr would be punished if anyone found out," he told her.

"For giving comfort to someone scared?" She couldn't believe that. What was wrong with these Tornians?

"The Emperor forbid any male to speak to the females. That Ynyr did broke Tornian Law."

Trisha understood the need to follow the law. She was a lawyer, after all. But she knew for every rule, there was an exception, which applied to what happened with Ynyr and Abby. "I'd say if they're happy together, then it's no one else's business. Love is hard enough to find without putting restrictions on how people find it. If your Emperor had allowed our females to meet with your males before shoving them out into that Joining Ceremony, they might have been more willing to Join with one. But then again, there's the whole 'kidnapping' thing."

"Yet as we speak, your females should be meeting with the Tornian males they have chosen," he told her.

"What are you talking about?!" Trisha demanded, sitting straight up.

"Queen Lisa didn't include this in the educator?" He didn't try to hide his surprise.

"No, she didn't. So, you tell me."

"It was decided, by Queen Lisa," he stressed, placing the blame where it belonged, "that as your females wouldn't be returning to Earth, they would choose the male they wished to Join with."

"Lisa is forcing them to Join?" Trisha couldn't believe that. The Lisa she knew would never do such a thing.

"No," Ull's honor wouldn't allow him to tell an untruth, not to Trisha. "She demanded the females be given two moon cycles to adjust to everything that had happened to them. During that time, the males interested in Joining with one of them would have to send in a written request. In this request, he must include a visual, an outline of his position in his House, where they would live, and, more importantly, why he wanted a female. The females would then review the requests, and then *they* would decide which males they wished to invite to Luanda to meet them."

"Oh my God," Trisha whispered. "It's Internet dating on a galactic level."

"I do not know this Internet dating," he told her.

Trisha shook her head, trying to come to terms with what she'd just learned. "It's basically what you just said except on a more individual level with both males and females submitting their preferences. They then either accept or reject those offered."

"This is common on your planet?" He couldn't believe Earth males and females met this way.

"I wouldn't say common, but yes, it does happen. Usually, with the younger generations."

"Younger generations?" Ull's gaze ran over her. She looked very young to him. "Aren't you part of that 'generation'?"

Trisha found herself giving a half-hearted laugh. "I guess in years, yes, but in life experience? There are days I feel decades older." Trisha couldn't believe Lisa had agreed to this. It didn't make any sense unless she was trying to make the best out of a bad situation. Lisa had always been very good at that. "Is female required to Join with one of the males she invited?"

"No, King Grim was very specific about that to our Warriors. Receiving an invitation does not mean a male would secure a female."

So, Lisa *had* given the women a way out. Trisha sighed with relief until the enormity of what she needed to do hit her. These women depended on her to get them home just as the Tornian males were relying on Ull to find them females willing to Join with them.

"So, could you?" Ull growled quietly.

"Could I what?" she asked, giving him a confused look, her mind still on the massive task before her.

"Find happiness with a Tornian warrior?" he asked.

"Me?" Trisha's eyes widened, totally caught off guard by the question.

"Yes, you."

"I… I don't know," she stuttered. "I suppose if I found the right male, but I don't expect that to happen."

"Why?" Ull demanded.

"Because I'm…" she cut herself off, shocked at what she'd been about to reveal to Ull when she wasn't even ready to admit it to herself. Quickly she corrected, "Going to be spending all my time negotiating between you, the Kaliszians, and Earth's leaders."

Ull didn't like her answer. *'What did you expect?'* the voice in his head whispered. *'She's Earthian, and no Earthian will ever want you.'*

"Then why do you continue to touch me?" he growled as that dark rage inside him began to rise again.

"Touch you?" She frowned at that, then looked down to find her hand resting on his muscled bicep. When had she done that?

"Females only touch a male if she is interested in Joining with him," he bit out at her.

"What?" She jerked her hand away and quickly rose, giving Ull her back as she put as much distance between them as the room allowed. What the hell was Ull talking about? Why hadn't Lisa included in the educator that touching between males and females was taboo for Tornians?

"Females only..."

"I heard you the first time!" Trisha cut him off as she spun around to face him. "I didn't realize you don't like to be touched. Is it the same way with Kaliszians?"

"No, and it's not that we don't like to be touched," Ull's growl deepened. "It's that our females refuse to allow it, outside of Joining."

"Thank God," she sighed in relief, recalling all the times she'd touched Jakob. They already had enough to deal with, without Jakob thinking she wanted to have sex with him. Then the rest of what Ull said hit her. "Wait. What? They don't touch you at all?"

"Not once turned over to our manno," he told her.

"Not even your *mother*?" Trisha found that hard to believe after what she'd learned about Isis.

"Maybe in passing," he admitted, "But not the way you do, or in the way Queen Lisa touches King Grim or her offspring."

Trisha rubbed her temples, trying to prevent the headache she felt coming on. She wanted to let this subject go, especially when she saw how much it upset Ull, but knew she couldn't. There was only so much time for her to learn what Earth females would be facing if they were going to negotiate with the Tornians in good faith. She also had to admit she wanted to know for herself.

"So how does Lisa touch Grim?" she asked quietly.

Ull's eyes narrowed, and he tried to decide if she was serious. Deciding she was, he finally said, "The way you have touched your tío and me."

"And your females don't do that outside of Joining?" She was finding that hard to believe. All beings need to be touched.

"No, they don't allow such intimacy," he growled. "It has also become known that the King and Queen rest together."

When his gaze sharpened on her, she realized he was waiting for her to be shocked by this. "Rest?" she questioned carefully. "You mean they sleep together? At night?"

"Yes," he nodded.

"I take it that's uncommon for Tornians too?" Trisha asked, and the headache she thought she'd staved off returned.

"It was until it became known that the Emperor and Empress also rested together," he told her.

"What about Abby and Ynyr?"

"They also share the Lord's Chamber, as my mother and manno now do." He grimaced as if he found that distasteful.

"I see." It seemed that was something humans and Tornians did have in common. Children didn't like to think about their parents having sex. "So, where did your mother rest before?"

"On her level, of course," Ull told her as if it should be obvious, but when she just continued to stare at him, he continued in a disgruntled tone. "A female always has a separate level above the male's, so she's protected. It is where she lives and rests until she chooses her next male."

"Well, that explains why your females don't let you touch them, outside of actually Joining," she muttered.

Ull gave her a confused look. "How does what I've said explain that?"

"No female wants to be *used,* Ull," she told him as if he should know that. "It doesn't matter if she's Tornian, Kaliszian, or Earthian. Why should they trust you enough to rest with you, to give you those gentle looks, touches, and kisses you seem to want, when you don't care about them and don't give them those things in return? They want to be loved and respected, just as much as you do, Ull."

"So, you aren't interested in Joining with me," Ull growled, finding that hurt, for a moment he'd thought…

'Thought what?' that dark voice whispered in his mind. *'That she would want to Join with one such as you? You are an unfit, unworthy male.'*

Trisha watched as Ull clenched his fists, his eyes darkening, becoming harder as if it were someone else looking at her, and for the first time, she wondered if she was safe with him.

"I'm not saying that," she told him carefully. "What I *am* saying is that Earth females touch other people all the time, both male and female, and it doesn't necessarily indicate that they want to Join with someone. It's something you and your males need to understand."

"Then what does it indicate?" Ull demanded, slowly standing, and while she saw him unclench his fists, the darkness still lingered in his eyes.

"It depends on who is touching who." She knew that was a hazy answer, so she expanded on it. "Touch...contact between humans is important."

"But it *can* indicate someone is willing to Join," he pressed.

"Well yes," she admitted, "but it usually takes more than a casual touch."

"You are referring to kissing."

Trisha looked at Ull in surprise. She'd assumed that since Tornians rarely touched that they didn't kiss either. "Well, yes, kissing on the lips usually means a closer, more intimate relationship."

"We were never taught kissing," he grumbled.

Trisha wasn't sure what to say to that. While she'd thought Lisa had included a great deal in the educator, there seemed to be more she'd left out. Was that on purpose? If so, why? How was she even supposed to ask, but it seemed her mind knew what it wanted to know, and her mouth followed.

"So, what *were* you taught?" she found herself asking.

"How to pleasure a female until she finds her release, of course," he gave her an arrogant look. "I am very good at it."

What Ull was saying had Trisha's heart starting to beat faster. Was he saying that Tornian males *always* went down on a female? That they made sure she had an orgasm before he had sex with her? Shit, she knew quite a few women who would eagerly Join with a Tornian if that was the case, as most men only thought of their own pleasure. Maybe Earth males needed to go to the same school Tornian males did. That thought had her frowning. "How are you taught to pleasure a female if you have so few of them?"

"With the Serai," he told her.

"Serai?" she questioned.

"They are animated sand creatures made on the planet, Creata. They…" he paused, giving her a hesitant look.

"Go on." She nodded encouragingly.

"They train a male on how to pleasure a female so her channel can become slick enough with her release so a male can then find his own," he told her.

Trisha just looked at him and tried to get the image out of her head of Ull going down on something like a blowup doll that responded like a woman, then fucking her. It was every teenage boy's fantasy, and yet it somehow still seemed so cold to her.

"You… enjoy this?" She was finally able to ask.

"It is the only way most Tornian males experience Joining unless they are willing to go to a Pleasure House."

The disgust in Ull's voice revealed to her what a Pleasure House was, and Trisha was sure few females ever found pleasure in them. "So, you've never been to one."

"A Pleasure House?" His eyes widened at her question. "No! It is unworthy of a Warrior to Join with a female when he knows she can't give him fit offspring."

Trisha felt the warmth that had begun to spread through her, as Ull denounced those who raped women, disappear as he expressed his reason why.

"What do you mean 'fit' offspring," she asked, hoping it didn't mean what she thought it did.

"Offspring that can become fit and worthy Warriors, of course," Ull told her. "Before the Great Infection, we were able to create such offspring with both the Kaliszians and Ganglians. Now such offspring are weak or deformed when presented, and therefore unworthy of being Tornian."

"So, it's not that the females aren't there willingly or raped," she let him hear the disgust and condemnation in her voice, "that stops you from going to a Pleasure House. It's the fact that they can't give you fit offspring."

"That is the reason for Joining," he told her but found her accusation bothered him. His manno had taught him that a worthy male always protected a female. He hadn't distinguished between Tornian and non-Tornian females, his manno had only said females. Shouldn't that include those in the Pleasure Houses? Had Queen Lisa been right when she'd disparaged them during the Joining Ceremony? Was their treatment of females the reason the Goddess had abandoned them?

"It's not the only reason," she fired back.

"What?" He jerked back from his confused thoughts.

"Having offspring is not the only reason for a male and female to Join," she spit out at him.

"What other reason is there?" he demanded.

"Loving and caring about the other person to start with," she told him. "Making love is an intimate act, Ull. You're trusting that the other person won't hurt you, not just physically, but mentally and emotionally. The way you describe your Joinings is more like a wham bam thank you ma'am type of thing." At his confused frown, she explained. "It's slang for when a male and female Join quickly, without any tenderness, then go their separate ways. Most likely, never seeing each other again."

"Earth males and females do this?" Ull couldn't hide his disbelief.

"Yes, when they don't care about the other person and just want the physical release. It's not about having offspring."

"They just Join for the release?" Ull was still struggling with the thought of that.

"Yes, isn't that why you use the Serai?" she demanded. "Because you enjoy it? It's not as if you can have offspring with it."

"That is truth, but…"

"But what?"

"I've just never considered that a female might want the same thing," Ull found himself admitting.

"If it's not for their enjoyment, why do you make sure they find their release before you Join with them?" Trisha questioned.

"Because it's the only way our female's channel can become slick enough, so she isn't harmed when a male Joins with her."

"It's because she isn't aroused," she told him.

"Aroused?" he asked.

"Excited about the Joining," she told him. "It's why touching and kissing are so important for Earthians. It arouses our body, a male's cock gets hard, and a female's channel gets wet."

"Without touching your pleasure nub?" Ull's eyes widened in shock.

"Pleasure nub?" It was her turn to be puzzled.

"Yes, when it's stimulated, your channel slickens, and you find your release."

"You mean my clit," she said, finally understanding what he was talking about.

"Clit," he tried the word out on his tongue and found he liked it.

"Yes," she told him, "and while stimulating it will cause a female to orgasm, other things can also excite a female enough, so her channel gets wet."

"Wet?"

"Slick enough to Join," she clarified.

"And touching and kissing do this for Earth females?" Ull's mind was racing. He hadn't realized this. Why hadn't his brother told him? Then again, why would Ynyr, with how surly Ull's attitude had been?

"Yes, and if your mother and father are now resting together, then I'd say it's the same for Tornian females." Trisha frowned as Ull just stood there for a moment. He then seemed to reach a decision, and his eyes locked with hers.

Trisha's breath began to quicken, her eyes widening when Ull slowly moved toward her with a lithe grace rarely seen in such a large male. He kept walking until their bodies were a hairs-breadth from touching. It forced her to tip her head up to maintain eye contact. "Ull?"

"You are truly beautiful, Trisha." Slowly he ran a knuckle along her jaw. "Your skin is so smooth and soft and your hair." He tucked a loose multicolored strand behind her ear. "It is unlike anything I've ever encountered in the Known Universes."

"I..." Trisha tried to make her suddenly dry throat work. While she found Ull attractive, she never believed he thought *she* was. Not after the way he'd treated her and talked to her. She was only a means to an end as far as he was concerned.

Ull closely watched every expression that crossed Trisha's face. He saw shock and disbelief, but beneath it all was fatigue.

He suddenly realized everything he'd put her through that day. How was it she hadn't complained? Not once after her initial shock, and he hadn't even thought to feed her. It had taken the Kaliszian Minister to do that. A Tornian female would never tolerate such abuse. Goddess, he was no better than Daco.

"I should leave," he murmured, yet he couldn't stop himself from cupping her jaw, or his thumb from caressing her lips. "You need to rest."

"I do," she breathed out, but she didn't move, her gaze remaining locked with Ull's.

"Before I do," Ull's voice was as low as hers, "I was wondering if I could experience my first kiss. With you."

The throat, Trisha had finally gotten to work, tightened up again. Dear God, to be Ull's first kiss. She couldn't believe how much she wanted that. You never forgot your first. It would further complicate an already extremely complicated situation, but God how she wanted to. Trisha knew she and Ull didn't have a future together. Still, she wanted him to remember her.

Slowly, she rose on her toes, bringing Ull's head down with one hand while the other rested on his chest. Tipping her head to the side, she brushed her mouth along his, surprised at how full and soft they were. Brushing them a second time, she couldn't resist lightly nipping at his lower lip. When Ull growled, she slipped her tongue inside to tease his.

“This is kissing?” Ull pulled back just far enough to whisper hoarsely. His eyes blazed into hers, his breathing ragged. Goddess, how had he not known such a thing was possible?

“One type, yes," she murmured back, her breathing just as ragged as she stared up at him.

"Show me more," he demanded, closing the distance between them.

Trisha willingly opened her mouth to him, her tongue teasing his, then retreating until he became an active participant. That's when she got lost in Ull, his touch, his taste, in how he made her feel like she was the most desirable female in the world.

But it wasn't true.

Ull would have responded just as passionately to any woman that kissed him.

That realization had her ripping her mouth from his. "Ull," she gasped, "we have to stop."

"No," he growled, trying to recapture her lips.

"Yes!" She turned her head to evade his determined lips. "Please, Ull," she pleaded. "Stop!"

Ull didn't want to stop. He wanted to continue this fantastic thing called kissing. Never in his life had he gotten so much pleasure from such a small act. Instinctively he knew there was more pleasure to be experienced, but the slightest sliver of fear in Trisha's voice had every one of his protective instincts kicking in. Breathing heavily, he slowly released her and took a step back.

"Did I harm you?" he asked gruffly, his gaze taking in her flushed cheeks and swollen lips. He didn't see any injuries, but she was so much smaller than him.

"No," she quickly reassured him, "but we both got carried away."

"Is that a bad thing?" he asked.

"It is when we're supposed to be working together for the betterment of both our people."

"Can't we do both?" he questioned.

"I'm not planning on leaving Earth, Ull. Are you planning on staying?"

"No."

"Then there's no reason to start something that can't go anywhere."

Chapter Eight

Trisha stared at the reflection in the cleansing room's mirror, taking in her towel-wrapped body, wet hair, and the lines of pain bracketing her eyes. Reaching into the toiletry bag, she'd brought, she pulled out the prescription bottle she'd filled the day before.

God, had it been just yesterday? That didn't seem possible. She'd planned on taking a little time to come to terms with what she'd learned, to decide what *she* wanted to do, and *then* contact her tío. But Ull's arrival had changed all that. Now what she wanted was secondary to the millions, no billions of lives that would be affected if she couldn't find a way for Earth to work with the Tornians and Kaliszians. Her tío, if he knew, would disagree. But she also knew if the situation were reversed, he'd do just as she was.

With a heavy sigh, she opened the container and popped one of the white, inconspicuous tablets into her mouth, swallowing it down with water from the sink. After she finished drying off, she pulled on the sleeping pants and top she'd packed and headed to bed.

Tomorrow was going to be a big day, and she needed her rest. So why was she staring at the ceiling, thinking about how amazing kissing Ull had been instead of sleeping? And how she wanted to do more than kiss Ull. She wanted to be more than his first kiss. She wanted to be his first everything. She wanted him to know he was special, that he mattered. It was something everyone deserved. Unfortunately, she also knew that *she'd* never be the one doing that for Ull, and *that* hurt her heart. So, while she couldn't guarantee Ull would find what other Tornians had with Earth females, she could do everything within her power to give him a *chance.* With that in mind, her mind quieted, and sleep claimed her.

∞ ∞ ∞ ∞ ∞

Ull stared at the ceiling above his bed, wearing only resting pants, his mind in turmoil. Goddess, he hadn't wanted to leave Trisha. He wanted to learn more about how to pleasure a female. No, that was an untruth. He wanted to learn more about how to pleasure *Trisha.* He wanted to know if his kisses had *aroused* her enough for her channel to slicken without him touching her pleasure nub. If it had, that would mean Trisha was as attracted to him as he was to her. He could then claim her, Join with her, make her his Lady.

'That will never happen. Trisha won't leave her backward planet, not unless you give her no choice. Give none of them a choice. You are a Tornian Warrior, a first male, and a future Lord. Force them to defer to you! Take what you want! It's the Tornian way!'

Every one of those thoughts was truth except the last one. It *wasn't* the Tornian way to take what they wanted, not even before the Great Infection struck. Ull had learned this in his studies. It was something his manno had told him all good Lords needed to know. That the way they were now is not the way they once were.

He wouldn't be a fit or worthy Warrior if he forced Trisha to do something she already said she wouldn't do. Trisha deserved better than that. All the females did, and it would be up to him to make sure his brother warriors knew it too.

∞ ∞ ∞ ∞ ∞

"What do you mean we can't all go?" Other voices quickly echoed Craig's question.

Trisha held up her hands to quiet the group. She'd asked them to remain in the eating area after first meal the next morning. She'd known this was how they were going to react and couldn't blame them. They wanted to get back to their lives and their families.

"I'm not saying you won't all be going home, Craig." Trisha looked to the leader from the male group. They had been the ones taken over eighteen months ago, and one of them had died while in captivity. The two women with them had become True Mates to a Kaliszian General and a Commander. "I'm saying you can't all go at the same time. The shuttle only holds ten, including the pilot and co-pilot, which means we have to go down in groups." Murmurs began to fill the room, and she knew what they were all wondering. Who got to decide who went when. "As President Garcia's representative, it's up to me to choose that. What I've decided is that *you* will decide. You've had enough taken away from you, and been forced to do things you never should. The decision will be yours."

Complete silence followed her statement, and from the back of the room, Ull's respect for her grew. Trisha had instinctively known that if she picked the groups, there would be resentment. By giving them that power, bitterness went away. The President had chosen his representative well.

"There are women who have young children. They need to get back to them as quickly as possible." Vanessa, the older female who had emerged as the leader of the second group, said stepping forward.

"There are men that do too, and they have been gone a great deal longer," Craig argued back.

"No matter who goes when," Trisha broke into the conversation, "You won't be reunited with your families until everyone has been cleared and interviewed."

"What do you mean?" Ull tensed as the Earth male Craig took a step toward Trisha. "Medically cleared? We're all fine." Craig looked around the room, and Trisha saw other heads nodding.

"While I've been told you are all healthy and carry no contagious diseases," she looked at Ull for a moment. "I'm sure you understand our doctors need to confirm that before you can be released. Not only for the safety of your families but for the rest of the world."

"But we *will* be released," Craig pressed, and Trisha suddenly understood their fear. An alien species had imprisoned them. They didn't want to be imprisoned by their own.

"Of course!" She let her gaze travel over the room. "The Tornians and Kaliszians are here because they want trade agreements with Earth. All of Earth. That means that soon everyone on Earth will know about them and what happened to you. In return for the agreements, the Tornians and Kaliszians will make sure that what happened to you doesn't happen to anyone else."

"Good," one of the women muttered, causing Trisha to smile. It said something about the human condition that even after everything that had happened to them, these people's spirits survived.

"It's why you also need to be interviewed. The President needs to know everything that happened to you, your treatment, and your opinions, so he can make an informed decision in his, and ultimately, the world's dealings with the Tornians and Kaliszians."

"But, our families will be notified we're alive?" Trisha knew why Vanessa was asking. Vanessa wasn't just a wife and mother; she was also a grandmother. Her family had been a major driving force in keeping her group's disappearance in the news.

"They will be, as soon as you are cleared." Trisha could see that didn't sit well with them, but it had been the guidelines her tío had given her when he contacted her earlier that morning. "The government has all their locations and will begin bringing them to North Dakota once everyone is cleared."

"North Dakota?!" nearly everyone questioned, and Trisha understood their confusion but just shrugged.

"That's what President Garcia ordered." She didn't see any reason to expand on that. "Now, I'm going to give you some time to talk amongst yourselves, so you can decide who will be on what shuttle."

"One more question." Trisha looked at Vanessa. "How long will it be between the shuttles?"

"One or two days, as long as the doctors don't find any problems when they examine you."

∞ ∞ ∞ ∞ ∞

"You handled that very well." Ull allowed his hand to brush against Trisha's as they leaned against the wall outside the eating area. He wanted to do more, wanted to feel her body pressed against his again, but knew he couldn't. Not with the Kaliszian present.

"You did," Jakob agreed, standing across from them.

"Thank you." While Trisha didn't want to, she subtly moved her hand away from Ull's. She couldn't think clearly when he touched her. Last night had proven that, and she needed to. Millions of lives depended on her. "They deserve to have control over at least some part of their lives again. Because once all this gets out, their lives, and the lives of their families, will never be the same."

"What do you mean?" Jakob asked.

"I don't know how it is in your world, but on Earth, we have the news media. It's a group of people that gather information and report it to the rest of the world via television, the Internet, and radio. They are all going to want to interview them to find out what 'really' happened to them."

"But, they will be telling your government that." Jakob frowned at her. "Won't your Government then inform this media of what they said?"

"They will, but that information won't satisfy everyone. Some will believe the government isn't telling them everything."

"Your people don't trust what your Leaders tell them?" Ull frowned at that. While he didn't always agree with Emperor Wray's decisions, he trusted his Emperor was doing what was best for his people.

"Some do. Some don't." She looked from Ull to Jakob. "Do you always believe what your Emperors tell you? Never wonder if there's something they're leaving out?" Their silence told her everything. "So, they will be interviewed to see what if anything the government didn't tell them. It will be crazy for them for a while. There's also going to be the problem of the media wanting to interview both of you." Her gaze moved between Ull and Jakob.

Ull growled his displeasure at that, while Jakob just asked. "Why would that be a problem?"

"Because you don't speak English and they aren't going to be able to understand Tornian or Kaliszian. Someone will have to be your spokesperson to the press."

"You," Ull growled.

"Most likely, yes." She nodded in agreement. "At least until more people can use your educator or you learn Earth's languages."

"I understand there is more than one." Jakob found that surprising. While every species in the Known Universes spoke their own language, there was a central language with slight variations depending on region and status.

"Thousands," Trisha informed him. "So, it's going to take a great deal of time before everyone understands why you're here and what that means for Earth."

Ull frowned at that. While he'd known he would need to spend some time on Earth, he hadn't believed it would take very long to convince Earth's leaders they needed them. Now, Trisha had him doubting that.

"Are you the only one that can pilot the shuttle?" Trisha's change of subject pulled Ull from his thoughts.

"What?" Ull asked.

"Are you the only one that can pilot the shuttle?" she repeated.

"No." His brow lowered as he looked at her. "Why?"

"Just trying to figure out the logistics of getting our people home while you and Jakob negotiate with the President and other world leaders."

"You believe he has contacted them?" It was Jakob's turn to frown. "Before we have an agreement? My understanding is that all the people taken were from your country."

"That we know of," Trisha corrected, "and yes, while the President of the United States can decide for the citizens of *his* country, an agreement of this magnitude affects the entire world, and therefore they will need to be involved with it."

Before either male could question her further, the door to the eating area opened, and the female called Vanessa stepped out.

"I believe we've reached an agreement."

"Wonderful." Trisha pushed away from the wall and followed Vanessa back into the room.

∞ ∞ ∞ ∞ ∞

Trisha sat next to Ull as the shuttle took off from the Searcher, loaded with the first to return. The returnees decided members from each group should go, so the President could get an accurate depiction of what they were facing as the two groups had such diverging experiences.

The men had been taken as slaves and survived horrific conditions in the mine they were found in. It resulted in the death of one of them and grievous injuries to both women they'd kept hidden.

The women, while terrified, had been treated relatively well compared to what Trisha had learned had happened to the Earth woman, Kim, who was now Empress of the Tornian Empire. The Kaliszians had discovered them on a Ganglian ship before they were sold or raped.

Still, only two men were on this shuttle besides Ull. The men had decided that while their captivity had been longer, and significantly harsher than the women's, the women still needed to return first. Jakob had stayed behind to care for those remaining and keep them informed of what was happening.

Trisha watched as the darkness of space turned to the blue of Earth's atmosphere. "Will it take long to get to the NACB?"

"No." Ull pushed a few buttons on the console. "Once we received the coordinates, the Searcher altered its orbit. It will now remain over our location so shuttle transport times will be minimal."

"And the Searcher will remain undetected?"

"Of course, as will the shuttle flights." Ull frowned at her. "Why would you think anything different?"

"With the President and other Leaders in residence, there's going be a great deal more surveillance and air traffic in the area."

"They will not detect us unless we want them to." The shuttle banked slightly, and Ull looked back to the console. Reaching into his vest, he pulled out his comm unit and handed it to her. "We are close. Let your tío know."

Trisha's gaze flew back to the window and saw they were flying over the flat land of the Northern Plains. Taking the comm unit, she pressed the button Ull pointed to and waited for it to connect.

"Representative Burke?" Her tío's voice came through almost immediately.

"Mr. President," she responded in English. It was something they had discussed earlier that morning. He wanted this to be thoroughly documented and understood by all on Earth, so they needed to communicate in an Earth language as much as possible. "We'll be landing shortly."

"Inform Warrior Ull that he will need to lower his shielding before landing."

That request surprised Trisha, and she looked to Ull.

"What?" Ull growled in Tornian.

"They want you to lower the shielding before you land." Trisha was finding it easier to switch between the languages.

"I will once we are overhead."

Trisha relayed that information as Ull pressed a few buttons. In moments, she felt the forward momentum of the shuttle end, and it began to descend.

∞ ∞ ∞ ∞ ∞

Aaron's eyes widened as he got his first look at the alien shuttle as it suddenly appeared hovering overhead. It wasn't the sleek silver ship depicted in so many movies or the round 'saucer' shape so popular in the 1950s. This ship was matte black and shaped like an arrowhead, and as it descended, Aaron realized just how much more advanced than Earth these Tornians were. While he could see the shuttle, it was utterly silent. It was only when it got closer to the ground that the air began to swirl, picking up dust and ruffling the clothing and hair of everyone present.

Three landing supports extended from the bottom of the shuttle just before it reached the ground, and whatever was powering it shut off. The air quickly calmed, and Aaron knew he would have thought it had been a freak wind if the shuttle were shielded.

Looking at the security and medical staff waiting with him, he saw they were just as shocked as he was, but were having completely different reactions. The Security personnel all braced for an attack, their hands tightening on their weapons. While the medical staff seemed filled with excitement for what they were about to see and discover.

The faintest of mechanical sounds had him looking back to the shuttle to see a doorway appear halfway down the side of the shuttle, and a ramp was descending from it. Security followed the President as he moved toward the ramp, along with the aerial drones in charge of recording every moment of this historic event.

∞ ∞ ∞ ∞ ∞

"Welcome home." Trisha smiled as she rose and faced those sitting behind her. Their expressions told her they weren't sure if they believed her, and she couldn't blame them after all they'd been through. "Warrior Ull and I need to step outside first and speak with the President. Once done, I'll return, and we'll get you off this shuttle so you can take your first steps in getting your lives back."

She'd explained all this to them before but wanted to make sure they understood and didn't panic. She wasn't sure how she'd react to being this close to home and still having to wait.

She nodded to Ull, who was now standing beside her, and he moved down the aisle between the abductees until he reached where she knew the door was. He touched a panel causing the door to open and a ramp to lower. As she looked out, she saw her tío standing there and knew she was the only one that saw the relief in his eyes. Calmly, confidently, with Ull just behind her, she walked down the ramp ignoring the gasps and whispers as everyone got their first look of an 'alien.'

"Mr. President." She formally addressed her tío in English and held out her hand as she stepped off the ramp.

"Representative Burke," Aaron replied, shaking her hand then addressed Ull in Tornian. "Warrior Ull, welcome to Earth."

"Mr. President," Ull growled back then crossed an arm over his chest in the Tornian greeting between Warriors and bowed slightly.

The President returned the greeting, then switched back to English and addressed Trisha. "Medical staff is ready to assist the abductees out of the shuttle." He gestured to his left.

"They..."

Ull's deep growl cut her off, and to her shock, he pulled out his sword and pointed it at the advancing group who instantly froze. The security detail didn't. They immediately raised their weapons and aimed them at Ull.

"No!" Trisha stepped in front of Ull, flinging her arms out, trying to make herself as large as possible, as she walked backward until she pressed against Ull's chest.

"Stop!" Aaron ordered shaking off those that were trying to pull him out of the line of fire. "Stand down! That's a direct order!"

Slowly the guards complied, and Aaron switched to Tornian. "That includes you too, Warrior Ull. Sheath your sword."

"No one other than Representative Burke shall enter the shuttle until we have reached an agreement," Ull growled back.

"Why?" Aaron demanded suspiciously.

"Do you allow unknowns onto your vessels?" Ull challenged, and Trisha suddenly understood the problem.

"Sheath your sword, Ull," Trisha said as she turned to face him. "I give you my vow that no one will enter the shuttle. You can seal it once everyone is off."

"My apologies, Warrior Ull. I should have realized, and I now understand your concern." The President switched to English and repeated what he'd just said, but Ull's gaze remained fixed on Trisha.

"Please, Ull." Her eyes pleaded with his.

"Only if you vow never to do that again," he growled.

"Do what?"

"Put yourself at risk to protect me. I am a male, and therefore, expendable. You are not!"

"You're not expendable, Ull." She placed a hand over his pounding heart. "Not to me."

"Vow it, Trisha," he demanded as he covered her hand with his.

"Fine," she sighed. "I vow it. Just make sure you don't do something like that again."

"I am a Warrior. I shall always protect my Empire and those under its protection, which includes you and those on the shuttle."

"The medical team wasn't a threat to the people on the shuttle." She couldn't believe he thought they would be.

Ull said nothing as he sheathed his sword.

"Representative Burke." Aaron waited until Ull sheathed the sword before he spoke. Still, he'd been intently listening to Ull and Trisha's conversation and found himself surprised at how protective the Tornian Warrior was of his niece. It was something he would discuss with her. Once they were alone.

Ull immediately missed Trisha's touch when she turned back to her tío. "Yes, Mr. President?"

"Are the abductees able to leave the shuttle on their own?"

"Yes." With that, she turned, and after giving Ull one last look, walked back up the ramp.

∞ ∞ ∞ ∞ ∞

If he could have, Ull would have followed Trisha up the ramp, tossed everyone else out, and taken Trisha back to the Searcher. His heart had nearly stopped beating when she put herself between him and the weapons the Earthian warriors had pointed at him. Seeing all those red targeting spots on her, he'd nearly lost his Warrior's control. Because of it, he'd nearly impaled her on his sword as she backed up. Only at the last minute had he repositioned his weapon so he could still defend them.

When she'd turned pleading eyes to him and willingly touched him in front of others, when she'd claimed that *he* wasn't expendable, he would have given her the entire universe. But he would never allow her to put herself in harm's way again. For anyone. She was too important, and not just because of what she could do for his people. That was what gave him the strength to not bend to her beseeching look. Or to follow her up that ramp.

Chapter Nine

"Representative Burke, you and Warrior Ull will follow me."

Trisha had just finished settling the abductees in the medical center of the NACB. It had been a little bumpy at first. The abductees had gotten used to speaking in either Kaliszian or Tornian. So, when the doctors had started questioning them in English, they'd struggled to answer them. It had the medical staff exchanging worried looks until Trisha had stepped in. She calmly reassured the doctors that nothing was wrong, and the abductees just needed to think to speak English again consciously, and they would. After that, things moved smoother, and the doctors began to compare the abductees' current health to their medical history.

Ull didn't understand what was said but took it all in without saying a word. Trisha wondered how this deep repair unit he talked about compared to Earth's medical procedures. She'd have to ask him, and when they were alone, she would. Right now, she needed to follow the President's directions.

"Of course, Mr. President." She gestured to Ull with her head, and he began walking beside her as she followed the President, his security detail closing in behind them.

Traveling through the building, Trisha was surprised at its size. It made sense if the countries of North America were going to be coming together because their leaders and support staff would need the room. But how had her tío been able to have it built without the media finding out and reporting it? After several more minutes, they arrived at a massive set of doors opened by more armed guards.

Ull's trained gaze quickly took in everything as he entered the room. Where every exit was, the armed guards defending each one, and how those individuals of most importance sat higher than where they were on the floor. It was like the chamber where the Assembly of Lords met but wasn't as intimidating. He realized that it was intentional. While there were warriors on Earth, its society wasn't built around them as the Tornian world was.

As they walked to the center of the room, the President gestured to two chairs. Between the chairs was a small table with several clear bottles and a small container.

"Warrior Ull. Representative Burke. You will sit here." He picked up the container and handed it to Trisha. "This will allow you to understand everyone." With that, he moved to where a guard had opened a door, then climbed the steps leading to his seat.

Trisha let her gaze travel around the horseshoe-shaped room taking in all those present. While she was no expert on all the world's leaders, because of Tío's position, she did recognize those elected to the new World Council, and they were all here. It was the reason for the earbud translator her tío had handed her.

"Is there a problem, Trisha?" Ull spoke quietly, so only she heard. If something concerned her, they would leave. He would not have her in harm's way.

"No." She turned to give him a small reassuring smile. "I was just surprised at the number of leaders here. I thought it would be just those from North America."

"This concerns you?"

"No. It's a good thing. It means decisions will be quickly made." Under her breath, she muttered. "Hopefully."

"Representative Burke." She looked up to where Tío sat. "Is there a problem?"

"No, Mr. President."

"Then would you and Warrior Ull please take your seats so we can begin."

Trisha nodded then translated for Ull, but before she could pull out her chair, Ull did it for her.

"Thank you," she told him, then opening the small case, pulled out the earbud, and placed it in her ear.

"What is that?" Ull growled.

"It allows me to understand all the languages that will be spoken here today," she reassured him.

"It will not harm you?"

"Of course not. My tío would never allow that." With a grunt, Ull sat.

∞ ∞ ∞ ∞ ∞

Aaron waited until Ull sat before standing to address the world leaders. "Esteemed colleagues. Thank you for responding so quickly to my request, especially as I could give you no specifics. You now understand why. Seated before you is Warrior Ull, a male that is obviously from another species, from another universe altogether, and while he made contact with the United States first, his reason for being here affects everyone on the planet."

Trisha expected there to be an outburst as she translated for Ull, and her tío paused, but she'd underestimated those gathered. They were the leaders of their Councils and countries for a reason.

"I know you all have questions, but first, let me make the proper introductions." He waited for Trisha to finish translating before continuing. "Chancellor Smyth representing the European Council." He gestured to the woman sitting the furthest away from him on the right. "Chancellor Abara representing the African Council." This male was seated next to Chancellor Smyth. "President Ochoa of Mexico." Aaron gestured to the man sitting closest to him then looked to a woman sitting to his left. "Prime Minister Gagnon of Canada. Beside her is Chancellor Nguyen of the Asian Council, and next to him is Chancellor Khatri from the Australian Council." He waited for Ull to acknowledge each leader. "Warrior Ull is the representative from the Tornian Empire."

"How is it you speak his language?" Chancellor Smyth questioned. "How long have you known of his existence, and who is the woman beside him?"

"I will get to how I now speak Tornian, but let me reassure you that I only became aware of Warrior Ull's existence two days ago through my niece, Representative Burke, who is translating our languages for him." He gestured to Trisha, sitting beside Ull.

"But how…"

"Perhaps it would be best if I explained?" Trisha interrupted the Australian Chancellor.

"Please," Chancellor Khatri encouraged.

As Trisha went to rise, Ull put a restraining hand on her leg. "What are you doing?"

"They want to know why you contacted us…me, first. I need to explain."

"You will not leave my side."

Trisha frowned at that but sat back down. If it made Ull more comfortable for her to remain at his side, then so be it. Looking back to Chancellor Khatri, she began.

"The reason Warrior Ull contacted me first is that approximately six months ago, a friend of mine, Lisa Miller, went missing along with her two daughters, Carly and Miki." She decided to leave out how it had been her fault, as she'd left the girls alone with their Uncle Peter. "I contacted my tío, or uncle as some of you call them, to see if he could help find them after the local authorities could find no trace." She let her gaze rest on her tío for a moment before continuing. "He couldn't. Two days ago, Lisa contacted me through Warrior Ull. She and her girls were taken from Earth and are now on Luda, a planet in the Tornian Empire, where they are happy and perfectly fine."

"How did they get there?" Chancellor Nguyen asked in Mandarin.

Ull's quiet, 'Tell them,' had Trisha looking at him in shock.

"You can understand Mandarin?" she demanded back in Tornian.

"I can understand every language you do if you and I are physically connected."

"Physically connected?" When she frowned, the hand he hadn't removed from her leg squeezed slightly. "Oh. Why didn't you tell me this earlier?"

"It didn't come up."

"Representative Burke?"

"I'm sorry." She looked back at Chancellor Nguyen. "Warrior Ull was inquiring about what you asked. If you would allow me to give you some background first, I will then explain how Lisa and the girls got to Luda." When the Chancellor nodded, she continued. "There are many different species in the universe, but the primary ones concerning us today are the Ganglians, the Kaliszians, and the Tornians. Each in their own way is on the brink of extinction."

"Why?" One of the leaders asked.

"Because of something they call the Great Infection." That comment had everyone surging to their feet and quickly backing away from Trisha and Ull.

"Calm down!" Aaron ordered over the melee. "It's not that kind of infection! Do you think I would have asked you to come here if it was?!"

"Then what is it?" Chancellor Abara demanded as slowly everyone began to settle back into their seats.

Trisha took back control of the room. "It's something that was caused by the actions of three males, one from each of the three species I just mentioned, over five hundred years ago. And while it has affected each species differently, it is also what has brought all of them to Earth."

"Explain," Prime Minister Gagnon demanded.

Trisha went on to explain how the Ganglians were now slavers who could only experience sexual release while inflicting pain. The Kaliszians could no longer produce enough food to feed their people. And Tornian males outnumbered their females two hundred to one.

"The Tornians knew nothing about Earth until approximately fifteen months ago when another Earth woman, by the name of Kim Teel, was discovered on a Ganglian ship by the Tornian Emperor, Wray Vasteri. Severely abused and barely alive, he not only saved her, but he fell in love with her and made her his Empress." Gasps were heard throughout the chamber. "That would have been the end of it, but when Kim became pregnant, all hell broke loose in the Tornian Empire."

"So that's why they're here. For our women." President Ochoa vocalized what all the other leaders were thinking.

"Yes." Trisha refused to lie to her people. The only way this was going to work was if everyone was upfront and honest. Or spoke truth as the Tornians would say. "They need our women, but only those willing to Join with a Tornian, and yes, that's what they call sex… Joining. But before you get fixated on that, there's more you need to know."

"And what's that?"

"There was another group taken before Kim. They, too, were taken by the Ganglians but were sold into slavery. The Kaliszians discovered them on one of their planets where another species had them mining illegally."

"Where are these people?"

"Two of them are in medical while the rest are still on the Tornian ship in space with Kaliszian Minister Ruskin. Minister Jakob Ruskin was charged with their care by his Emperor, Liron Kalinin. Once they are all back on Earth, Minister Ruskin will appear before you to negotiate the agreement the Kaliszians wish to make with Earth."

"To feed their people," Chancellor Khatri spoke, showing her understanding of what was happening.

"Yes," Trisha nodded.

"How does entering into an agreement with either of them benefit Earth?" Chancellor Smyth questioned.

"The Tornians and Kaliszians will, in exchange for us assisting them, protect Earth from the Ganglians who are stealing, abusing, and enslaving our people."

"How do we even know these 'Ganglians' exist?" Chancellor Abara questioned.

"I believe once you speak with the abductees, you'll have no doubt. And before you say anything else, there is a third group that the Kaliszians discovered in their Empire and this one I know you have all heard of. It is the women that went missing from the Global Petroleum Corporation."

A shocked silence filled the room. A worldwide search had been conducted as Global Petroleum was an international corporation, and the missing women hadn't just been from the United States.

"They were found in the Kaliszian Empire?" Chancellor Abara's hushed query was easily heard.

"Yes, on a Ganglian ship that planned on selling them on the black market to Kaliszian males who are desperate to continue their bloodline."

"Emperor Vasteri is searching for those unworthy males, and once they are found, they will be punished." Ull had trusted Trisha would know the best way to explain things to her leaders but now felt he needed to speak, so they knew this was unacceptable to the Tornian Emperor. "A female able to give a Tornian male fit and worthy offspring is the most valuable thing in the Tornian Empire. They are cherished and protected. Anyone who harms one is ended."

Trisha translated and watched the shock and disbelief that crossed the leaders' faces.

"That still doesn't mean we should offer up our women in exchange for this so-called protection. How do we know you aren't the ones taking the females?" President Ochoa had a good point, and Trisha wasn't sure how to address the fact that the Tornians *had* taken Earth females and had no intention of returning them, but she also knew that the Earth needed their protection. Not only from the Ganglians but from the Regulians, who they hadn't even addressed yet.

"President Ochoa…" Aaron began, only to pause when Ull reached inside his jacket as a strange beeping sound filled the room.

"What is it, Veron?" Ull growled.

"We've discovered a Ganglian ship orbiting Earth, and they have a shuttle heading toward the surface."

"How in the name of the Goddess did you not detect them approaching?!" Ull's eyes shot to Trish at her shocked gasp.

"Our current location isn't optimal for monitoring the entirety of space," Veron fired back.

Ull growled his displeasure but knew this wasn't Veron's fault. They would need at least four ships encircling the planet along with multiple deep space satellites before the Earth would be adequately protected. But that couldn't happen until they reached an agreement with Earth. "Can you calculate their destination?"

"Yes. If they continue on their current course, they will land in the mountains to the west and north of you."

"How long until they reach the surface?"

"Twenty-five minutes."

"What's happened?" Aaron demanded in Tornian.

"There is a Ganglian ship orbiting this planet. They've launched a shuttle, and it's heading toward the surface."

Trisha translated for the rest of the assembly as the President contacted the head of NACB security, putting it on speaker. "Admiral, are our radars picking up any incoming spacecraft?"

The President had thoroughly briefed Admiral McDonald before Ull's arrival. Aaron had known the man hadn't wholly believed his Commander-in-Chief, but seeing Ull and his ship suddenly appear had changed that. "Spacecraft?"

"Yes, Warrior Ull has been notified there is a hostile ship heading toward Earth."

"One moment, sir."

"You won't detect it," Ull told the President.

"Why?"

"Because while Ganglian ships have only the most rudimentary of shielding, it will still be undetectable with your primitive systems."

"But you can?"

"Yes, and once they are close enough, you will be able to see them with the naked eye."

"Sir, there are no unknowns on any radar." Admiral McDonald's confirmation had Aaron frowning.

"Keep scanning, Admiral." Aaron's gaze remained locked with Ull. "Can you track them, Warrior Ull?"

"Yes, President Garcia. If they maintain their current course, they will be landing in the mountains to the northwest of here."

"In my country?" The Canadian Prime Minister demanded.

"Unknown at this time," Ull responded, understanding the female leader because his hand was still on Trisha's leg.

"How long until you know for sure?" Trisha asked.

"Veron, are they maintaining course?" Ull demanded knowing the Captain was listening.

"Yes, they're currently heading toward you."

"Transmit the coordinates to the shuttle."

"Ull, what are you doing?" Trisha demanded placing a hand on his arm when Ull rose. She'd translated everything between Ull and Veron, but she didn't know what Ull was planning.

"What I was trained to do. I will not allow them to abduct any more of your people. To do that, I need to intercept the Ganglians."

"But..."

"Warrior Ull, you will take members from the Earth's military with you."

"That won't be necessary, President Garcia."

"It wasn't a request, Warrior Ull." The power in the President's voice was undeniable. "Our men need to know what we are facing."

"I agree." The Canadian Prime Minister said after Trisha translated the conversation. "We cannot fight what we do not know."

"But, they won't be able to understand Warrior Ull." Trisha reminded them.

"Then you will just have to go with them," the Asian Chancellor told her.

"No!" Ull and Aaron growled together.

Trisha understood their concern, and if she were honest with herself, she didn't want to go. From what the abductees had told her, these Ganglians were genuinely terrifying. But there was no way Ull would be able to communicate with anyone without her there.

"I'll go," she said over the rising voices.

"You will not," Ull growled down angrily at her.

Trisha just ignored him and looked to her tío. "May I recommend that whoever you send speak English? It would allow me to translate more expediently."

Aaron wanted to argue that it was too dangerous for her to go. She was his niece, and he'd promised his sister he would always protect her. But as the President of the United States, he knew the only way this would work was if Trisha went with them.

"Are there any objections that those going come from the NACB security force?" Aaron asked, looking around the room when no one protested he looked back to Trisha. "Then so be it. Admiral McDonald."

"Yes, Mr. President." McDonald instantly responded as the President had left the line open.

"Gather…" Aaron switched to Tornian to ask Ull. "How many men can you take?"

Ull angrily glared at the President. How could this male allow any female, let alone one under his protection, get anywhere near a Ganglian? Didn't he understand how vicious they were or how precious Trisha was? If he didn't, Ull did, so *he* would make sure Trisha was protected.

"Warrior Ull?"

"Eight," Ull bit out.

"Don't you need more than that?"

"It is the number the shuttle will hold." Ull wasn't going to reveal that with the humans' smaller size, the shuttle could hold more. Still, with their inability to directly communicate, these Earthians never having encountered a Ganglian before, and Trisha being there, he wasn't going to allow more than that. When he saw the President open his mouth again, Ull snapped out. "If you wish to prevent the Ganglians from abducting more of your people, we need to leave immediately." With that, Ull spun on his heel and headed for the door.

"Admiral McDonald, send your best eight men to the Tornian shuttle immediately. Fully armed. They will receive and follow the orders from Warrior Ull once they are in the air."

"Yes, sir."

Trisha and her tío shared one last look before she turned and ran to catch up with Ull.

∞ ∞ ∞ ∞ ∞

Trisha didn't say a word as she followed Ull, partly because she didn't know what to say and partly because she was becoming breathless with how quickly they were moving. When they were back in the open area where they'd landed the shuttle, she saw eight soldiers already there.

They were all dressed in the black high impact body armor all elite soldiers wore, including the helmets that conformed around their necks protecting that vulnerable area. The dark reflective visors that generally covered their faces were retracted, and each carried an armada of weapons, the largest being the automatic rifle in their hands.

One of the men stepped forward as they approached. "Captain Anderson, reporting as ordered."

Trisha translated then asked. "Do you know why you are here?"

"No." While he remained still, the Captain's gaze followed Ull as he walked up to the shuttle. He couldn't see what the alien did, but whatever it was caused the ramp to lower and the hatch to open. "We were told Warrior Ull would inform us."

Ull just grunted and moved up the ramp as Trisha translated.

"I'm sure he will once we are on the shuttle," Trisha told them quickly, moving up the ramp. Once inside, she found Ull already at the controls. "You need to talk to them, Ull. They're here to help you."

"I don't need help."

"Then why the hell did you even bother coming to Earth?!" she demanded, running an exasperated hand through her hair.

Ull gave her a confused look. "You know why."

"Because you need us, and we need you."

Ull didn't like it put that way. After all, Tornians were the most feared warriors in the Known Universes, but he couldn't deny her words were truth. "Truth."

"Then you must know you have to work with *everyone* on Earth, including our men, because there's going to be a great deal of outrage when they learn what you want in return for your assistance *and* that you've already taken some of our females… just like the Ganglians did."

Ull growled his displeasure at what she was saying, but again it was truth.

"You need to start building bridges, Ull. So why not start now?"

"Build bridges?"

"It's a reference to attempting to span the gap between you and the men of Earth," she explained.

Ull realized this was what he'd been sent to Earth to do. To 'span the gap' as Trisha called it, and he suddenly realized it something he'd been trained to do his whole life. After all, he was the first male to a Lord, and a great deal of a Lord's job was resolving disputes. It was time he started acting like one. Swiveling his seat around, he found the eight Earth soldiers silently watching him.

"I am the Tornian Warrior, Ull Rigel, first male of Oryon and Isis Rigel, Lord and Lady of the Planet Betelgeuse." Ull wasn't sure why he'd included his mother in that statement, but it had just come out, and it felt right to acknowledge her. "A species called Ganglians are on their way down to the surface of your planet to abduct females. We will stop them. Know this, the Ganglians are larger than you, faster than you, and stronger than you. They also show no mercy and thrive on inflicting as much pain as possible. When you see one, end it. Do not hesitate. For I tell you truth, that it will not."

Ull let his gaze travel over each male, and while he saw several eyes widened slightly; no other expression showed.

"How do we recognize these… Ganglians?" Anderson calmly questioned.

"They are large. Almost as tall and wide as me." Ull had positioned his knee, so it touched Trisha's when she'd turned her seat so he could directly understand what the Earth males were saying. "They secrete an offensive odor and are covered in long filthy hair."

"They look like Big Foot," Trisha told them.

"Big Foot?" one of the male's huffed.

"I know it sounds crazy." Trisha's eyes went to the soldier that had spoken. "But that has consistently been what the abductees have said. They look like Big Foot, and they stink to high heaven."

A beeping from the consul had Ull turning back to find Veron had sent the flight path of the Ganglian shuttle. "Strap into your seats," Ull growled as his fingers moved over the controls starting the shuttle's engines. "The Ganglians will be landing in ten minutes."

"Where?" Captain Anderson demanded as he took the seat closest to Ull.

Ull touched a few buttons and a holographic projection of where they were and where they were going.

"We'll never get there in time to intercept!"

"No, but we won't be that far behind." Ull didn't see the disbelieving look Anderson gave him, but Trisha did.

"Tornian ships travel a great deal faster than ours, Captain."

"But that's over eight hundred miles away in Canada." Anderson's next words were cut off as he was pressed back into his seat as the shuttle surged forward. After several moments, the pressure eased, and leaning forward, he was astonished to see how fast the land beneath them was passing by, and before he knew it, the Canadian Rockies were rising before them.

"Are these Ganglians able to travel this fast?" he asked, looking to Ull.

"No, although by your standards, they are extremely fast."

Anderson frowned, his gaze going to Trisha when Ull responded without Trisha translating his question. "I thought you were here because he couldn't understand English."

"He can't," Trisha told him then gestured to where her and Ull's knees touched. "I have to translate for him unless we're physically connected."

"You can't be planning to go as we hunt the Ganglians!"

"Of course not," she denied before Ull could say anything. "I'll be staying in the shuttle. Warrior Ull will relay through me what he wants you to do." At least that's what she assumed. Looking at Ull, she saw him nod.

"Tell them we will arrive in three minutes." After she did, he continued. "Ganglians have long claws on both their hands and their feet, and they won't hesitate to use them to eviscerate you. Stay out of their reach. The easiest way to kill one is to cut off its head, but as none of you carry a sword," he absently reached back to touch the hilt of his resting against his spine. "I would recommend you bring them down by shooting them multiple times in the chest then blow their heads off."

Trisha paled at the violence of Ull's words as he landed the shuttle, but she translated what he said to Anderson and saw his men nod. God, what type of men readily accepted the use of such violence and what type of male was Ull to be able to suggest it.

Chapter Ten

As they approached the clearing where the Ganglians had landed, Ull slowed the shuttle. The Ganglians had chosen well. This was a secluded area, but his instruments told him it wasn't that far away from a group of humans. He didn't know what they were doing this far out, but he knew they were what attracted the Ganglians to the area.

Trisha took in the Ganglian shuttle as Ull landed on the opposite side of the clearing. It was the same shape and matte black color as the one she was riding in, but that was where the resemblance ended. The Ganglian shuttle was covered in dents and scratches like the ones on a child's abused dump truck. The thought of traveling through space in something that damaged scared the crap out of her.

"Are there Ganglians in there?" She found herself almost whispering when she saw the open hatch and extended ramp.

"No. They have already left." Ull pulled up a different holographic map showing multiple dots in two distinct colors. "These are the Ganglians." He pointed to six black dots that were moving parallel to one another. "And these are your people." He pointed to a cluster of several dozen red dots that seemed to be stationary.

"It's a campsite," Anderson told him, standing up to take a closer look.

"Campsite?" Ull gave him a questioning look.

"Yes. It's where a group of people sleep and eat while they hike the trails and explore the area around them."

"Males *and* females?" Ull couldn't believe a male would risk his female that way.

"And most likely children. Many families like to camp together. Can your equipment differentiate any of that?" Anderson looked to Ull.

"No, just the number of beings."

Anderson turned back to his men. "There are several dozen civilians in the area, some of whom may be children. Fire accordingly." The soldiers grunted their understanding.

Ull opened a comm to the Searcher. "Veron."

"Here."

"I'll be leaving this comm open. Representative Burke will remain on the shuttle. If the unthinkable were to occur, you will remote pilot her to safety."

"Ull!" Trisha looked at him in shock

"The Ganglians will never touch you, Trisha."

"What's wrong?" Anderson demanded, his gaze moving from Ull to Trisha.

"I..."

"I need one of the Captain's communications devices," Ull interrupted. "I need to sync it to the shuttles comm center."

Anderson removed his own and handed it to Ull once Trisha translated, and they both watched as Ull put it on a glowing circle. Several moments later, a beep sounded, and Ull handed the device back.

"You will now be able to relay my instructions to them," Ull told her. "And relay any questions they have to me. All you need to do is listen then press this," he pointed to a button, "to communicate with me and this one with them." He pointed to another switch.

Trisha nodded her understanding, and after Ull put in his own Tornian earpiece, they tested the connections and found they worked.

"I will be sealing you in the shuttle, and it will remain shielded," Ull told her as he rose then addressed the men standing behind him. "Once we exit the shuttle, we need to move quickly to intercept the Ganglians before they reach your citizens. Remember what I said about engaging a Ganglian."

Ull waited for every male to acknowledge his order once Trisha translated, then moved to the door and unsealed it. With one last look at Trisha, he turned and went to end the immediate threat against her and her people.

∞ ∞ ∞ ∞ ∞

Trisha had to bite her lip to stop from calling Ull back to the shuttle as the door slid closed. God knew she hadn't wanted to be here, but she definitely didn't want to be here alone. What had she been thinking agreeing to come? She should have listened to Ull.

As if feeling her panic, Ull's calm deep voice came through the comm. "Trisha."

"Yes, I'm here," she quickly responded.

Ull's jaw clenched at the anxiety he heard in her voice. Goddess, while he knew she was safe inside the shuttle, he wished he were there with her. Somehow she'd come to be very important to him and not because his people needed her to help them reach an agreement.

"How far are we from the Ganglians?" He forced his mind to remain focused on the mission. The sooner he completed it, the sooner he could get back to her.

Knowing he couldn't see it, she still gave the comm an exasperated look. "How would I know that?"

"Look at the map I left up. How many gridlines are there between the Ganglians and us?"

Looking at the holographic map, she suddenly realized that faint lines were running horizontally and vertically on it. She also saw the eight red dots along with the green one leading them, two lines behind the six black dots. "They're two grid lines ahead of you."

"Good, then we're closing on them."

Trisha didn't think that was such a good thing. Not after the way Ull had described the way Ganglians liked to kill. But then she was a lawyer, not a warrior.

Ull used a hand signal to direct Anderson's men to spread out to his left and right before he remembered they wouldn't understand. But to his surprise, they did, and he began to realize these Earth warriors weren't that different than Tornian warriors. It had him wondering what else they might have in common.

Trisha's eyes remained glued to the screen as their group gained ground on the Ganglians. Suddenly one of the Ganglians reversed direction. Frantically pushing both buttons, she told them. "One of them has turned around. He's heading back your way. Fast!"

Ull had no more than heard Trisha's warning when he smelled the Ganglian moving toward them. Ull wasn't sure who was more surprised when the Ganglian burst out of the underbrush, the Earth warrior third down on Ull's right, or the Ganglian who'd skidded to a halt. But it was the Ganglian that recovered first. With a vicious snarl that alerted the other Ganglians there was trouble, he attacked the much smaller Earth male.

Even as the Ganglian attacked, Ull was drawing his sword and charging to intercept, but even with his Tornian speed, he wasn't in time. The Ganglian swiped his claws across the male's chest, penetrating the body armor the Earthian wore as the warrior fired his weapon. The blasts drove the Ganglian back far enough for Ull to detach its head from its body.

"Gallagher!" Anderson was immediately at his fallen man's side, quickly assessing the amount of blood covering his shredded body armor. How the fuck had the Ganglian been able to do that? They were wearing the most advanced body armor on the planet. Bullets couldn't penetrate it, and it could absorb and dissipate even the most powerful of energy blasts. And yet this Ganglian had been able to destroy it with just its claws.

"You need to get him back to the shuttle," Ull growled, knowing Trisha would translate. "He needs the repair unit."

"Jones. McGuire." Anderson motioned to the two warriors closest to him. They immediately knelt next to their fallen comrade. One taking his legs the other his arms.

Trisha's eyes were glued to the map in front of her. While she couldn't see what was actually happening, she could visualize it from Ull's enraged growl, the snarl of the Ganglian, someone's cry of pain, and the distinctive sound of a pulse rifle firing. God, who was hurt?! When Anderson named one of his men, her heart began to beat again, at least until she realized all the other black dots were heading Ull's way. "Ull, the rest of them are heading your way now."

"Get him back to the shuttle," Ull growled at Anderson's men then turned to face the oncoming assault. It didn't take long.

Anderson and his remaining men took up defensive positions on either side of Ull, Trisha having informed them of the incoming attack. "Suppressive fire!"

Ull watched as the Earthians' weapons struck the Ganglians. They were good, targeting the Ganglians heads and chests as he'd instructed them, and while it stunned and slowed the Ganglians down, it didn't stop them. Instead, the Ganglians pulled their own blasters and began to fire. Ull moved forward, swing his sword, deflecting the Ganglian blasts until he was close enough to one to remove his blaster from his hand by slicing it off. It didn't stop the Ganglian as it thrived on pain. Instead, it slashed at Ull with the claws he still had. Ull ducked, then spinning around sliced through the Ganglian's thick neck muscles with one stroke removing its head from his body. Ull then quickly moved on to the next Ganglian.

Anderson winced as he took a blaster strike. Damn it, that wasn't supposed to penetrate his armor like that. Looking to his men, he saw Deen fall when simultaneous blasts hit him. Firing rapidly at the Ganglian, he moved to the down man, helping him to his feet. "Ull!"

"Go!" Ull ordered as he began attacking the Ganglian from behind. "Get back to the shuttle." While these warriors were good, their weapons weren't powerful enough to bring down a Ganglian, not even with multiple head and body shots. Moving to the next Ganglian, Ull quickly separated him from his head too.

Trisha's gaze kept moving from the clearing outside the shuttle to the map. She could see all eight of the red dots getting closer, but they still hadn't re-entered the clearing yet. She could also see that one by one, the black dots disappeared whenever Ull's green dot got near them until there was only one left.

Suddenly Anderson and his men burst into the clearing. Two were carrying another by his arms and legs, while a third was helping another, who was bent over at the waist and limping.

"Veron!" she cried out, knowing Ull had left the channel open.

"What is it, Trisha?" Veron immediately responded.

"I need you to open the shuttle door."

"Not until all the Ganglians have been eliminated." Veron had been monitoring what was happening through the shuttle's systems and knew Ull would end him if Trisha were hurt.

Before Trisha could argue, her mouth dropped open when the remaining Ganglian burst into the clearing. Dear God, they really did look like the legendary Big Foot. How long had they been coming to Earth? And just how many people had they taken and killed?

Ull quickly appeared behind him, and she gagged as the Ganglian's head went bouncing across the clearing.

"Now, I will open the door. They are going to need the portable repair unit."

"The what?" she choked out; her gaze still fixed on where the head had landed.

"The portable repair unit. It's a smaller version of our deep repair units. It's in the survival bag on the floor in the cabinet next to the door. Take the bag to Ull. He'll know how to use it." Nodding, Trisha was immediately on her feet and rushing to follow Veron's directions.

∞ ∞ ∞ ∞ ∞

After eliminating the last Ganglian, Ull rushed across the clearing, frowning when the shuttle's ramp began to lower. How in the name of the Goddess had Trisha figured out how to activate it? Then he saw the survival bag she carried and realized Veron must have been communicating with her.

"Put Gallagher down. Strip off his armor," Ull ordered knowing Trisha would translate.

"We need to get him back to base," Anderson argued.

"Captain..." Blood surrounded that single gurgling word Gallagher expelled. He knew he wasn't going to make it to the base.

"He won't make it that far." McGuire set his friend down. He and Gallagher had served together for the last five years, and they'd promised each other that they'd never bullshit one another. He'd seen the extent of his friend's wounds as he'd carried him to safety.

Ull grabbed the bag from Trisha and shoved the other men aside, but once he knelt beside the wounded warrior, he couldn't figure out how to get his armor off. McGuire, who was on his knees on the other side of his friend, shoved Ull's fingers aside and quickly undid the armor.

Ull inspected the injury. It was severe, and the delay in treatment hadn't helped, especially not with how frail these Earthians seemed to be, but he knew a portable repair unit had saved the Empress when she'd been near death. He just hoped it would help this warrior too.

Setting up the unit, he activated it then looked to the warrior across from him. "Don't touch him." The male seemed to understand, clenching his hands on his thighs.

Trisha bit her lip as the device traveled over the soldier's mangled chest before a stream of light appeared. God, she hoped it helped him enough for them to get him back to their doctors. To her amazement, the bloody bubbles that had formed with each breath Gallagher took disappeared, and the streams of blood seemed to slow. After a few minutes, the gashes across Gallagher's chest were nearly closed, and the machine shut off. Ull removed the device.

"Gallagher?" McGuire leaned down to help his friend, who was struggling to sit up.

"I'm good, man," Gallagher responded, his gaze moving from the machine to Ull. "That thing is amazing. I owe you."

Ull frowned at that. While he knew Earth didn't have portable devices like this, he'd assumed they had something similar. "If I hadn't used the repair unit, what would you have done?"

"Watched me die," Gallagher told him after Trisha translated. When Ull's eyes widened in shock, he asked. "Do you not lose warriors in battle?"

"We do, but only those with the most extreme injuries."

"And this wasn't extreme?" Gallagher gestured to his still bloody chest.

"Without your armor, it would have been. It prevented the Ganglian's claws from penetrating deeply enough to shred your internal organs. If they had, not even the portable repair unit could have saved you." Ull looked back to the other warrior who was still bent over, holding his side and lifted the unit. The male nodded and began removing his armor.

∞ ∞ ∞ ∞ ∞

Trisha remained silent as Ull moved around the clearing. He'd healed the heavy bruising along Deen's stomach, and side then put the repair unit away. Now he was moving toward the decapitated Ganglian.

"What are you doing?" Anderson asked, following him.

"Do you wish your people to find the bodies? I'm sure the sound of blaster fire has drawn their attention."

Anderson realized the Tornian was right. Humans were curious people, and while some would stay back to protect the women and children, most of the men would want to investigate. If they were lucky, none of the campers' phones would have reception this far out.

"Do you know where they are?" Anderson looked to Trisha.

"Give me a minute to get inside, and I'll let you know." Trisha turned and ran back into the shuttle. In moments she reported what she saw. "Looks like half the dots are still in camp, the other half are moving our way."

"Ull. Gallagher. Deen. Remain here. Gather up the remains of the Ganglians while we intercept those campers," Anderson ordered.

"What are you going to tell them?" Trisha demanded.

"That they've stumbled on to a training exercise and need to immediately exit the area."

Trisha thought about that for a moment then nodded even though no one could see her. "That should work. We can't have anyone finding out about the Ganglians until the world leaders are ready. It will only cause mass panic." She relayed everything to Ull and, through the front viewport, saw him nod his agreement.

"Trisha, you will remain in the shuttle." Ull seemed to know she would argue even before she opened her mouth. "Captain Anderson will need you to guide him toward the humans."

With a small huff, Trisha sat back down, knowing Ull was right. Looking at the screen, she began to direct Anderson and his men.

∞ ∞ ∞ ∞ ∞

While she gave Anderson directions until they met up with the campers, Trisha watched Ull, Gallagher, and Deen repeatedly disappear into the forest only to return with either the body or head of a Ganglian. She understood the necessity of gathering up the bodies, so there was no 'evidence' of them being there, but what were they going to do with the other shuttle?

By the time all the body parts were gathered up, Anderson and his men had returned to the clearing.

"How did it go?" Ull growled, but Anderson didn't need Trisha to interpret what he asked.

"Good. We escorted them back to their camp, helped them pack up, and sent them on their way."

Trisha translated that as she exited the shuttle and headed across the clearing to the men. "What are we going to do about the Ganglian shuttle?"

"I've changed its remote frequency. Veron will now be able to pilot it." As Ull spoke, the Ganglian ramp retracted, and its engine started.

"What's going on?" Anderson demanded, and Trisha explained. "Those bodies need to be taken back to base so everyone can see what we are facing."

After a moment, Ull growled his agreement and informed Veron. He then gently took Trisha's arm and led her back to their shuttle. Even though he knew the Ganglians were dead, he wanted to get Trisha as far away from them as possible. It was still possible that there was another shuttle on the Ganglian ship. Unlikely, but possible. Which meant they could send it down to see why they'd lost contact with the other crew. Veron would notify him if that happened, but it still made him uneasy. Trisha was too precious to risk.

It only took him moments to prep the shuttle and for them to lift off. "It will take us longer to get back."

"Why?" Anderson demanded.

"The Ganglian shuttle is an old model that is not capable of the speeds this one is. It is also more difficult to remotely pilot."

The Captain nodded his understanding after Trisha translated, and they all settled in.

The ride back to base was quieter than the one out. Everyone seemed to be digesting what had happened. Trisha knew these were highly skilled, experienced soldiers. They had to be, or they never would have been given their current assignment. Still, she knew they had to be shocked at how ineffective their weapons and armor had been against the Ganglians and how effective just one Tornian had been. If it hadn't been for Ull and his sword, they'd all be dead, and they knew it. What would have happened if the Tornians had decided to attack, taking what they needed instead of coming to negotiate? The Earth owed Lisa and Kim more than they knew.

Trisha let her gaze travel over Ull, taking in his strong, stoic profile and how skillfully he piloted the shuttle. She'd only known this male for a short time, during which he'd mostly pissed her off, yet she still found him to be an honorable male, and she felt safe and protected around him. Yes, he could be gruff and surly, but he'd opened up to her on the Searcher. He'd explained how Tornian females always left their male and their offspring and how envious he was that his brother's female, Abby, had already refused to do either. Ull was a proud male, a product of his upbringing and society. It had to be hard for him being at the mercy of a species so much weaker than he was. To know the survival of his people depended on the decisions of others.

She wasn't sure the people of Earth would be so restrained if the situation were reversed.

Looking forward again, she was surprised to see they were closing in on the base. "I thought you said it would take us longer to get back."

"It did. It took an additional ten minutes."

"That's not really a *much longer*."

"It is for a Tornian."

"I need to notify the base that another shuttle will be landing, so they don't shoot it down." Anderson interrupted from behind them.

"Oh, right." Trisha undid her safety strap and rose from her seat.

"Where are you going?" Ull demanded as he put a restraining hand around her wrist.

"Captain Anderson needs to notify the base about the extra shuttle. I'm just giving him my seat so he can do that."

Ull growled his displeasure but released her wrist. "Strap into his seat. We'll be landing soon."

Nodding, she switched seats with Anderson and strapped in as Ull opened the channel for the Captain. Several minutes later, the shuttle began to descend, and she felt it touch down.

Chapter Eleven

A stunned silence filled the Council chamber as Captain Anderson replayed the raw footage that his vest recorder had captured of the Ganglian attack and the ineffectiveness of their weapons against them.

"This actually happened?" the Asian Chancellor asked, and the tone of his voice told Trisha he was hoping the answer would be no.

"It did, Chancellor Nguyen." Anderson stood at attention as he addressed him. "If it hadn't been for Warrior Ull's skill, we would all be dead, and who knows what would have happened to those families in the forest."

"Would our more powerful weapons be successful?" This question came from the European Chancellor.

"I don't know, Chancellor Smyth."

"It is something you will only learn if you strike the Ganglians before they disappear again," Ull growled as Trisha had been translating. "And right now, you can't even detect them entering your atmosphere, let alone know where they will be landing."

"Which is what you are offering," Chancellor Smyth countered.

"No, we are offering to make sure they never come near your planet again."

"In exchange for us supplying you with our women," President Ochoa fired back.

"In exchange for *willing* females that wish to Join with a Tornian warrior," Ull stressed.

"There's something else you need to see," Captain Anderson quietly but firmly interjected.

Trisha looked away as Captain Anderson advanced the recording to Sergeant Gallagher lying on the ground, revealing his horrific injuries. She only looked back when she heard the surprised gasps as they saw Gallagher's injuries miraculously heal.

"We would, of course, be willing to include repair units in our negotiations if you wish." While the Emperor hadn't authorized this, Ull knew he would be agreeable. After all, repair units were standard in the rest of the Known Universes.

"The unit that healed Sergeant Gallagher is the same deep repair unit you spoke of to me before?" President Garcia asked. "The one that all the abductees have used?"

"No, this was a portable repair unit. All warriors have one close by, especially in battle. It quickly heals life-threatening wounds until he can get to a deep repair unit, which is a much larger stationary unit."

"Would we also be able to obtain those?" Trisha's eyebrows drew together slightly at her tío's carefully spoken words. She knew his little nuances and facial tics. Something was going on here. Something important.

"I'm sure the Emperor would be agreeable."

"Very well." Aaron looked around the room then looked back to Ull after receiving nods from the other leaders and continued. "Thank you, Warrior Ull. You have given us a great deal to think about and to discuss. We'll meet again tomorrow after you've brought down the next group of abductees."

Ull nodded, but as he turned to leave, Captain Anderson stepped in front of him and extended his hand. "My men and I owe you a debt."

Ull didn't need to be able to understand the other male's words to know what he was saying. Reaching out, he clasped the male's forearm just below the elbow as he would any respected brother warrior, and he did respect this male. When he realized how outmatched they were, he hadn't panicked. He'd fought on, and because of that, they were all alive.

The difference in grips surprised Anderson for a moment, but he instantly found he liked the way this Tornian acknowledged another warrior. It seemed to be a stronger, more binding act.

∞ ∞ ∞ ∞ ∞

Ull stood outside Trisha's quarters, holding a tray full of food. It hadn't been until he'd passed the eating area that he'd realized Trisha hadn't eaten anything since they'd left the Searcher earlier that morning.

Goddess, how had he not realized that sooner? The fact that they'd either been meeting with the Earth Council or fighting Ganglians was no excuse. Trisha's well-being should always come first. No wonder she'd been so quiet during the return flight. Or that she'd chosen to go directly to her quarters instead of meeting with the other abductees first.

If she'd been a Tornian female, his lack of care and attention never would have been allowed. A Tornian female would have screamed and shouted and made him pay dearly for the oversight, most likely refusing to assist him in negotiations further. But not his Trisha, and that's how he was coming to think of her, as *his*. Could he win her affections when he hadn't been able to win those of any other female, Earthian or Tornian? She'd already willingly kissed him. Could he convince her to Join with him? To return to Betelgeuse with him and be his Lady? To be *only* his?

There was only one way to find out.

With that thought, he balanced the tray on the one hand and knocked.

∞ ∞ ∞ ∞ ∞

Trisha ignored the way her hand trembled as she took the medication her doctor had prescribed. He'd stressed she needed to take it consistently three times a day to stay ahead of her symptoms. But she'd forgotten the bottle on the Searcher. Her doctor had also stressed she needed to eat regularly and get enough sleep to slow the disease's progression. She huffed out a humorless laugh knowing neither of those things was going to happen until these negotiations were over. So, without her meds and not eating, by the time they'd flown back to the Searcher, her symptoms had returned, and it was all she could do to get to her quarters without Ull noticing.

Now she needed to lie down, let the meds take effect, then go and get something to eat. After that, she needed to meet with the other abductees to keep them informed on what was happening. Maybe then she could get some sleep.

Leaving the cleansing room, she paused when someone knocked on her door. Sighing, she straightened her shoulders and forced her facial muscles to relax. When the door slid open, her eyes widened at what she saw.

"May I come in?"

"What… oh! Yes, of course." Stepping back, she allowed Ull to enter with the large tray he carried. "What's all that?"

"Last meal," he told her moving to set the tray on the table.

"Last meal?" Trisha couldn't believe Ull had done something like this.

"Yes. I suddenly realized that with everything that occurred today, I never made sure you were cared for."

"I had breakfast… I mean, first meal."

"That was hours ago. I should never have allowed you before the Council again until you had eaten."

"Allowed?"

Ull completely missed the iciness of her tone. "Yes. You are female. Your needs will always take precedence over anyone else's, including your Council."

"There are females on the Council," she reminded him.

"They are not my concern. *You* are." Ull's gaze captured hers, his grey eyes blazing.

That gave her pause. When was the last time *her* needs had come first? Oh, she knew her mamá had put Trisha's needs first when Trisha had been growing up, but as a single mamá, there were only so many hours in the day. Her mamá had to work to finish putting herself through school. The military benefits she received after her father's death went only so far. After that, there had been the long hours she'd put in to get tenure as a professor to provide a better life for her daughter. Trisha had never felt deprived or abandoned, but she'd also always known her mamá had other responsibilities that sometimes had to take priority. Then her mamá had gotten sick, and their roles had reversed.

Now Ull seemed to be saying that for him, *she* would always come first. Was that true, or was he talking in general about *all* females?

"What did you bring?" she asked, the fantastic scent pulling her from her thoughts. Walking toward Ull, her gaze traveled over the heaping plates he'd uncovered.

"A variety as I wasn't sure what you would like. This is sicin." He pointed to a plate. "I believe it is similar to something you call chicken." He went on to describe several more meat dishes along with a variety of Tornian fruits and vegetables. Some were odd-looking, but she'd never been a picky eater.

"There's way too much here for just me. Will you join me? You haven't eaten yet, have you?"

"You wish to share a meal with me?"

Trisha didn't understand what she heard in his voice. "Yes, unless it's something not done in Tornian society… males and females eating together."

"It is rare." Ull pulled a chair out for her once he finally spoke.

"But, it does happen."

"Yes. Until recently, it was mostly between males and females before they Join, but now families are beginning to share meals." Ull moved around the table, taking the seat across from her. He wanted to see her reaction to what he said next. "I've even heard that King Grim and his family now share a weekly meal with his warriors. It is something that my brother and his Lady are also doing, along with my parents."

"On Earth, it's common for families to eat meals together and sometimes with guests." Just then, her stomach loudly growled, and she gave him a sheepish look. "I guess we'd better eat. What should I try first?"

"You would allow me to choose?"

"In this? Yes, after all, this is food from your world."

Slowly, Ull began filling a plate with all his favorites, reminding her of what they were and how they tasted as he did. There were tender slices of sicin, several thick, crispy pieces of rashtar, tart endary berries, and little bits of bread drizzled with hunaja.

"Thank you," she said, taking the plate from him but didn't begin to eat.

"Why aren't you eating?"

"I'm just waiting for you to fill a plate."

Ull wondered if this female would ever stop surprising him. She was hungry, yet she still insisted on waiting until he filled *his* plate before eating. Quickly he filled his plate so she would begin to eat.

The sounds of eating filled the room for next several minutes. Ull kept a close eye on what Trisha seemed to enjoy most and put more of it on her plate. When he attempted to give her even more, she waved him off, then leaned back in her chair and rubbed her stomach.

"No, thank you. I couldn't eat another bite. It was all delicious."

"You're sure?" Ull held up a cluster of endary berries trying to tempt her.

"I'm sure."

Setting the cluster back down, Ull let his gaze travel over her. Her color looked better than when he'd arrived. He'd first noticed it on the return flight to the NACB, but assumed it had to do with the violence she'd witnessed. Tornian females were always shielded from unpleasant things in life, but he hadn't been able to do that with Trisha. He'd needed her to communicate with the Earth Warriors, to guide them to the Ganglians, but he'd never expected her to witness him ending one. That last Ganglian had slipped passed him while he'd been engaging two others. By the time Ull had caught up to him, the Ganglian had made it to the clearing. Now he realized it had been more than that. Trisha had been hungry. He would make sure that never happened again.

'You will fail.' that dark voice whispered through his mind. *'Just as you always fail.'*

"What?" she asked when his gaze darkened as he continued to stare at her silently. "Is there something stuck in my teeth?" She ran her tongue over them, not feeling anything.

"No." Ull didn't' want her to know his dark thoughts. "You said it is common for males and females of the same bloodline to share a meal on Earth?"

Trisha frowned slightly at his abrupt change in the subject but let it go. She'd already learned that if Ull wanted her to know what he thought he'd tell her. Sometimes bluntly.

"Families, yes." She wasn't sure if Ull understood that on Earth, you didn't necessarily have to share the same blood to be considered family.

"But not males and females from different bloodlines." Ull gestured from himself to her.

"They do. Sometimes it's casual, or it can be a date."

"Date? What is a date?"

"It's when a male and female, who are romantically interested in one another, share a meal to get to know each other better. A great deal like we just did." She gestured to the table between them.

"Alone?" Ull didn't even try to hide his shock. A Tornian male was never alone with a female until they had agreed to Join. "And the female's manno allows this?!!"

Trisha couldn't help but laugh at that. "After a certain age, a father usually doesn't have a say over his daughter's life. That includes who she dates."

"But what if the male is unfit and abuses her?"

That immediately ended her laughter, and her eyes turned serious. "I'm not going to lie. It happens. That's why the first few dates are usually done in public or with another couple."

"If your females stayed under their manno's protection, it wouldn't happen at all," Ull growled, forcefully throwing his napkin down on the table.

"Really? How did that work out for Emperor Berto's young females?" Trisha asked quietly and saw Ull jerk back in his seat as if slapped.

"That son of Daco was an abomination!"

"What does Berto's father have to do with it?" Trisha's brows drew together in confusion. Lisa hadn't included anything about him in the educator.

Ull looked at her in shock then shook his head in disbelief. It seemed Queen Lisa had left out a great deal in the educator.

"Daco isn't Berto's manno. He is a lower God that was cast into darkness after he stole the Great Goddess from her mate and attempted to force her to Join with him. Tornian Warriors prevented that from happening, which is why the Goddess promised that for every warrior born, there would be a female created specifically for him…his mate."

"And after Emperor Berto abused his daughters, she withdrew that promise," Trisha said quietly.

"Yes," he growled deeply.

"But you are beginning to discover your mates again," she reminded him. "You and the Kaliszians."

"With Earth females, yes."

"Are you sure you can't mate with any of the other species? Lisa included something about a species called Auyangians in the educator. That there was a Tornian male on Luda who had two talented offspring with one. She also said you were once able to have fit offspring with the Kaliszians."

"And with the Ganglians," Ull grudgingly admitted.

"You once Joined with the Ganglians?!" Trisha didn't even want to think about what that must be like, or the offspring created.

"They were once a fit and worthy species that had honor." Ull didn't know why he was telling her this, but he found he couldn't deceive her, even by omission.

"Until the Great Infection changed everything for everyone."

"Truth."

"So maybe if it's changing for you, it can change for them too."

"After all the pain and suffering they've caused? That would be highly unlikely."

"While I don't disagree with that, how is it any less egregious than what your people have done? You've basically turned the females you have into breeders, and then even before you were certain you could create healthy children with Earth females, you kidnapped a group of them."

"It is about our survival." Ull couldn't believe she still believed what they did was wrong.

"What about the Ganglians' survival?" The lawyer in Trisha couldn't help but argue in the Ganglians' defense even though it sickened her.

"The sooner they cease to exist, the better the Known Universes will be," Ull growled.

"Maybe they feel the same way about you… after all, it was *your* Emperor's abuse of his daughters that caused all this to happen."

Ull surged to his feet, his chair skidding across the floor. He couldn't believe she could say something like that. "You *dare* insinuate we are *anything* like the Ganglians!"

The widening of Trisha's eyes was her only reaction to Ull's anger. She knew she'd hit a nerve with that comment, but she couldn't let Ull slide on this. Yes, the Ganglians were horrible and were doing awful things, but the Tornians weren't innocent in all this. They were abducting women for their own selfish needs too, and until Ull recognized that, admitted it, and corrected it, there was no way her tío would agree to a treaty with the Tornians.

"Aren't you also abducting women?" she demanded.

"They aren't being abused!" Ull growled back.

"That's *your* opinion. Theirs might be different." Trisha slowly rose and walked around the table until they were standing nearly chest to chest. "You had no right in taking them, Ull. No right in forcing them to choose a Tornian warrior with which to Join. Those women weren't involved with a man at the time of their abduction, but that doesn't mean they don't have families. Mothers, fathers, brothers, and sisters who love, care for, and miss them. Who think they are dead and are grieving for them. *You* could stop their suffering if you wanted to."

"That isn't going to happen."

"Then, you're going to have a problem getting the treaty you want, because no one is going to let you get away with enslaving our women."

∞ ∞ ∞ ∞ ∞

Veron paused as he entered the exercise room, where he found Ull violently sparring with their training droid. The best way to learn was to spar with a live warrior, not a droid. But watching the speed, skill, and power behind the clashing swords, Veron knew no warrior on the Searcher would survive Ull's onslaught, Veron included. The droid couldn't either as Ull dropped to block the droid's blow before spinning and slicing off the droid's sword arm. That should have ended the match, but it seemed Ull wasn't satisfied. He continued attacking until the droid was on the floor, minus all his extremities and his head. And still, Ull continued to attack, dropping to his knees to repeatedly plunge his sword into the torso as his enraged battle roar filled the room.

"Feel better?" the captain asked when Ull finally rested his forehead on the pommel of his sword, the blade still embedded in the droid's body. He nearly took a step back at the dark rage swirling in Ull's eyes, making them look blacker than gray.

"No," Ull growled but rose to his feet, jerking his sword out of what remained of the droid before moving toward the wall to sheath it.

"You know you'll have to account to the Emperor for this." Veron moved toward the destroyed droid pulling out its energy crystal so it would stop snapping and sizzling.

"It should have been programmed better."

Veron didn't comment that this particular droid was one of their most advanced. The Emperor personally sparred with it when he was on the Searcher. "What happened with the Earth Council that has you taking your frustration out on a droid?" Ull hadn't given him a report on the second meeting.

"It has nothing to do with the Council," Ull snapped.

"If not the Council, then what? The Ganglians?" Veron found that hard to believe. Fewer Ganglians in The Known Universes made it a better place.

"How can she think we are anything like them!" Ull swung around to face Veron, his fists clenching and unclenching. The rage that had faded by destroying the droid returning with a vengeance.

"Like who?" Veron was confused. "Who's 'she'?"

"Trisha!" Ull spits out. "She claims we are no different than the Ganglians because of the females we aren't returning."

"I see." Veron ran a hand through his hair as he turned away from Ull, his voice full of resignation and regret. "It would appear King Grim's initial belief was right."

"What belief?" Ull couldn't understand Veron's reaction or his words. Even though injured, King Grim was the strongest, most feared warrior in the Tornian Empire. With his discovery of Earth, his return with unprotected females, and his subsequent Joining with one, Grim had become a legend.

"That the taking of females made us no different than the Ganglians, and it might be the thing that finally ends us."

"Grim said that?" Ull looked at him in disbelief. "When?"

"Right after we secured the last female. Queen Lisa."

"If he truly believed it would have such dire consequences, then why did he secure them?"

"Because his Emperor ordered him to."

Ull instantly understood it was as simple as that. A fit and worthy warrior, the first male of a Lord or King, always followed his Emperor's orders, whether he agreed with them or not. That King Grim had doubts about that order only gave Trisha's words more weight.

"Our warriors need those females," he quietly told Veron what he already knew.

"Truth," Veron agreed, "which is why you must make sure the keeping of them doesn't interfere with us obtaining this treaty."

"Trisha says that isn't possible."

"You have to convince her and the Earth Council otherwise. Now the Emperor is waiting for his daily update." With that, Veron left the room.

Chapter Twelve

Ull watched as Trisha led the second group of Earthians up the shuttle ramp the next morning. He'd been up all night replaying her and Veron's words in his head.

Did she genuinely believe Tornians were no better than Ganglians?

That *he* was no better?

He could have harmed her last night. Could have forced himself on her. After all, they'd been alone in her quarters. He was a highly-trained warrior, the first male of a Lord. He could have prevented her from calling out for help if he'd decided to abuse her.

That had him drawing in a sharp breath.

Abuse her?!

He would never harm any female, never abuse one. Especially not Trisha.

But wasn't taking one away from all she knew to fulfill their own needs a type of abuse?

How had he not realized that before?

When he'd been in the room and heard the stories the Earthians had told Trisha about what had happened to them, he hadn't listened or, in truth, *cared,* mainly when the males spoke. What fit and worthy male allowed himself to be captured by a *Ganglian*? Yet he'd found the Earthian warriors fit and worthy, courageous even, especially after they continued to fight against a superior foe.

Not all Tornian males were suited to be a warrior. Their skills lay in other areas, but that didn't make them unfit or unworthy. Perhaps it was the same for Earthian males. If that were the case, then there was no dishonor for these males. They'd gone to great extremes to protect the two females taken with them, a truly honorable thing to do.

"Are you planning on returning to the planet, or am I taking them down?" Veron asked as he walked up to Ull.

"I am," Ull growled, refusing to let the Emperor's Captain know he'd startled him. "Why do you ask?"

"Because the second group has been in the shuttle for five minutes, and you're still standing here."

Giving Veron nothing more than a grunt, Ull walked toward the shuttle.

∞ ∞ ∞ ∞ ∞

Trisha kept up the light and easy chatter as they waited for Ull to enter the shuttle. She'd seen him silently standing there on the other side of the landing bay, so she didn't know what was taking him so long. She knew she'd upset him last night, but she'd hoped he'd be over it by now and not take it out on the abductees who were anxious enough returning home. They didn't need Ull adding to it. She was just about to find him when he entered the shuttle.

Ull felt the mood of the shuttle immediately shift once he entered and closed the hatch. Even though there was underlying tension, he'd heard her light banter as he walked up the ramp, and the ease in the replies she received. Now there was only tension, and he knew it was because of him.

"My apologies for the delay," he couldn't prevent himself from saying even though a first male never apologized.

"Was there a problem?" Trisha asked, knowing the others wanted to know.

"No, I just needed to discuss something with Captain Veron before we left." Ull moved to the pilot's seat as he spoke, and after strapping in, started the engines and looked over his shoulder. "You'll be back on your planet shortly."

Trisha remained silent as Ull piloted the shuttle down to the NACB, but she discreetly watched him. There seemed to be something different about him, but she wasn't sure what. When he glanced her way and held her gaze, she felt her heart begin to beat faster.

"Is there something wrong, Trisha?" he asked quietly.

"No," she responded just as quietly, not wanting anyone else to overhear their conversation.

"You are sure? You are staring at me."

"Maybe I just like what I see." She couldn't believe she just said that and quickly looked away.

"Do you?"

The insecurity in the question pulled her gaze back to his. "You know I do, Ull."

"Even though you believe I'm no different than a Ganglian?"

"That's not what I said." She quickly glanced behind them to make sure no one could overhear them before continuing. "I said your *actions* were no different, not that you weren't. I know you would never abuse me or any other female. It's not who *you* are, Ull."

Her absolute belief in him was easily heard and drove the lingering darkness from his mind. When was the last time someone expressed that much faith in him? It had him quickly facing forward and blinking rapidly.

"Ull?" She placed a hand on his arm.

"I need to concentrate on landing."

The gruffness of his tone had Trisha jerking her hand away. Again, Ull pulled back the moment she believed they were becoming closer and were beginning to understand each other. "Then, I'll let you get to it."

Ull heard the cold distance in Trisha's tone and knew his curtness had hurt her. That hadn't been his intention. He just needed a moment to figure out how to deal with the unusual feelings she brought out in him.

∞ ∞ ∞ ∞ ∞

"Are you alright, Vanessa?" Trisha asked, surprised to see the woman in medical when she entered with the second group of abductees. Vanessa had initially planned on staying on the Searcher until the last group came down, but it had been Zandy, the youngest one taken, that had convinced her to be in the first group. With Vanessa's age and health conditions, Zandy felt she needed to go first. The rest of the group had agreed even though Vanessa claimed to be feeling fine, even without her high blood pressure medication.

"I'm fine. Really." She squeezed Trisha's arm reassuringly. "I'm just here to greet and reassure the next group."

'You're sure?"

"Yes, the doctors gave me a clean bill of health."

"That's great."

"It is." She looked over Trisha's shoulder, and seeing Ull standing there, moved around Trisha to stand in front of him. "In case I don't get a chance to see you again, Warrior Ull, I want to say thank you for bringing us home. I know it wasn't your first choice and that you have other reasons for coming to Earth. But thank you anyway. You'll never know what this means to our families and us." With that, Vanessa did something Trisha knew shocked Ull. She gave him a massive hug before stepping back. "Now, I'm going to go see if I can help settle some nerves."

Trisha watched the older woman hurry to where Kara, the young mother of two, sat sobbing. Knowing there was nothing for her to do here, she looked to Ull. "Let's go."

∞ ∞ ∞ ∞ ∞

When Trisha and Ull again entered the Council chambers, the mood was vastly different. She hadn't had the chance to talk to her tío alone yet, so she wasn't sure what was going on.

"The second group has been settled in medical?" President Garcia asked once she and Ull settled.

"Yes," she told him.

"And our remaining citizens on the Searcher?"

"They are doing fine. Anxious to return home and get back to their lives, of course, as I'm sure you can all understand." She let her gaze travel around the room. "The Kaliszian representative, Minister Ruskin, is also looking forward to coming down and meeting with this esteemed Council to negotiate for his people."

"We look forward to meeting with Minister Ruskin," President Garcia told her, "but we need to deal with the Tornian issue first."

"Tornian *issue*?" Trisha wasn't exactly sure what her tío was talking about.

"Yes, Last night, I met with the other world leaders to explain to them how I can speak and understand Tornian, and the full extent of the situation in the Tornian Empire."

"I see." That explained the change in the world leaders' mood. They'd learned that the Tornians had also come to Earth and taken females but had no plans on returning them, and the leaders weren't happy about that.

By his low growl and with his knee touching hers, she knew Ull had realized that too. She'd told him this was going to be an issue, but it seemed he hadn't believed her.

"I'm sure you do." The President shifted his gaze from his niece to Ull. "The other leaders have expressed interest in using your educator, as I have, so we might all speak directly to you and Minister Ruskin. Would that be possible?"

Trisha looked to Ull when he didn't immediately respond. "Ull?"

"I will arrange that," he finally replied, his gaze slowly traveling over the leaders. "Although it will take some time."

"Why?" the African Chancellor demanded suspiciously.

"Because there is only one educator available, and each session will take several hours and need supervised."

"Are you the only one qualified to do that?" the Chancellor questioned after Trisha translated.

"No. Captain Veron and Minister Ruskin are also qualified."

"Then I move we start these sessions as soon as possible." A volley of agreements filled the room at the Chancellor's motion.

"It seems we are all in agreement." President Garcia looked back to Ull. "Warrior Ull?"

"I will bring the educator down tomorrow when we return with the last of your people."

"Why not now?" the Australian Chancellor asked. "Don't you have another shuttle?"

"There is another shuttle on the Searcher," Ull acknowledged.

"Then why can't this Captain Veron or Minister Ruskin bring it down?"

"Minister Ruskin isn't qualified to fly a shuttle, and while Captain Veron is, it would leave the Searcher without anyone to fly it, putting those on board at risk."

That had Chancellor Khatri leaning back in her seat. "Well, we don't want that."

"So, are we in agreement that the next time Warrior Ull returns, he will bring the educator with him?" Aaron looked around the room, and once all the other leaders nodded their agreement looked back to Ull. "Then, with that settled, we need to move on to a more concerning issue. The *Tornian* abduction of our females."

All eyes zeroed in on Ull, including Trisha's, but he remained stonily silent.

"Warrior Ull?"

"Yes, President Garcia?"

"Were you going to respond?"

"To what, Mr. President? I heard no question."

Trisha winced internally at Ull's tone and the way her tío's eyes narrowed in response to it. Tío didn't get to be President by taking crap from anyone, but he especially hated being condescended to, which was what Ull was doing.

"Then let me speak words you *can* hear. When will you be returning the women *your* people abducted?"

"We won't be."

Ull's short, succinct answer had Trisha wanting to pound her head on the table. No, wait, she wanted to beat Ull's on it. Didn't he know this was *not* how you negotiated with someone you needed? He was a first male, for God's sake.

"Then, you're going to have a problem with this Council."

Ull had argued against allowing Queen Lisa to include that they had taken more than just her and her offspring in the educator. This is why. What the Earth rulers didn't know they couldn't hold against them. The Emperor and King Grim had disagreed, so now *he* had to deal with the fallout.

"Those females are vital to the survival of my people. They have been well treated and have their choice of every interested Tornian male. Just as every other Earth female shall once we reach an agreement."

"That is not acceptable," the President argued.

"Then you will continue to have your females taken," Ull fired back.

"That makes you no different than the Ganglians."

Trisha watched Ull bristle at the accusation and fully expected him to react as he had when she'd said the same thing. Instead, he took a deep breath before calmly replying.

"If that were truth, then my Emperor would have sent ships full of Tornian warriors. We would have easily conquered your world and just taken what we needed. And we both know there would be nothing you could have done to prevent it." Ull's eyes glittered as his gaze traveled from one leader to the next, letting that sink in. "That is what many wanted to do, but my Emperor is a fit, worthy, and honorable male. He refused to allow it. Instead, he sent me to negotiate a mutually beneficial agreement. One where your females voluntarily Join with the Tornian male *they* choose while we protect your planet from the Ganglians." Ull paused, his gaze moving to Trisha. "It is my understanding you already have something similar to this on your planet called Internet dating."

Trisha's eyes widened, but she continued to translate Ull's words. She hadn't thought he had been listening when she'd told him that. Not with everything else happening.

"This would be the same," Ull continued. "Except the male would be Tornian."

"It would not be the same," President Garcia argued. "Internet dating most often is a one-time meeting between two individuals. It's not permanent."

"But isn't that what these 'individuals' are looking for? Something permanent?"

The President had no answer to that.

"There are things that still need to be worked out, of course," Trisha entered the conversation for the first time. "But at its essence, that's what this program will be. Internet dating just on an interplanetary level."

"That still doesn't address the issue of the women you already took against their will."

Trisha spoke before Ull could. While she didn't agree with what the Tornians had done, she was beginning to understand it. She also knew Lisa wouldn't allow any of those women to be forced into something they didn't want. "Perhaps that is something that we can address at a later date?" She asked as she made eye contact with each leader, trying to gauge their thoughts. "I know that at this time, those women under Lisa's and King Grim's protections aren't forced to Join with any Tornian male. They are going through something similar to internet dating on Luda."

"And if they chose to *never* Join with a Tornian?" the President demanded.

"It would be up to the Emperor if they would be allowed to return to Earth." Ull took back control of the conversation. "But I can vow to you that will *never* be allowed unless *willing* females are allowed to Join with a Tornian."

"President Garcia," the Prime Minister of Canada spoke up. "While I understand and respect the concern you have for your citizens, I believe Representative Burke is correct. The return of the females taken from your country needs to be set aside, for now, so we can decide what is best for *all* the citizens of Earth."

Trisha watched as her tío gave Prime Minister Gagnon a shocked look. "You can say that? When only yesterday it was a group of *your* citizens at risk?!"

"It's because of that that I *can* say it." The Prime Minister argued with a voracity that surprised Trisha, and she could see it had her tío too. After a moment, the powerful woman composed herself and continued. "I contacted my husband once you briefed us on the exact location where the Ganglians landed. Our daughter and her family traditionally vacation in the Rockies in Southern Alberta.' Trisha felt her heart clench at what she somehow knew was coming. "Philip contacted her, so it didn't go through official channels, and learned they were fine but forced to leave early." The Prime Minister's gaze went to Ull. "So, I would like to personally thank you, Warrior Ull, for keeping my daughter and her family safe."

Ull dropped his head slightly, accepting the Prime Minister's gratitude before speaking. "I'm glad I could be of assistance. While Tornians are a warrior race, we still hold all life sacred, especially the lives of females. Which is why I don't understand why you allow so many of yours to be unprotected."

"Our females... women," President Garcia corrected, "*aren't* unprotected. They are independent creatures that have the right to live their life as they see fit. Just as our males do."

"That makes no sense. Females are the most important resource in all the Known Universes. For without them, there would be no life. To not ensure they are safe from harm is irresponsible."

Stunned silence met Ull's statement, and that included Trisha. While Ull had said something like that to her before, he hadn't been nearly this intense. Although she wasn't sure, she liked being referred to as a 'resource.'

"Are you saying that Tornian females are allowed to participate in your society?" Chancellor Smyth leaned forward as she asked, clearly profoundly interested in Ull's answer.

"Define participate."

"Do they hold positions of power as I," she gestured from herself to the other female leaders, "Chancellor Khatri and Prime Minister Gagnon do? Are their opinions heard and taken seriously?"

Trisha looked to Ull finding she wanted to know the answers to those questions too. Lisa hadn't included much about that in the educator, but Trisha had gotten that Tornians pretty much cloistered their females away. God, she hoped Ull knew how important his answer was going to be. It could make or break these negotiations.

"All a female's wants and needs are taken seriously," Ull began slowly. While he refused to tell an untruth, the look in Trisha's eye told him to choose his next words carefully. "But no, until recently they had no voice in the Assembly of Lords."

Trisha could feel the world leaders' displeasure at Ull's admission. It had taken centuries of struggle and repression for all the women of Earth to receive the same rights and protections as men. None of these leaders were going to allow them to subjugated again. She had to do something.

"Until recently?" She quickly posed the question. "What's changed?"

Ull tipped his head to the side and gave her a strange look as if that should be obvious. "Earth females arrived."

"And that's changed things for females in the Tornian Empire?" Prime Minister Gagnon pressed. "How?"

Ull turned his attention to the Prime Minister. "It began when King Grim declared the Earth female he'd Joined with his Queen." Knowing he would need to explain further, he continued. "Since the Great Infection struck, no Tornian female has accepted a male's claim except for the Empress, who must."

"I don't understand," Gagnon said.

"For a female to accept a male's claim means she has agreed to Join with him, and only him, until they meet the Goddess. Our females no longer agree to do such a thing. Once they present offspring to a male, they expect another male to entice them away by offering them more for giving *them* her gift of offspring. When that happens, she takes everything the first male has given her and moves on, leaving behind her offspring. If she accepts a male's claim, as Queen Lisa has with King Grim, it means she can no longer do this. Another Earth female, Lady Abby, has also accepted the claim of her male, Lord Ynyr."

"But, there are no Tornian females that accept the claim?"

"There is one, Lady Isis. She has been with her male, Lord Oryon, for more than twenty-five years and presented him with four fit and worthy males."

"She is also Warrior Ull's mother," Trisha quietly told the Council.

"This is truth. Since this has happened, Empress Kim, Queen Lisa, Lady Abby, and Lady Isis have taken very active roles in their Houses and have also addressed the Assembly of Lords."

"So, they are only respected because they are with important *males,*" Smyth said in disgust.

"They are respected because *they* are important," Ull corrected, stressing the word 'they.'

"I am the only one who has spent any amount of time with Tornians, and as the Representative appointed by President Garcia, I want to remind this esteemed Council that it wasn't that long ago in our past when others held Earth women in esteem only due to their social status or to whom they were married. Our society changed, and I believe, from what Warrior

Ull has just said, that the Tornian society can change too. It's already begun to, thanks to the influence of Earth females."

"Any applicant would have to be made aware of this difference."

"Of course, Chancellor Smyth."

∞ ∞ ∞ ∞ ∞

"Representative Burke, a moment, please?"

Trisha turned at her tío's request and waited for him to catch up to her and Ull. "Of course, Mr. President."

"Alone?" The President spoke in Tornian so Ull could understand.

"I will wait for you in the shuttle," Ull told her and continued down the corridor.

"My offices are this way." Aaron gestured down a different hallway, and with bodyguards in front and behind them, they silently moved toward it. Once there, one of the guards opened the door for them to enter, then closed it and left them alone.

Trisha let her gaze travel around the room, taking in the plush carpeting, warm wooden walls, and the understated opulence that, while fitting for the President of the United States, surprised her.

"How long has this facility been in the works?"

"Since I was first elected."

"So, you've known the countries of North America were going to merge into a Council for nearly four years?" She moved toward the chairs facing the desk, but he gently gripped her elbow, guiding her to a couch along a wall.

"Not all the countries, just Canada, Mexico, and the United States. The rest are worried their voices would be drowned out by three such large countries. Can I get you something to drink?"

"Water, please," she said, sitting down. "But each country would have an equal vote. That's how it was in every other Council, so why would these other countries think it would be different?"

"That was stressed, but to no avail." He went to the mini-fridge tastefully hidden in one of the cabinets and pulled out two bottles. Returning, he handed her one as he sat down beside her. "Change takes time, and they are considering forming a Central American Council. They feel it will better represent their wants and beliefs."

"That is their right." Taking the bottle, she twisted off the lid and took a much-needed sip.

"It is. Now enough about that. Tell me how you're doing. Honestly. Are you all right?"

"What do you mean?" She didn't understand the question. Why was he asking? He couldn't possibly know. "I'm fine."

"Look, I know how heavily the disappearance of Lisa and her children weighed on you. Now all this is going on. Maybe I was wrong choosing you as Earth's Representative."

"With all due respect, Tío, you didn't choose me, Lisa did. And I'm not going to let her down again."

"You've lost weight and aren't sleeping well." He reached out to gently run his thumb over the faint bruising under an eye.

"It just takes time to adjust to sleeping on a spaceship and eating alien food." Thank God, that's what he was talking about. She wasn't ready to reveal her condition to him, not with everything else going on.

"Well, thankfully, this will be the last night you'll have to do that." Lowering his hand, he opened his bottle.

"What?" She gave him a confused look as he drank deeply. "What are you talking about?"

"After tomorrow, all our people will be back on the planet," he told her, screwing the lid back on his bottle. "So, there will be no reason for you to return to the Searcher. Warrior Ull and Minister Ruskin can travel back and forth alone."

"I… I guess I hadn't realized that. As Earth's representative, I just assumed I would need to be readily available to both Ull and Jakob. Meaning I'd be remaining on the Searcher."

"No, I want you on the planet."

"If that's what you and the other world leaders decide is best, then, of course, that's what I'll do."

"This is my decision, Trisha."

"What was it you once said to Mamá and me about choosing a political life? *'That in serving for the betterment of the people, one must sometimes make decisions that aren't always in your own best interest.'* It's one of the reasons you said you'd never marry. You didn't want the woman you loved always to take second place."

Aaron's eyes widened in astonishment. "That was over fifteen years ago. I can't believe you remember that."

"It stuck in my mind. During election years, you were often asked if you would get engaged to the woman you were dating at the time. Now might be one of those times, Tío, when what's better for the people of Earth isn't going to be better for you."

"I promised your mamá that I would always keep you safe."

"I know, but the truth is, no woman on Earth is safe unless we stop the Ganglians from abducting them, and we can't do that without the assistance of the Tornians and Kaliszians."

"I know that. I just love you so much, Trishy."

"I love you too, Tío."

Chapter Thirteen

Trisha leaned back in the copilot seat of the shuttle and released a tired sigh. God, it had been such a long day but a productive one.

"Are you alright, Trisha?"

Looking to Ull, she took in his unique profile. When she'd first met him, she'd thought his features strange with his flatter nose and sharper cheekbones, but now they seemed to fit him perfectly. He was just Ull, and the thought of not seeing him again hurt, especially when he looked at her with those unusual gray eyes of his, full of concern.

"Why does everyone keep asking me that? Do I look that bad?"

"You are beautiful. Who has dared to say otherwise?!" Ull demanded, and she watched rage fill the eyes that only moments before had been full of concern.

"Calm down." She reached out to put a soothing hand on his bare arm. "No one insulted me. Tío Aaron just asked me the same question you did, and I'll tell you the same thing I told him. I am fine. A little tired, that's all."

"Then you will rest more." Ull looked forward as if the subject was settled and began to land the shuttle.

Trisha opened her mouth then closed it, knowing it would do no good, and really why start an argument when after tonight Ull wouldn't know if she was resting enough or not.

∞ ∞ ∞ ∞ ∞

"How did things go today?" Jakob asked in the way of greeting as she exited the shuttle.

"It went well." Trisha knew the Kaliszian Minister was anxious to get down to the planet and negotiate for his people. That he'd put the needs of those under his protection first said a lot about the male and the Kaliszian people. "There were some tense moments, but in the end, I think we have a good plan going forward."

"Wonderful."

"The Council seems very interested in trading with the Kaliszian Empire."

"May the Goddess hear," Jakob prayed quietly.

Trisha gave him a small, understanding smile. "Has anything happened with the remaining abductees that I need to know about?"

"No, they are just impatient to return to their home."

"Understandable, I'll go reassure them that it won't be much longer."

"You need to rest, Trisha," Ull growled.

"What? Why? Are you ill, Trisha?" Jakob ran concerned eyes over her.

"I'm *fine,*" she stressed, giving Ull an exasperated look. "I'm just a little tired. I'm not used to all this space travel. Once I talk to my people, I'll go get some sleep."

"You're sure?" Jakob knew it was selfish of him, but this female held the future of his people in her hands. If she were to become ill from helping them, there would be little chance of there being an agreement between their people.

"I am." Reaching out, she gave Jakob's arm a reassuring squeeze then left.

As soon as Trisha left the hangar, Jakob rounded on Ull, shoving the larger male. Jakob might be a Minister, but he'd started as a Kaliszian Warrior, and while he may have had to defer to Ull, he wasn't intimidated by him. "What happened down there? Why is Trisha so exhausted? You can seal the fates of both our people without her. Don't you realize that? What. Did. You. Do?"

"Never. Touch. Me. Kaliszian." Ull growled, shoving the Kaliszian male back. "I did nothing to Trisha. The sessions with the Earthian Council exhaust her. Other than her tío, she's the only one of them who currently understands either of our languages. Trisha must continually translate all the conversations. I have tried to assist her by making sure we are always physically joined, but that isn't always possible. On top of that, she is continually checking on the Earthians that have returned."

"She is doing too much." While Jakob didn't back down, his hostility level did.

"She is. She..." Ull trailed off, unable to come up with the right word to describe Trisha. She was strong and brave while still being soft and gentle. She understood even the things she disagreed with, and while he had kidnapped her, Trisha was doing everything she could to help them. "She needs more rest. Hopefully, she will start getting it tomorrow after all her people have returned."

"I will be traveling down with you tomorrow."

"That is the plan, Minister Ruskin. Now I need to contact my Emperor."

∞ ∞ ∞ ∞ ∞

Trisha sagged back against the wall of her cleansing unit. The coolness of the wall was in sharp contrast to the heat of the water pounding down from above. She felt as drained as the water flowing down the drain at her feet. The meeting with the remaining abductees had taken longer than she'd planned.

They'd been full of questions, most they already knew the answers to, but a few were new concerning how those already on the planet were doing. She'd answered the questions the best she could, but she also knew nothing could honestly calm their fears until *they* were back on Earth.

Back on Earth.

She shook her head at that phrase. A few days ago, that phrase hadn't even been a possibility. Now, thanks to the arrival of the Searcher, it was. Now, so many previously unknown things were possible.

Traveling to an alien planet.

There being 'aliens' who were more like us than they were different.

Having feelings for one of those aliens when nothing could ever come of it.

Sighing heavily, she straightened and motioning for the water to shut off, stepped out of the shower and began to dry off. Several minutes later, dressed in sleeping pants, she heard a knock on her door. Sighing heavily, she tossed the towel back into the cleansing room, then answered the door.

"Ull." It was a little bit like déjà vu seeing him there holding a tray.

"May I come in?" he asked when she just stood there.

"What? Oh, yes, of course," she said, stepping back. "Please come in."

"I noticed you didn't join the rest of your people for last meal."

"No, I wanted to shower first."

"And to rest." He gestured with his head to what she was wearing as he went to set the tray down.

"Truth," she chuckled, sitting down in the chair he pulled out.

"You will eat before you do that."

"Well, as you've brought more than enough," she said, her gaze traveling over the plates then back to him, "I hope you planned on joining me." She was surprised at how much she wanted to share last meal with Ull. Especially when this could be the last time they were ever alone again.

"I would very much like that." This time though, instead of sitting across from her, he took the chair beside her. After being so close to her all day on planet, he found he didn't want to be separated now. "I selected the things you seemed to most enjoy last night."

"Thank you, but I hope they are things you enjoy too."

Ull's gaze traveled over the items he had selected just because she liked them. He now realized they were also some of his favorites. "They are all items I would have chosen for myself."

"Good." The next several minutes, they selected what they wanted and settled down to eat. Trisha watched as Ull picked another piece of what passed for Tornian bread and smothered it with hunaja. "You must have a sweet tooth."

"Sweet tooth?" Ull gave her a confused look.

"You seem to *really* like the hunaja. It's like something we have on Earth called honey. It's sweet." She watched a ruddy flush spread across Ull's pale, pearly face.

"Hunaja is a rare substance in the Tornian Empire. It is found only on my home planet of Betelgeuse, so I grew up on it."

"Then I'm glad they included it with the supplies on the Searcher. Everyone deserves to have something that reminds them of home."

"Is this… honey on your planet a rare thing?"

"There was a time when it was. The bee population suddenly began to decline because of several factors, but thankfully we were able to address them. Now the honeybees thrive, so we have an ample supply of honey."

"Just as you have an ample supply of females."

"I don't think I ever thought to compare the two, but in a sense, yes." Carefully she set her silverware down. "I want to say something to you while I can, but I don't want it to sound condescending or for you to take it that way."

Ull set the hunaja smothered treat aside. "You can say whatever you want to me, Trisha, and I will listen."

"When I first met you…"

"When I kidnapped you," Ull corrected.

She gave him a small smile. "When you kidnapped me, I honestly believed you were the most arrogant, stubborn, unlikeable 'alien' I had ever met."

"I was the only 'alien' you had ever met."

"True." Who knew Ull had a sense of humor? "Now, stop interrupting me."

"My apologies."

"I also believed that if you were the best your Emperor had to send, with your abrupt and aggressive attitude, then there was no way to reach an agreement."

'See, she doesn't believe in you. She never believed in you.' Suddenly that dark voice was back in his mind, and he stiffened.

Trisha noticed how his eyes began to darken and put a hand on his arm. "You said you would listen."

"Continue," he growled.

"As I said, you were abrupt and aggressive and seemed to take offense when I intended none. But as I got to know you, how you were raised, and got to learn about your society, I began to understand."

"Understand what?"

"That while our societies are very different, as are many of our attitudes and beliefs, we are more alike than any of us thought."

"In what way?"

"When you strip everything else away, all we want is to be loved for who we are. Not for who our family is, or the position we hold, but for who *we* are, as individuals."

"This would be truth, but it seems you believe that can never happen for me."

"What?! What are you talking about? I never said that!"

"You said that with my abrupt and aggressive attitude, no female will ever be willing to Join with me, let alone remain."

"That's *not* what I said or implied." Slamming her fists on the table, she surged to her feet. "But I left out pigheadedness, which is what you are exhibiting right now! God, men are so infuriating, especially when all you're trying to do is compliment them!"

Ull rose when she did and was about to storm out of the room until her words stopped him. "Compliment?"

"Yes. Compliment, you big cabrón!"

Ull quickly moved across the chamber and pulled her up against his chest. Leaning down, his lips nearly brushing hers, he murmured, "What compliment were you trying to give me, my Trisha?"

"That… that I was proud of you today," she whispered, her hands coming up to rest on his chest. "You listened to the leaders' concerns and found solutions. Maybe not perfect ones, but solutions. You were honest with them, even when it wasn't to your advantage. You told them what they and you were up against, and you never lost your temper. Your Emperor chose exactly the right male to send to Earth."

"You no longer consider me to be arrogant?" He placed the faintest of kisses over one corner of her mouth. "Or stubborn?" He did the same to the other corner. "Or to have an aggressive attitude?" With that question, he captured her lips in a deep, hard kiss, lifting her off her feet as he did so.

Trisha's fingers instinctively dug into Ull's chest as he lifted her off her feet and let herself sink into the kiss. God, just moments ago, she'd thought he was walking out of her life forever, but now he was kissing her as if he'd never let her go, and she never wanted him to.

Sliding her fingers up over the hard, bulging muscles of his chest, then along his broad shoulders, she finally sunk them into his hair, increasing the pressure of the kiss. God, she wanted this, wanted to get lost in this kiss and Ull. She needed to forget about everything and everyone else. But she couldn't. Not because of how it would affect everyone else but because of how it would affect Ull.

God, she wanted this, wanted to get lost in Ull and what he was making her feel and forget about the rest of the world. Was it too much to ask? For her to grab for a bit of happiness.

∞ ∞ ∞ ∞ ∞

'I'm sorry, Steve, but I have to end this.'

'What?! Patricia, why? We're good together, and Trisha likes me.'

'I know, and you're right. My baby does, but I can't give you what you want. I care about you, Steve, I do. But Martin will always be the only man I love, and you deserve better than that. You deserve to find someone who loves you like that because I know she's out there. You're too great of a guy for there not to be.'

∞ ∞ ∞ ∞ ∞

Trisha ripped her mouth away from Ull's gasping at the memory. She'd been eight when her mamá had begun dating Steve Able, a fellow lawyer. They'd dated for nearly a year, and it had seemed like a happy time through Trisha's young eyes. Her mamá and Steve went on dates together, but there'd been just as many that had included her. Trisha even thought her mamá might marry Steve until the night when she'd gotten up for a drink of water and overhead that conversation.

She'd slipped back into bed, and Steve had disappeared from their lives. When she'd asked her mamá about it, all she would say was that Steve's work schedule had gotten hectic, but one day, they'd see him again.

And they had, nearly a year later.

She and her mamá had been in the park when Steve had walked by, his arm around another woman. He'd stopped and introduced the woman as Shelly, his fiancée. Her mamá had congratulated them and wished them well.

After that, Trisha never saw Steve again, not until the day of her mamá's funeral. He, his wife, and their three children had come and paid their respects.

None of that would have happened if her mamá hadn't been honest with Steve and put his wants and needs before her own. She'd known true love, and she wanted him to have it too.

"Trisha?"

Ull's concern-filled tone pulled her from her memories. "What's wrong? Did I harm you?"

"No," she reassured him but still slid her fingers from his hair and lightly pressed them against his chest, silently requesting to be put down. "But we can't do this."

"Why?" he growled, refusing to release her.

Trisha stared up into his beautiful gray eyes and couldn't stop her hand from reaching up to caress his cheek. "You are so handsome."

Ull's eyes widened at that. No one had ever said something like that to him before, and for it to be Trisha, made it mean even more. Turning his head, he gently pressed a kiss into her palm.

"And loving," she whispered. "I don't want to see you hurt again."

"Again?"

"Not being chosen during the Joining Ceremony, then again when Abby chose Ynyr, hurt you." She watched his eyes darken with pain. "Those things happened for a reason, Ull, because none of those women was the right one for you. But she is out there, just as your Goddess promised."

"You do not believe she is in my arms right now?"

In the quiet question, Trisha could hear all his hope, and it broke her heart. "Can you put me down? We can sit and talk."

Instead of doing as she asked, Ull carried her to the Tornian-sized couch. Sitting down, he arranged her, so his bulging erection pressed against her already throbbing clit.

"Tell me why it can't be you," Ull growled, his fingers sinking into the flesh of her ass, keeping her close.

Knowing Ull wasn't going to let her move away, she allowed her hands to caress his chest gently.

"Talk," he growled.

Trying not to let the thought of how amazing that huge cock would feel inside her, of how completely it would fill her, she began.

"I told you about my father… manno."

"That he was a Warrior and met the Goddess because of it."

"Yes, and even though she was only twenty-two at the time, my mamá never got over losing him, or at least never allowed herself to."

"I don't understand."

"There was a time, six or seven years after my dad died when Mamá met another man. He was a good man, Ull. A fit and worthy man who loved Mamá and wanted to claim her and me the same way Grim claimed Lisa and the girls. But unlike Lisa, my mamá refused to open her heart to Steve, even though I know she cared about him."

"Why?" Ull didn't understand that. From what he had observed of the Earth females, they were among some of the most open and giving beings in the Known Universes.

"Because she knew he deserved someone who could love him with her whole heart. Not someone who continually compared him to her first love."

"You are saying there is another male in your heart?"

She knew if she told Ull there was he would let it go, but she couldn't lie, wouldn't lie, not to him. "No, there's only one male who will ever fill my heart." Reaching up, she gently caressed the cheek of that male. "But I can't have him, at least not forever, because I can't be what he needs. This is why before we Join, I have to make sure you understand that."

"You would Join with me without expecting anything else? What you referred to as a wham bam thank you ma'am Joining."

"No!" She jerked her hand away from his cheek. "Never. That's people who don't care about each other. You *know* I care about you. I wouldn't be here in your arms if I didn't, especially not when this is probably the last time we'll be alone together."

"What do you mean?!" Ull growled, his arms pulling her even closer as if to protect her from the possibility.

"After we return the last of the abductees tomorrow, I've been ordered to remain on the planet."

"By who?!"

"Tío Aaron, as the President of the United States."

Ull hadn't considered this. He'd been looking forward to the Earthians leaving, wrongly thinking that would give him more time alone with Trisha. Instead, it was taking her away from him.

"Then, if this is all I can have with the one the Goddess promised, I will have it all," Ull vowed and gripping the back of her head, crushed her lips to his.

Trisha knew there were arguments and understandings she still needed to make, and Ull to accept. She was a lawyer, after all. It was something her mamá had always stressed to her, but now Trisha saw those lessons in a different light. And she wasn't her mamá. Trisha was going to do something her mamá never could. Embrace everything life offered her while she could.

Decision made, Trisha flattened her upper body against Ull's as she rose on to her knees and wrapped her arms around his neck, returning his kiss just as ravenously.

∞ ∞ ∞ ∞ ∞

Lost in Ull's sweet hunaja taste, Trisha never even realized they were moving until her back met her bed with Ull's weight covering her. Wrapping her legs around his hips, she pulled him closer, rocking her hips against his.

Ull growled at how the movement nearly caused him to lose control. Ripping his mouth from hers, he rose on his forearms and glared down at her. "You must cease doing that!"

"Why?" she asked, giving him a knowing smile as she rolled her hips again. "It feels so good. You feel so good."

"You need to stop, or I will find my release before you receive yours."

"If that happens, then we'll just have to start all over again," she teased, but when she tried to repeat the movement, Ull bore the full weight of his lower body down on her, preventing it.

"I will have your release first, my Trisha. I will have all of you." With that, he slowly pulled down the thin straps of her tank top, revealing two amazing mounds of flesh, each crowned with dark areola and already taut nipple. Goddess, he'd never seen anything so beautiful. They were so much more generous than the Serai. Leaning down, he captured one, sucking it deep into his mouth.

"Ull!" Gasping, she arched up, offering him more, which he greedily accepted. With a pop, he released her nipple then turned his attention to the other, his hands continuing down to slide under the waistband of her pants to cup her ass, grinding her against his shaft the way he refused to allow her.

"Please, Ull, more," she begged.

Finally, Ull released the succulent flesh of her breast so he could continue his way down her flat, taut stomach, kissing, and sampling the entire way. Shifting her legs to his shoulders, his knees hit the floor as did her pants, revealing to him the glistening curls that hid her sex.

Inhaling deeply, he let her unique scent fill him and knew he would never forget it. Carefully his thumbs parted her curls, revealing plump, tender flesh that beckoned him. Already aroused for Joining, he hadn't used anything he'd learned with the Serai to give her pleasure. It was time he did. Lowering his head, he tasted her for the first time and nearly released. Her nectar was sweeter than the rarest hunaja found on his planet, and he intended to consume her. Exploring further, he discovered her berry and latched on to it.

Breathing heavily, Trisha propped herself up on her elbows to watch Ull explore her. She'd never been the absolute center of a male's attention or had his complete focus on seeing she found pleasure first. When he latched onto her clit, she nearly screamed.

"God, Ull!" She sunk her fingers into his hair, guiding him exactly where she needed him, her hips instinctively moving.

Ull's gaze bore into hers when he pulled back, his lips glistening. "You enjoy this?" He growled as the rough, thick pad of his thumb continued to tease her berry.

"You know I do," she growled back.

"Shall I give you more?"

"Yes!"

Sliding his fingers through her slick folds, Ull coated them before finding her woman's opening and pressing two fingers inside. Goddess, she was so much tighter and softer than the Serai.

"Please, Ull..." Trisha wasn't too proud to beg. She was so close. The feel of his fingers stretching her felt amazing, but she needed more. "I'm so close."

Her admission caused him to thrust his fingers as deep as possible before twisting and withdrawing them before rapidly filling her again and again. At the same time, his mouth returned to her clit, lightly biting it.

"Oh, God, yes!" She exclaimed as that last bit of pain sent an orgasm tearing through her body.

∞ ∞ ∞ ∞ ∞

Ull rose from between Trisha's thighs and ripped open his pants. He'd watched her the entire time he'd pleasured her to make sure she was enjoying everything he was doing. Goddess, she was so open and honest with her responses that several times he'd nearly found his release before her. But now it was his turn to finally know what it felt like to release into a real female.

The head of his shaft at her entrance, he paused, his eyes shooting up to her. He had to be sure.

"Yes," she told him quietly. "Fill me, Ull. I need you."

That was all the encouragement he needed and with one powerful thrust impaled her on his shaft as he had done with the Serai.

Trisha's back arched up off the bed, her scream lodged in her throat at the sudden intrusion. She'd known Ull would be massive. She'd seen the outline of his cock often enough and, thanks to Lisa, knew they were compatible. Still, she hadn't thought it would feel like this like he split her in two.

"Trisha?" Ull immediately froze. Goddess, how could he be so stupid? Trisha wasn't anything like the Serai, so why would he treat her as if she were?

'Because you are a weak, unfit male. She knows this. It is why she refuses to be yours.'

Ull wanted to rant and rage at the voice, but he knew doing so would further harm Trisha and that he would never do. Instead, he slowly began to withdraw.

"No!" Trisha wrapped her legs around his hips, keeping him in place. "Just give me a minute," she whispered even as a tear disappeared into her hair.

"I am harming you," he growled. "I need to get a portable repair unit."

"I won't deny that hurt, but only because you're very well endowed."

"I'm what?"

"You've got a big cock, Ull, a lot bigger than Earth males." She watched the expressions that quickly crossed his face. Shock. Pride. Then shame. It had him lowering his head and his voice deepening.

"I should have taken more care."

"Perhaps, but it's done." She refused to let him take the blame for what she'd encouraged when, as they spoke, her body had grown accustomed to the intrusion. A pleasurable throb replaced the burning pain as her hips started pumping against his.

"Trisha..." he growled, gripping her hips to stop the movement.

"Please, Ull..." she continued to try and move her hips. "Join with me. Let me give you as much pleasure as you've given me."

Ull's chest heaved at the thought, to find pleasure within Trisha's body, to release inside her, to have her want it. It was something he wouldn't deny either of them. Slowly he withdrew until only the head of his shaft remained inside her before carefully pushing back. He'd watched her expressions when he'd pleasured her before, had memorized them, as he did now. Seeing only pleasure, he repeated the action.

"Yes," she moaned, gripping his wrists as she arched up into him. "More, Ull. Harder.

"No," he growled, maintaining slow, measured thrusts. He would not hurt Trisha again, even though he could already feel his balls tightening so his seed could burst forth and fill her. No, he would hold onto his control because he didn't want this incredible experience to end.

Realizing she wasn't going to change his mind, Trisha decided to use it to her advantage. Releasing his wrists, she ran her hands up and over his sweat-soaked body, exploring each bulging muscle and recognizing the strength he held ruthlessly in check.

Trisha would never claim to have that type of strength, but using her legs wrapped around him for leverage, she lifted herself to capture one of his nipples.

It broke the control he'd just regained, and with a roar, he caged her beneath him and, with one final thrust, exploded.

Chapter Fourteen

With his weight braced on his elbows and his shaft still embedded inside Trisha, Ull's head dropped into the crook of her neck as he tried to regain control of his mind and body. When Trisha's arms wrapped around him and her fingers began to run through his hair slowly, everything within him settled, and a feeling of peace flowed over him, unlike anything he'd ever experienced before.

Goddess, was this what his brother experienced with Abby?

What the Emperor, King Grim, and even his manno had with their females? If so, no wonder they refused to give them up. He owed them the gravest of apologies.

"What has you thinking so hard?" Trisha murmured, never opening her eyes. God, Ull had just given her two earth-shattering orgasms. She couldn't move even if the Ganglians attacked.

"You," he admitted his lips caressing her bare skin, "and the other males who have Joined with Earth females. I now understand why they are so committed to them."

"And why's that?" she asked lazily.

"Because they complete them as the Goddess intended." Slowly Ull lifted his head to gaze into her eyes. "The way you complete me."

"Ull…"

He watched her eyes go from soft and luminous, to sharp and full of regret. Her hand slid from his hair to his cheek.

"You know we can't be together. Not the way Lisa and Grim are."

"Why?" he demanded gruffly.

"Because my place is *here,* on Earth helping my people. While yours is on Betelgeuse taking care of yours. Ull, you will be an amazing Lord. It's what you were born to be." Stretching up, she gently kissed his lips, whispering, "But we have tonight."

Ull refused to acknowledge she was right. He was a first male and future Lord. There wasn't supposed to be a problem he couldn't solve. This one would just take some time. Until then, growling lowly, he took over the kiss and thrust until they both released again.

∞ ∞ ∞ ∞ ∞

Picking up her bag, Trisha turned and gave her quarters one last look. It was still as drab and colorless as when she'd arrived, but now it was filled with memories she would treasure forever. Of Ull. Of the meals they'd shared and of the love they'd made. Inhaling deeply, she gave herself one last moment with those memories, then spinning on her heel left the room. It was time for her to get back to doing her job, helping those anxious people who were waiting to return to Earth.

"Good morning, Jakob," Trisha greeted as they met in the corridor.

"Good morning to you, Trisha. Did you rest well?" He ran a critical eye over her as he took her bag from her. He'd been surprised when she hadn't already been in the landing bay when he'd arrived with the remaining abductees. So, he'd come to make sure she was well.

"I did." She couldn't prevent the faint blush that crept across her cheeks and quickly changed the subject as his eyebrows drew together. "How about you? Are you nervous about meeting Earth's leaders?"

"Not really, especially not with you at my side." He gave her a small smile.

"Thanks for your confidence, but I'll only be repeating what you and others say."

"It will be more than that, and you know it. It's how you do it. Ull informed me of how you assisted him in understanding what was said and how to respond effectively. I hope you will do the same for me."

"It will be my honor to do so, Jakob." Entering the landing bay, she saw the remaining abductees standing next to the shuttle and Ull a few feet away, holding the box containing the educator. She'd forgotten all about needing it until Ull had mentioned it as they lay together in the early hours of the morning. God, she hadn't wanted him to leave, hadn't wanted the night to end. It meant the return to real life, a life without Ull.

Forcing a smile she wasn't feeling, she crossed the bay. "Good morning, Ull."

"Trisha." He bowed his head slightly to her.

"Why do you have the educator?" Jakob asked.

"Did I not tell you?" Ull honestly couldn't remember if he had. He knew he had informed Veron and sent a comm to the Emperor about it. "The Earth Leaders wish to be able to speak directly to us."

"That is an encouraging sign."

As they spoke, Trisha moved to the remaining group, which consisted primarily of the men who had been the first taken. She'd sat with them, heard their horrific stories, and couldn't believe they'd only lost the one. "Let's get you home."

It didn't take long for her to get them all settled. They'd all traveled on several different shuttles during their time with the Kaliszians and knew how to work the restraint system. She had planned on sitting with them, allowing Jakob to take the copilot seat, but Ull gently gripped her elbow and guided her forward.

"You will sit next to me," he told her lowly. He hated leaving her earlier. The Earthians had waited this long to return home, and they could have waited another day. But his honor wouldn't allow him to suggest such a thing, especially as he knew Trisha would never have agreed. Still, that didn't mean he wouldn't keep her close. Ull *needed* to keep her close for as long as he could.

The flight down was as uneventful as the previous two, except this time she knew it would be her last. Looking to Ull, she let herself memorize his unique profile against the blackness of space. It was a stunning contrast.

Feeling her gaze, Ull looked to her and was stunned by what he saw in her eyes; awe and respect. No one had ever looked at him that way before. Not even his manno and Ull wanted to make sure that never changed.

"Are you alright?"

"Yes, just enjoying the view."

Ull frowned at that and looking around the cockpit, found nothing unusual. Suddenly he realized she was referring to him and felt himself begin to flush. "The view from my seat is the most stunning I have ever seen."

"That is because you have a view of the Earth." Jakob's words broke the spell Ull's words had spun around her. She'd been about to lean forward and kiss him, having forgotten where she was.

"Yes." Trisha made herself look away from Ull to her planet. "It is amazing, isn't it. Is it that different than the planets in the Kaliszian Empire?"

"Every planet in the Kaliszian Empire is different but beautiful in its own way. My homeworld, Kalbaugh, looks a great deal like Earth from space with its blue water and green vegetation, but very little of it is edible. Pontus, on the other hand, became a desert planet after the Great Infection. There is very little water there, and nothing lives or grows." Recently, he was informed this was changing, but he couldn't reveal that. It could take years, centuries even before Pontus returned to the fertile planet it had once been.

∞ ∞ ∞ ∞ ∞

Once again, Trisha found herself before the world leaders, this time between Ull and Jakob.

"Esteemed leaders, may I introduce to you Minister Jakob Ruskin of the Kaliszian Empire, sent by his Emperor, Emperor Liron Kalinin." Trisha gestured to Jakob then switched to Kaliszian. "Minister Ruskin, may I introduce you to Earth's leaders. Representing the European Council, Chancellor Smyth. From the African Council, Chancellor Abara, and Chancellor Nguyen of the Asian Council. Chancellor Khatri represents the Australian Council. President Ochoa of Mexico. Prime Minister Gagnon, the leader of Canada. And President Garcia of the United States of America."

Ruskin bowed to each leader as she introduced them, the beads interspersed in his braids catching the light. "It is my great honor to be here," he replied once Trisha finished, "And to be able to return your people taken by the Ganglians."

"It is my understanding that not all of our people returned," President Garcia said in the way of a greeting.

"This is truth." Ruskin wasn't thrown by the lack of greeting, for he'd been a Minister for too long. "Unfortunately, one of your males met the Goddess before we discovered the Zaludians illegally mining on Pontus. But if you are referring to the two females, Ashe Mackenzie and Ashe Jennifer, it was their choice to remain on Pontus with their True Mates."

"True Mates?" Prime Minister Gagnon questioned.

Jakob lifted a group of his braids to show the beads placed in various locations. "Kaliszians wear their bloodline, their status, and their accomplishments for all to see. Overall our beads are called Suja beads, but each one represents something more specific. First, the bead at the end of every braid is an Elemental bead." He touched one of his. "They maintain our braids. The beads above them are called Attainment beads and reflect my accomplishments or milestones I have achieved in my life. The height of the bead on the braid indicates the worthiness of that accomplishment or milestone." Releasing those braids, he held up the one closest to his face. "These are my Bloodline beads. I received them during my naming ceremony. This one," he touched the first and largest bead, "represents my mother and her bloodline, which now runs through me. This one represents my manno." He pointed to the second bead just above his mother's before moving to the third. "And this one represents me, the new bloodline created by the Joining of my mother and manno. A portion of this bead has passed on to each of my offspring, claiming them forever as mine."

Releasing that braid, he held up the first one on the other side of his face. "This braid holds my True Mate bead and the Dasho bead given to me by my Ashe when she agreed to commit to me. It is my understanding you have something similar called wedding bands." He saw heads of several leaders nod. "I never wish to deceive this esteemed body. The Kaliszians are as much a warrior race as the Tornians. It is our nature to fight for what we want and to defend what we have. That hasn't changed because of the Great Infection. What has changed, besides us not being able to properly feed those we love most, is that our True Mate bead no longer transfers."

"Transfers?"

"Originally, Kaliszians only had our Ashe and Dasho beads to exchange. It caused problems when more than one male offered his bead to the same female. They would then fight to prove who was most worthy. Many fit and worthy males died during those challenges leaving a great deal of pain and heartbreak in its wake. Finally, the Goddess took pity on us and gifted us with the True Mate bead." He reverently touched the large swirling bead on the braid. "It can't be given or received the way our other beads can. It appears as a Kaliszian reaches maturity then transfers to one's True Mate as an outward and irrefutable sign of who belongs to whom. It stopped the conflicts, at least until the Great Infection struck."

"So, is that *your* True Mate bead or your Ashe's?" Prime Minister Gagnon asked quietly.

"This is mine." Everyone in the room heard the sadness in the Minister's voice as he rolled the bead between his fingers. He'd had high hopes for him and his Ashe after hearing about the General's and Commander's beads. "While I love and am committed to my Ashe, as she is to me, our True Mate beads have never transferred."

"I'm sorry," Gagnon said. "You said your True Mate beads have begun to transfer again?"

That seemed to bring Jakob back from his thoughts. "Yes, Prime Minister, and while there are rumors of one transferring between Kaliszians, the only verified ones I know of are between Ashe Jennifer and General Rayner and Ashe Mackenzie and Commander Kozar."

"I'm sorry, Minister Ruskin, but I don't understand," Chancellor Nguyen spoke. "Earth women don't have True Mate beads. So how can they be exchanged?"

"It was surprising for us too, but as I stated before, our True Mate beads are a gift from the Goddess and appear when she wills it, as they did with Ashe Mackenzie and Ashe Jennifer. Few non-Kaliszians have ever received the gift, but it did happen before the Great Infection."

"So, these two Earth women can't ever leave these Kaliszians?"

Ruskin frowned at that. "The bead does not control them, Chancellor Nguyen. It represents the deep bond between them. I believe Ashe Mackenzie once referred to Commander Kozar as her Soul Mate, something rare on Earth."

"It is," President Garcia admitted.

"I hope that settles your question on your citizens remaining in the Kaliszian Empire."

"So, you are saying that they could return to Earth if they wished," Chancellor Abara pressed. "To visit their family."

"If that is their wish. But it is my understanding Ashe Mackenzie has no family on Earth. Ashe Jennifer, who is the True Mate to the Supreme Commander of Kaliszian Defenses, General Treyvon Rayner; her only relative, her sister, now resides in the Tornian Empire as its Empress."

The gasp that filled the chamber told Trisha none of them had made that connection.

"This has strengthened the already strong bond between our Empires."

"Do you agree with this statement, Warrior Ull?" President Garcia asked.

"Yes, Mr. President. I met with Ashe Jennifer and Ashe Mackenzie while on Pontus. They were both helping with those returning and seemed happy and content. They also had every opportunity to join us if they wished."

"Esteemed leaders," Trisha spoke for herself. "I have spoken in depth to those taken with Jennifer Teel-Neibaur and Mackenzie Wharton. They have assured me both women freely chose to stay on Pontus, and I feel that we should believe those that know them best and move on."

"Well said, Representative Burke." President Garcia looked to the other leaders and saw they were all in agreement. "Representative Ruskin, it is our understanding that besides returning our citizens to us, which we thank you for, you wish to enter into trade agreements with Earth for a variety of foodstuffs to feed your people. In exchange, you will also help protect Earth from the Ganglians."

"That is correct, President Garcia, but my Emperor is also aware that more is needed and has also authorized me to offer you energy crystals in exchange for the foodstuffs as we do with the Tornian Empire."

"Energy crystals?"

"Energy crystals are what power most of the Known Universes. They can provide light and heat and power all modes of transportation and weaponry."

"Are they why your blaster was able to bring down the Ganglians when ours could not?" Chancellor Khatri directed the question to Ull.

"Yes, Chancellor."

"How dangerous are these energy crystals? What pollutants do they produce?" Chancellor Nguyen demanded in quick succession.

Trisha saw Jakob's eyes widen slightly at the demand and excitement in the Chancellor's voice, but his tone didn't reflect his surprise.

"Energy crystals on their own are harmless. They interact with their environment, nurturing it. They release no toxins."

"On their own?"

"Energy crystals occur in nature wherever life is found. Our ancestors learned how to harness their energy, and it advanced our civilization, as it did for the Tornians and every other civilization in the Known Universes. Things that cause harm can use them, such as blasters, but the crystals do not cause harm."

"There are energy crystals outside the Kaliszian Empire?"

"Of course. As I've said, where there is life, there are energy crystals. One only needs to know how to harness their power."

"If the Tornian Empire has energy crystals, why would they trade for yours?" Chancellor Abara demanded.

"Because Kaliszian energy crystals are some of the most powerful in the Known Universes."

"Is this true, Warrior Ull?" All eyes looked to Ull at Abara's question.

Ull hated admitting that the Kaliszians had something his people needed. It made them seem weak, but he also wouldn't tell an untruth. "While the Tornian Empire does have and uses energy crystals mined from our planets, it is truth that those found in the Kaliszian Empire are extraordinarily powerful and slow draining. Which is why they are the preferred crystals for use in ships and weapons."

"Would you be willing to share your technology with us in exchange for foodstuffs?"

"That isn't something my Emperor has authorized, but once I contact him, I'm sure he will be agreeable."

"Thank you, Minister Ruskin," President Garcia said. "I believe we all look forward to knowing his answer. Until then, as the other world leaders wish to hear from you directly, I believe we should adjourn so they can use your educator."

∞ ∞ ∞ ∞ ∞

Trisha frowned, looking to her tío when they went to Medical.

"There are concerns about what the educator does, and we decided that our medical personnel should monitor the procedure."

Chancellor Smyth was going first, but both Ull and Jakob frowned at the equipment being attached as Trisha translated.

"What's wrong?" Trisha asked.

"We do not know what these machines do or how they operate," Jakob told her.

"Or if they could somehow interfere with the educator and causing harm," Ull finished.

"You think that's possible?" Trisha couldn't keep the alarm out of her voice, and it had her tío moving toward her.

"What is wrong, Trisha?"

Looking at him, she found all eyes in the room were now centered on her, Ull, and Jakob. Switching to English, she spoke so all could either understand or have it translated for them.

"Representative Ruskin and Warrior Ull are concerned that the monitoring equipment could adversely affect the educator causing it to damage someone."

"What? Why?" The questions filled the room.

Ull didn't need to understand the words to know the questions. "The educator is powered by an energy crystal. The power source from your medical equipment isn't."

Trisha translated and then directed a question to the doctor who seemed to be in charge. "Have any problems been found in the returnees?" She refused to call them abductees anymore. "They've all used the educator, some more than once."

A doctor stepped forward. "We've found no ill effects from their experience physically. They are incredibly healthy."

"And mentally?" President Garcia demanded.

"We did brain scans on them and found nothing unusual, although many are suffering nightmares."

"I'd say that is understandable," Trisha murmured.

"I agree. I have extensive experience with hostages, kidnapping, and trauma victims, and I have to admit I'm surprised they aren't having more problems." He turned his gaze to the two aliens. "I don't know who is responsible for that, but I thank you. These people went through something terrible, but your treatment of them went a long way to helping them heal."

Jakob bowed slightly to the doctor once Trisha translated.

"I understand how you would want to understand how the educator works, Doctor…" Trisha trailed off.

"Monroe," he supplied.

"Dr. Monroe," she acknowledged, "but as there have been no adverse side effects found in any of the returnees, wouldn't it be prudent not to change how they administer the educator? To listen to the concerns of those trained in using it? Especially when we don't understand the technology?"

Dr. Monroe was silent for several moments then slowly nodded. "I can agree with that. While all the returnees were from the United States, they had diverse ethnic backgrounds. That leads me to believe that while this device did not harm anyone, our attempts to study it while in use might."

"Then may I suggest that we allow Warrior Ull and Representative Ruskin to direct where and how the educator is applied."

"As long as my staff may observe."

Trisha turned to them and translated.

"That is fine as long as that is all they do. The educator must power down before removed, or it may cause harm." Trisha made sure everyone understood that then nodded to Ull. Removing the educator from its case, Ull then walked over to the Chancellor carrying the educator. "Are you comfortable in this position?"

After the translation, the Chancellor replied. "Yes."

"Then close your eyes and relax. My vow, it will cause you no harm."

Taking a deep breath, she released it, and after doing as Ull requested, he placed the educator over her eyes.

"How long will this take?" Chancellor Abara asked.

"It depends," Ull informed him.

"On what?"

"The person. The educator first assesses them to determine how quickly they can absorb the information, then transmits it at the optimal level. Besides language, this educator contains a great deal of information on both the Tornian and Kaliszian civilizations for your better understanding. It will take some time."

"How long did it take President Garcia or Representative Burke?"

"Several hours for each."

For a time, everyone remained and watched what Ull did, which was nothing once the educator was applied, except to closely watch the Chancellor. Doctor Monroe had asked several in-depth questions about how the educator worked, but once it became clear, Ull didn't know those answers, stopped.

"Come. Let's sit." Aaron said, guiding her to several chairs. "You don't need to be standing there the entire time."

"I might need to translate."

"If you do, you can hear it from here. Or I can. Now, did you bring your things with you?"

"You mean from the Searcher?"

"Yes."

"They're on the shuttle."

"I'll send someone to get them."

"They won't be able to get in. Ull sealed it."

"He still doesn't trust us?"

"Would you? If our technology was so much more advanced?"

"I suppose not."

"Trust takes time. It has to be earned, not given blindly. Isn't that what you've always told me?"

"Sometimes, you listen too well, Chica."

"It's the only way to learn. Something else you've always said."

"True, and here's something else that's true." He turned her, so they were staring directly into each other's eyes. "I am very proud of how you've handled all this."

"It's not like I had a choice."

"Of course, you did. You could have refused. Lisa. Warrior Ull. Me. But you didn't. You've shouldered this weight for the entire Earth and, in doing so, made things easier for all of us."

"I don't see how. You and the other leaders are doing all the negotiating."

"True, but you've gotten to know Warrior Ull and Representative Ruskin, despite the way you met. You've made us see them as well, human, and been able to explain and bridge the gaps when we haven't understood one another. You don't realize how important and rare that is, especially in politics."

"I…thank you."

"But I don't like the toll it's taking on you."

"I told you..."

"I know what you've said, but I also know it's not true. Or not the whole truth," he corrected and, at her shocked look, smiled slightly. "I've known you since you were born, Trisha. I even changed a few of your diapers. I know when you're happy, when you're sad, when you're telling the truth and when while you're not lying, you're not completely honest. Something has been bothering you, more than just Lisa and her girls disappearing."

"Isn't that enough?"

"It is, but there is still more."

Trisha sighed. While others wouldn't notice, her tío knew her too well. "There is something I've meant to talk to you about, but it can wait." She looked to Ull, who was still standing next to Chancellor Smyth's bed. "We have more important issues to deal with."

"Nothing is more important than you, Trisha."

Smiling, she leaned her head against his. "I know, Tío. I know."

Seeing Ull go to remove the educator, she quickly rose and went to his side as did her tío and every other person in the room. The Chancellor remained unmoving for several moments that seemed like hours, but finally, her lashes began to flutter, and slowly she opened her eyes.

"How are you feeling?" Ull asked in Tornian.

"I..., I feel fine."

"You are sure?" This time Ull spoke Kaliszian.

"Yes, maybe a little woozy, but otherwise fine." Her eyes sharpened and locked on Ull's. "Did it work?"

"What House is Emperor Wray from?"

"House Torino, on the planet Tornian," she snapped as if it were a stupid question. Her eyes widened when she realized she didn't know that before and that she wasn't speaking English. Her gaze went to Trisha, who gave her a reassuring smile.

"I'd say it worked."

"You will want to rest for a while," Jakob told her. "It will give you time to realize everything you now know."

"I would prefer you to do that here so that we can monitor you." Dr. Monroe looked to Ull and Jakob. "That shouldn't cause any problems now, should it?"

"No," Jakob answered. "There will be no chance of interference now."

Aaron gave Trisha's arm a reassuring squeeze then followed Chancellor Smyth. He felt since he had already gone through the process, he would be the best one to assist her and answer any questions.

Trisha looked to the remaining world leaders. "So, who's next?"

Chapter Fifteen

Six hours later, Ull and Jakob finally called a halt. It was getting late, and while they had been taking turns monitoring the educator, it had been a long day, and they were both tired. The final two leaders would use the educator in the morning.

"Would you like to stay and have dinner with us?" President Garcia asked. "It would just be myself and Trisha, so you wouldn't need things translated."

Jakob replied, "While I greatly appreciate the offer, President Garcia, it would be best that I return to the Searcher so I can contact my Emperor about the questions raised during the Council meeting."

"You are in direct communication with your Emperor?" Aaron couldn't believe that given the great distance between their planets.

"Not direct as instantaneous, but I can send communications. It will take several hours for it to reach Luda, then relay to my Emperor. Once he reaches a decision, he will respond. I hope to have his answer before we reconvene tomorrow."

"Then, by all means, that is the priority."

"Unfortunately, that also means Warrior Ull will be unable to attend as I can't pilot the shuttle."

"Of course." Aaron looked to Trisha. "I guess it will be just you and me. I can't remember the last time that happened."

"It's been a long time," Trisha agreed, "but I need to walk back to the shuttle with Ull and Jakob and get my bag first."

"I can send one of the guards."

"No," she quickly refused. "After sitting and standing all day, I want to stretch my legs. I assume your quarters are by your office?"

"It is. I'll go there and catch up on some work. Meet me there."

"Alright." Rising on her toes, she kissed his cheek. "I'll be there soon."

∞ ∞ ∞ ∞ ∞

Ull remained silent as Trisha walked between him and Jakob. He'd known her leaving him was coming, but he never thought it could hurt this bad. He was a Tornian Warrior, trained to ignore pain, but he couldn't ignore this.

Reaching the shuttle, he punched in the security code, and the ramp lowered. When Trisha would have followed Jakob, Ull put a restraining hand on her arm.

"Are you sure you wish to remain here? You could return with us and come back tomorrow." He prayed to the Goddess that she would. He wanted another night with her.

Looking up at him, Trisha knew there was nothing she wanted to do more. One more night with Ull to fill all the lonely nights to come, but she knew she couldn't. It wasn't fair to Ull. *He* wanted a female that would go to Betelgeuse with him, who would be his Lady, and give him offspring.

She wasn't that female.

She was the female that would be responsible for *finding* that for him.

But God, it hurt.

Reaching up, she let her fingers graze his lips. "I can't. You know that." When he opened his lips to argue, she pressed her fingers lightly against them. "This is the way it has to be."

Ull growled his displeasure but didn't say anything. Instead, he pulled her body flush against his. Letting her feel how much he wanted her to return with him.

"Trisha, I..." Jakob came to an abrupt halt on the ramp seeing Trisha in Ull's arms. "I brought you your bag."

Slowly Trisha pulled out of Ull's arms, her fingers lingering as long as possible on his lips before walking over to take her bag from Jakob. "Thank you, Jakob. I'll see you tomorrow."

"Trisha, wait!" Ull growled, moving toward her holding out a comm unit. "Take this in case you need to contact me."

Slowly Trisha took the comm, making sure not to touch him again, and forced herself to walk away from the only man she knew she would ever love.

∞ ∞ ∞ ∞ ∞

"What, in the name of the Goddess, do you think you're doing?!" Jakob burst out once the shuttle door finally closed. "We *need* her. Both our *people* need her, and you're treating her like a female from a pleasure house?!"

Ull rounded on Jakob so fast that it had Jakob stumbling back. "Never. Ever. Compare her to one of those females. Trisha is the fittest, worthiest, most beautiful female in the Known Universes, and if you insult her that way again, you will meet the Goddess. Minister or not." With that, Ull went to the Captain's chair and started the shuttle.

Carefully Jakob slid into the copilot's seat, never taking his eyes off Ull. He barely got his harness fastened before the shuttle shot straight up at combat speed. "Ull!" he gritted out through clenched teeth.

Ull knew he was overreacting. Ull also knew he'd pushed the shuttle to its limit, but he needed to get away from Trisha before he *did* do something that ruined his brothers-in-arms' chance to find females. Slowly he reduced speed and leveled out the shuttle.

"My apologies, Minister Ruskin. I should not have done that."

Jakob took in the tension in Ull's body, the clenching of his jaw, and the pain that filled his eyes. "You truly care about Trisha," he murmured, astonished at the thought.

When Ull's jaw only tightened further, Jakob tried again. "If you truly care about her, you need to tell her."

"I have," Ull ground out. "She has refused me."

"I..." Jakob knew he should let it go, but he couldn't. "I'm sorry, Ull, but are you sure? I saw how she looked at you. How she openly and willingly touched you. Females don't do that unless they care about a male."

"I didn't say she didn't care. I said she refused me."

"But why?"

"Because she refuses to leave Earth. She says her place is here, helping her people while mine is on Betelgeuse."

"She does speak truth, but that doesn't mean she can't still be yours. Not if you truly want her."

Slowly Ull turned his head, his eyes blazing to demand. "Explain."

"Goddess willing, it will be many years before you become Lord of Betelgeuse. By then, Trisha may be willing to leave Earth."

"So, you expect me to wait for *years* before I claim her? Leaving her unprotected?!"

"No, what I'm saying is you should claim her now. If she is willing, of course."

The tiny spark of hope the Kaliszian's words had brought him died. "I already told you she refuses to leave Earth."

"Then, *you* remain here with her."

"Remain?! I am the First Male of a *Lord*. My place is at *his* side."

"An idiotic Tornian attitude," Jakob muttered. "A male's place is at his female's side. *She* should be more important to him than any current or future position. She should even come before a male's family because only *she* can give him a family of his own if the Goddess so blesses them."

"Statements like that are why Kaliszians can't feed their people."

"And your belief is why the Goddess doesn't bless you with more females," Jakob fired back.

These were long-running insults Kaliszians and Tornians threw at each other, but neither could deny the other was right, so they both remained silent. After landing the shuttle, they found Veron was impatiently waiting for them at the bottom of the ramp.

"Was there a problem at NACB?" Veron immediately demanded.

"No. Why?" Ull asked, coming to a stop in front of the Captain.

"Then why in the name of the Goddess did you take off like that?"

Ull had the decency to look abashed. "I was in a hurry to return."

Veron frowned. "You knew the Emperor sent an urgent comm?"

"What? No. What's happened?"

"I don't know. The comm was for you."

"I need to send a comm to Emperor Liron," Jakob told him.

"Then come. You can send your comm while Ull listens to his."

∞ ∞ ∞ ∞ ∞

"So, how is it on a spaceship?" Aaron asked as he and Trisha settled down to eat.

"Not too bad. I suppose it's like being on any military ship. Sparse, colorless, and without a lot of extra comforts besides the bed and a couch. All Tornian sized, of course." She took a bit of the perfectly cooked steak and hummed her enjoyment.

"And the food?"

"There was a little Earth food," she told him after swallowing. "It seems Jennifer insisted they sent some of what they'd found on a Ganglian ship on the Searcher, but I left that for the returnees and tried the Tornian food. It was pretty good. Different but good. Like going to another country and eating only local fare. Some of the textures and tastes aren't what you expected but still flavorful. They have what they call hunaja, which tastes just like honey. They even spread it on their type of bread."

"Interesting, so we have more things alike than we thought."

"I'd say we have a great many things alike. We all want to survive while making sure our families are safe, healthy, and protected. That makes Tornians, Kaliszians, and humans more similar than different."

Aaron leaned back in his chair and let his gaze take her in. He could still see her smiling at him with her two front teeth missing. Could see her running full out across the park stubbornly trying to get her kite to fly on a windless day. And he remembered how strong she'd been during her mamá's illness and how devastated she'd been when Patricia finally passed. Now she sat across from him, a beautiful, strong, poised woman who had taken on something no one else ever had and made it look easy.

"You have grown into a truly amazing woman, Trisha."

Trisha felt herself blush at her tío's compliment. "Thank you. I've tried to live up to what you and Mamá expected of me. You set the bar high."

"There was never a bar, Trishy. We only ever wanted you to be happy in whatever you chose to do."

Setting her silverware aside, Trisha placed her elbows on the table, her chin resting on her clasped fingers. "And are you, Tío? Happy that is, with what you've chosen?"

"Most of the time, yes," he told her honestly. "Are there times I wished I had a wife and family of my own? Yes, but I had your mamá, and I have you so that more than makes up for what I sacrificed to make sure you and the rest of the world were safe and protected."

Reaching across the table, she squeezed his hand. "You've done wonderfully in both cases."

"I wasn't able to protect your mamá, not from our parents' reaction to her marriage, not from Martin's death, and not from cancer that killed her."

Trisha felt her throat tighten. "No, but no one could have done that. What you did do was make it easier for her. You were there for her at the wedding. You were there for her at the gravesite and the hard times that came after. And you were there, holding her other hand as she slipped away to join Dad in heaven."

"I am the President of the God-damn United States. I should have been able to save my sister."

"But you couldn't. Maybe that's our Great Infection. Cancer. We can cure some, drive others into remission, but it still takes too many."

"It does. You've been going to your annual screenings, right?"

Trisha knew what he was asking. Because of her history, her mamá's medical history, she was at a higher risk of getting cancer, which she had. She'd only missed one screening, but that seemed to have been enough. Trisha hadn't told him yet. Oh, she'd planned on it, once she'd come to terms with it herself, just like her mamá. Trisha took the oral meds her doctor had prescribed and meant to tell him, but then the Tornians had arrived. "Had one just over four months ago."

"Good."

"Now enough about me, tell me about the returnees. When are they going to be reunited with their families?"

"We've started, very discretely, to bring the families here. The first ones will begin arriving later tonight."

"That's such good news. Are the families going to have to stay here long?"

"Only until we resolve the trade agreements and can announce to the world in a way that won't cause a panic."

Trisha's eyebrows drew together. "But that could take *months*. Haven't these people been through enough?"

"I realize it may be inconvenient for them but compared to the best interests of the world… it's a small thing."

Trisha just stared at Tío. This was why he was the President and not her. He saw the bigger picture and was willing to take the hard, sometimes painful and unpopular steps to make it happen.

"Then I'd better get working on the matching program for the Tornians so everyone can go home."

"You think the other world leaders will approve it?" Aaron raised a questioning eyebrow at her.

"Of course, not without some complaining, but they will. What else can they do? We need Tornian protection from the Ganglians."

"But if the Kaliszians supply us with these energy crystals and tech, we could do that ourselves."

"Maybe in a decade or so. Is anyone willing to be at risk for that long? To take the chance the Tornians won't just invade? They are facing extinction." Trisha held up her hand to stop her tío from speaking. "Yes, the Kaliszians would come to our defense because they need us too, but that means they'd be starting a war with the Tornians. Another race that helps support them *now.* Are you willing to start an intergalactic war over females who are *willing* to Join with a Tornian?"

Aaron slowly smiled. "God, you're just like your mamá. I rarely won an argument with her either."

"Well," she shrugged her shoulders, "when you're wrong, you're wrong."

"Hey, I'm not wrong. I never said I was against the Tornians' proposal. I just wanted to hear how you justified it."

"Which is what you'd always say to Mamá, so you didn't have to admit you lost." As they shared a smile at the memory, the comm Ull had given Aaron went off.

∞ ∞ ∞ ∞ ∞

While Jakob sent his comm to his Emperor, Ull listened to the one from his own in the other room. It was short and to the point.

"Warrior Ull, you will return to Luda immediately. I will explain more once we are in direct communication. Emperor Wray out."

Ull looked at Veron and saw the Emperor's Captain was just as surprised as he was. "You don't know what's happened?"

"No, but it must be important for Wray to want us to return. I'll ready the ship."

"Ready the ship?" Jakob asked, walking over.

"Yes, Emperor Wray has recalled the Searcher."

"But I can't leave. You can't leave." He gave Ull a pleading look. "We are still in negotiations."

"My Emperor has ordered my return. I will not disobey him," Veron told him.

"Well, mine hasn't, and I won't leave until he does," Jakob argued back.

"Then, Ull can transport you back to Earth, and you can continue without us."

"But, I'm waiting for a response from Liron!"

Veron sighed. "I will launch another relay satellite into Earth's orbit. That way, you can send and receive transmissions from Earth. It will still only be verbal and not as secure as going through the Searcher, but it will be something until we return."

"That will have to do," Jakob grumbled. "Do you know how long you will be gone?"

"No, Wray refused to say until we could communicate directly."

"I'll go ready the shuttle and contact President Garcia while you pack, Jakob."

"Thank you, Ull," Jakob said, giving him a somewhat shocked look. "It shouldn't take me long."

∞ ∞ ∞ ∞ ∞

"What is it?" Aaron answered the comm in Tornian without a thought.

"I will be returning shortly with Minister Ruskin. My Emperor has recalled the Searcher. We will be leaving as soon as the shuttle returns."

"What about negotiations?"

"Minister Ruskin will continue with his, and I will discuss the inclusion of Tornian technology along with the necessary Tornian steel needed to use it."

"And the repair units?"

"I have already contacted the Emperor about those, and they will be on the next ship that comes to Earth."

"Do you know when you'll be returning?"

"No, we've been ordered to Luda, which is a two-week journey from here. Once there, it will be up to Emperor Wray as to when we return."

"So, a minimum of a month, one of your 'moon cycles.'"

"Yes."

"Alright, I'll make sure rooms are made available for Minister Ruskin."

"We'll be down shortly."

Trisha had sat in stunned silence as Ull, and her tío spoke.

He was leaving.

Ull was leaving.

Yes, she'd known that eventually, he would be, but not today, not now. She'd thought she still had some time to see him, hear his voice, and maybe casually touch him. Now she didn't.

"Trisha, are you okay?" Aaron asked after ending the comm.

"What?"

"You seem pale all of a sudden."

"No, no, I'm fine, just trying to rearrange things in my head."

"Nothing has changed. Tomorrow Minister Ruskin will oversee the use of the educator for Prime Minister Gagnon and President Ochoa. Once they've had some time to recover, we will convene the Council and continue negotiations with the Kaliszians."

"I was thinking more along the lines of helping Jakob adjust to our world and our foods."

"I'll leave that to you as you have experience in what he is used to consuming."

"I'll go meet Jakob at the landing pad." Wiping her mouth, she rose. "Should I bring him back here?"

"Yes, and I'll have several guards meet you there."

"Guards?"

"Because I'm sure the Minister will have luggage, not because I don't trust him," he quickly told her.

"Oh. Well then, that would be great. Also, how late is the cafeteria open?"

"You want to take him there?"

"Yes, I doubt Jakob has had time to eat, and it will allow him to see the variety of foods the Earth has to offer. After all, with the other leaders here, I'm sure you've had something from every region prepared for their support staff."

Aaron just shook his head. "You are a born politician."

"Hey now, no reason to get nasty." But she returned his smile. "I'll see you in a little bit."

∞ ∞ ∞ ∞ ∞

Trisha rapidly blinked, so her tears didn't fall. Ull hadn't even gotten off the shuttle. He'd landed, lowered the ramp, and Jakob had exited carrying two large bags, one in each hand. Jakob had hardly stepped off the ramp before it retracted, and the shuttle lifted off again to disappear rapidly.

"Did you get dust in your eyes?" Jakob asked. Setting his bags down, he stepped in front of her, blocking the worst of the still swirling dust.

"What?" Trisha pulled her gaze from the sky and forced a smile on her lips. "Oh, no, just thinking." She looked to the guards. "If it's alright with you, I'll escort you to where you'll be staying."

"That would be wonderful." Turning to retrieve his bags, he found them already in the hands of two warriors.

"They can carry those for you," she told him as she linked her arm through one of his. "Did you have last meal before you came down?"

"No." Looking over his shoulder, he realized that no one would understand what they were saying, so he told her what he knew. "Everything happened rather quickly once we landed. Emperor Wray recalled the Searcher without giving any reason."

"Do you think there is trouble in the Tornian Empire?"

Jakob had given that a great deal of thought on the way down. "I don't believe so. Wray is a fit and worthy Emperor who has earned the trust and respect of his fellow warriors. I'm hoping to hear something about it when my Emperor responds to my transmission."

Trisha came to a halt and turned to look at him. "Damn, I hadn't even thought about that. Can you communicate with him when the Searcher's gone?"

"Captain Veron placed a communications satellite into Earth's orbit so I could still send and receive comms. It's not ideal but will do until we deploy permanent, advanced comm satellites. Then we can communicate directly back and forth both visually and verbally."

"We'll actually be able to see the person we're talking to? Even this far away?"

"Once a network of satellites is set up, yes."

"How amazing," she murmured as they began to walk down the corridor again.

"You are going to find there are many amazing things in the Known Universes. I'm almost envious of your people discovering them all for the first time."

"There are also many terrible things."

"This is truth, but hopefully we will be able to help you recognize them, so you don't learn the hard way as we did many times."

"I'm sure that will be appreciated." Stopping, she knocked on a door.

"Enter."

"These are President Garcia's rooms," she told him as they entered. "He wanted to escort you to yours personally."

"Welcome, Minister Ruskin." The President rose to greet him. "I have to say I'm excited to have you staying with us. It is an opportunity for everyone to get to know you as a person."

"That will be a benefit, yes."

"I wasn't exactly sure what you are accustomed to, so I hope what we have will be suitable. I did have the bed changed out, as Trisha said everything on the ship was Tornian size, which I assume is also a Kaliszian's preferred size."

"It is, thank you."

"Wonderful, then let me show you where you'll be staying." Both Trisha and Jakob stepped back, allowing the President to exit first then followed. "I hope you don't mind. I put you in my area."

"Of course not."

They walked for several moments, passing a corridor. "I thought you'd be more comfortable across the hall from Trisha. That way, if you have any questions or problems, she's near."

"That was most considerate, Mr. President."

All this was news to Trisha. She hadn't been to her quarters yet, although a guard took her bag there.

"This is Trisha's quarters." He gestured to one door then to the one across from it. "And here is yours." Pulling a key card out of his jacket, he pressed it against the reader, and they heard the locks turn. Reaching out, the President pushed down the handle and walked in, the lights immediately coming on. "I'm going to let Trisha show you around as she knows better than I the difference." He handed Jakob the key card. "I'll see you in the morning."

"Goodnight, Tío Aaron." Stepping forward, she hugged him. She knew it wasn't the proper thing to do in the presence of others, but Trisha didn't care. After everything that had happened today, she needed the contact.

Aaron didn't hesitate to return the hug, even going as far as placing a kiss on the top of her head. "I'll see you in the morning too." With that, the President left.

Trisha smiled at Jakob as the guards put his bags in the bedroom then left, the door closing behind them. Looking around the room, she wondered what Jakob thought.

"It's not like on the Searcher, is it?" she asked.

Jakob's gaze traveled around the room, taking in what, compared to the Searcher, were lavish accommodations. The stone floor was familiar, but on top was a rug even thicker than the one in his own home. Several chairs appeared comfortable, but a tight fit for him. The couch was deep enough. But what caught his eye was the sizeable Kaliszian-size desk.

"I'll see that you receive larger chairs."

"That would be appreciated."

"This is your resting room, as you refer to it," she said, walking over to the only other door in the room. There was a massive bed in the room, as per her tío's orders, with Jakob's bags sitting on it.

"Is that wrong?" Jakob asked. "Do you not rest in this room?"

Trisha smiled. "We do, but because of the bed, we usually call it the 'bedroom.'" She went on to explain the rest of the room. "Like in your office, the lights come on automatically, but you can also control them by voice. Lights off," she commanded, and the room went dark. She then ordered, "Lights on. Once you use voice commands, the only way for them to be automatic again is to touch a pad." She gestured to one by the door and then walked over to the one by the bed. "There is also a sensitivity level, so at night the lights won't turn on if you're just rolling over."

Jakob nodded his understanding and took in the controls, the bed, and the few pieces of furniture with again the thick rug on the floor. It all offered warmth and comfort.

"And in here is your cleansing room. There are handless controls for the sink and shower as on the Searcher, but the temperature adjustment is manual." She showed him the levers for both. "There are towels here," she pointed to the ones hanging on the rails then opened a cabinet. "And more in here if you need them."

"I'm surprised the President was able to accommodate me so quickly."

"To be honest, so am I," she admitted. "I never knew this facility was here. I doubt few do. But my tío gets things done."

"He certainly seems to."

"He'll do his best for you and your people, Jakob. You will get the food you need."

"I'm actually starting to believe that. Thank you, Trisha."

"I didn't do anything but translate for you. But speaking of food should we get some? Ull's comm interrupted my meal, and you didn't get any. I could return your kindness to me on the Searcher and try to describe what things are and taste like."

"I would like that."

Chapter Sixteen

Several hours later, after a delightful meal, where she enjoyed watching Jakob's reaction to the staggering variety of foods available and their different tastes and textures, she was finally alone in her quarters.

God, she was so tired. It felt like she hadn't slept in days, and she hadn't. Her night with Ull hadn't involved much sleeping. More like passing out from pleasure. She'd never known anyone with Ull's stamina and recovery time. She'd had more orgasms during the night with him than she'd had in her entire life combined and that included the ones she gave herself. Just thinking about it had her getting wet and the tender flesh between her legs throbbing in anticipation.

Forcing her thoughts away from Ull and the pleasure he'd given her, she moved into her bedroom, where her small bag sat on the bed. She needed to talk to her tío about cleaning what clothes she had and getting some more. When she'd packed, Trisha hadn't taken into consideration how long she'd be gone, probably because she'd still been shocked by the arrival of 'aliens.'

Sighing, she opened her bag and pulling out her sleeping pants, tank, and toiletry bag, headed for the bathroom. She needed to wash away the day, and hopefully, the heat of the water would relax her enough to sleep. Fifteen minutes later, she waved off the water and stepped out into the steam-filled room. Grabbing a towel, she began drying her hair as she opened the door, letting in the cooler air from the bedroom.

By the time the mirror had cleared, her short hair was nearly dry, and she wrapped the towel around her body. Pulling what she needed out of her toiletry bag, she brushed her teeth, and then her hair before reaching in for her pill bottle. Not finding it, she set her brush aside and gripping each side of the bag, opened it wider peering inside. She immediately saw her moisturizer, the makeup she rarely wore, and her manicure set.

But no pill bottle.

With her heart beginning to pound, she upended the bag, dumping its contents onto the counter and started frantically searching through them.

No pill bottle.

Gripping the edge of the counter, she closed her eyes and thought back to the last time she *knew* she'd had it. It had been that morning on the Searcher. She'd showered after Ull had left, taken her morning dose, then put everything into the toiletry bag for the return to Earth. Could it have fallen out?

Rushing into the bedroom, she began pulling all her clothes out of her travel bag, then flipped that over and shook it vigorously.

No pill bottle.

Ignoring the mess she'd made, she slowly sat down on the bed and tried to figure out what happened. Either she didn't put the bottle in the bag, or it fell out, and she didn't notice it. But none of that mattered now. What mattered was what was she going to do now? She could have just contacted Ull and had him bring the bottle down with him tomorrow if the Searcher wasn't recalled. It wouldn't have been ideal, as she wasn't supposed to miss any of her doses, but it wouldn't have been earth-shattering either. But the Searcher had been recalled, and it had been hours since it left.

What was she going to do?

If she told her tío, not only would he freak out, he might remove her from the negotiations, especially since they would all be able to communicate directly. She couldn't let that happen. Lisa had pleaded for *her* to help the Tornians, and she'd be damned if she'd let her friend down again.

She couldn't call her pharmacy and have them send more medication. She was in a top-secret facility. It had no address, at least not yet.

Maybe she could talk to Dr. Monroe. Chances were slim that he would have the exact medication prescribed for her, but with them not knowing the condition of the returnees, maybe he had something similar. Looking at the time, she realized it was too late to contact him tonight. She'd have to do it in the morning.

Cleaning up the mess she'd made in the bedroom and bathroom, she dressed in her sleepwear and crawled into bed. Within minutes, despite this new concern, she was asleep.

∞ ∞ ∞ ∞ ∞

Ull's knuckles whitened as he gripped the edges of the back viewport of the Searcher and continued to stare out, even though Earth had disappeared hours ago. Goddess, he hadn't wanted to leave her, not like this, not without a proper goodbye. He'd seen her standing there on the landing pad waiting for *Ruskin*. Not him. And he knew if he got off the shuttle, he would have kidnapped her…again. So he'd forced himself to leave as quickly as possible.

He was doing what all fit and worthy warriors did, following his Emperor's order. But if it was the right thing, then why did it feel so wrong. The Kaliszian had been right. A male's place was at his female's side. It's where he wanted to be but didn't know how he could get there. It had him wanting to rip the Searcher apart. Turning away from the viewport, he went to the only place that might soothe him.

The lights automatically came on as he entered the quarters Trisha had once used. He'd never given much thought to quarters before, on the Searcher or off. They only needed to serve a warrior's needs. But when Trisha had been here, they'd become more, more interesting, with more warmth, and more alive. Now, this room was back to being the cold, grey, and uninviting place it had always been.

Entering the resting chamber, he took in the disheveled bed, a testament to what they had done in it. Moving toward it, he lifted a pillow to his face, taking in his Trisha's unique scent. The circulation system had removed it from the rest of the room, but here it still existed.

Goddess, he missed her.

And not just for Joining.

She openly challenged him when she thought he was wrong. Not with tears and tantrums the way Tornian females did when they didn't get their way, but intellectually, arguing her point. She made him see things differently, like how wrong they had been in kidnapping those females. If something like that happened to his Trisha, he'd destroy the Known Universes to get her back.

The ringing of his comm jolted him from his dark thoughts.

"What?"

"It's your shift for piloting," Veron told him.

"I'll be right there." Leaving the pillow on the bed, he turned on his heel and strode into the outer chamber. As he headed for the door, something on the floor near the cleansing room door caught his eye. Frowning, he walked over and picked up an amber-colored bottle. Rolling it in his hand, he could see there was writing on it, but he couldn't read it. It had to be Trisha's.

Putting the languages of Earth into the educator so everyone could understand one another, no matter the dialect they spoke or wrote, needed to be addressed quickly once negotiations were over.

Tucking the bottle into his vest so he could return it to Trisha, he left her quarters and headed to the control room.

∞ ∞ ∞ ∞ ∞

"What is the name of the drug?" Dr. Monroe asked Trisha early the next morning. Trisha pronounced the medication the best she could and saw Monroe's eyebrows shoot up. "That's a potent drug." He paused, then continued. "It's only used for extremely aggressive late-stage cancers."

"I know," she told him. "The President doesn't know, and I'm trusting you to keep it that way."

Monroe let his gaze travel over the young woman who'd played a significant role in getting their kidnapped people back home. She was instrumental in the negotiations between the Tornians, Kaliszians, and Earth and had been this sick while doing it?

"I will say nothing to the President."

"Thank you. And the prescription?"

"I don't carry that specific drug. Let me do some research to see if a combination of what I do have can be substituted until we can get your prescription here."

"Is that even possible? This is a secret facility."

"Which has to be restocked from time to time. I'll put in a special request to be resupplied sooner and add your prescription to it. That should keep it under the radar."

"Thank you."

"Don't thank me yet, not until I get it here." He pointed his finger at her, "And I expect you to tell me immediately if the medication I prescribe doesn't help. We can't let this get out of control."

"I will," she promised.

∞ ∞ ∞ ∞ ∞

Trisha was returning to her quarters when Jakob stepped out of his. "Good morning, Jakob. Did you sleep well?"

"I did, thank you."

"Interested in getting first meal together? There will be a different variety available this morning."

"Truth?"

"Truth." Smiling, she linked an arm through his. "Come on. I'm hungry."

Last night Jakob had been surprised by the variety and amount of food. Trisha had encouraged him to try a little bit of everything, stating it would help him to know what to negotiate for, so he had. Jakob felt guilty afterward, knowing that the majority of Kaliszians had less than a tenth of what Jakob had sampled for last meal. Entering the same room now, he came to a stunned halt.

"Jakob? What's wrong?"

Jakob's gaze traveled over the food area that last night he'd thought was full but realized it had only been one of five sections now open. "You have such an abundance of food," he murmured.

Trisha's gaze followed his and realized he was right. It was something she'd never really given much thought. While they hadn't completely wiped out hunger yet, they had come a very long way. She couldn't imagine what if felt like to know the majority of your people went hungry.

"We do, and soon your people will too. Come on." She started him moving forward again. "You need to sample again. For the betterment of your people."

"You are just trying to make me not feel guilty."

"That may be, but it's still the truth. Kaliszian tastes probably vary as much as humans, but hopefully, you will know what appeals most so we can get those sent first."

"Minister Ruskin, it's wonderful to see you again." Vanessa walked up to the Minister who had taken in her and the other females. He'd treated each of them with respect and consideration she would never forget.

"Ashe Vanessa," Jakob took the hands she held out. "How are you doing?"

"I'm fine. In fact, I'm wonderful. Dr. Monroe gave me a clean bill of health even though I have high blood pressure and am diabetic. But never mind that. I want you to meet my husband, Dasho, Collin." She looked to the well-built, grey-haired man whose hands rested on her waist as if afraid she'd disappear. And while he smiled, Trisha could tell by the haggard expression on his face that his wife's abduction had taken a toll on him. "Collin, this is Minister Ruskin, who took care of us on his planet and made sure we had everything we needed returning home."

"I can't thank you enough, Minister Ruskin," he said as he stuck out his hand. "I don't know what I would have done if I'd lost my Nessie forever. These last few months have been hell."

Trisha translated as Vanessa burrowed into her husband's chest.

"The honor was mine, Dasho Collin." He shook the male's hand as he knew humans did. "I only regret the circumstances that allowed me to meet your amazing Ashe. My own Ashe Piri enjoyed her time with Ashe Vanessa immensely."

"While there is still a great deal for Collin and me to catch up on, perhaps one day it will be possible for us to come to visit Kalbaugh."

"You and your Dasho would be most welcome."

"Jakob and I were just going to get first meal, have you and Collin eaten yet."

"Yes. We had just finished and were going back to our rooms when I saw you."

"Then we'll let you do that. I'm sure your husband still has a great many questions."

Vanessa looked up over her shoulder at him. "You're right. It's going to be a while before he lets me out of his sight again, not that I mind." With that, the couple walked away arm in arm.

∞ ∞ ∞ ∞ ∞

Trisha sighed in relief as Prime Minister Gagnon sat up from using the educator, the last one to do so, answering Jakob's questions correctly and saying she felt fine.

"I would still like you to rest for several hours," Dr. Monroe told her.

"I agree," Jakob said once Trisha translated.

"Then we will convene the Council after lunch," President Garcia said, looking to Dr. Monroe. "You will let me know if there are any problems."

"Of course, Mr. President."

"Good, then I have some work to attend to and will see you all at one o'clock." With that, the President left the room, followed by the other leaders, while Dr. Monroe began to run some tests on Prime Minister Gagnon as he had with everyone who had used the educator.

"Would you like to go for a walk, Jakob?" Trisha asked. "See more of what Earth is like?"

"I would very much like that, but first, I must return to my quarters to see if Emperor Liron has responded yet."

"Representative Burke," Dr. Monroe spoke up. "Could I speak with you for a moment?"

"Of course." Trisha looked to Jakob. "Do you remember how to get back to your quarters?"

"I believe so."

"Then how about I meet you there in about twenty minutes if that gives you enough time."

"That should be sufficient. I will see you then."

Trisha waited until Dr. Monroe finished speaking with the Prime Minister then followed him into his office, where he closed the door.

"I did some research, and while these aren't a perfect substitute, they are what I have." He held out two bottles. "These will help curtail your cancer's growth. You need to take both three times a day."

"Three?" she frowned at that. "I only had to take the other twice."

"I know, but these aren't as long-acting, so you'll need to maintain your levels. They also offer no pain relief, so you'll need to take this." He handed her another bottle. "Take it when you do the others, but if you need more, you can take it."

Trisha released a heavy sigh as she took the third bottle. "Alright. Any side effects I should know about?"

"Fatigue, nausea, possibly some blurry vision, and lightheadedness. You need to get as much rest as you can and eat as much as possible." He ran a critical eye over her. "I haven't seen your charts or known you long, but you seem to have lost some weight since we first met."

"I've been sampling Tornian and Kaliszian food for the last few days, and while it was good, I wasn't sure how my system would react to it, so I probably wasn't eating as much as usual."

"I see," Dr. Monroe hummed, obviously not wholly believing her. Loss of appetite was a later symptom of this cancer. "Well, now that you are on Earth, I expect you to start eating more. Your body needs it."

"I will, and thank you again for helping me."

"No thanks needed. I wish I could do more. The returnees have all told me how much you helped them."

"I didn't do anything but listen and answer their questions the best I could."

"Which is what they needed. You made the return home easier for them and my medical staff."

Trisha felt her eyes mist at that. All she'd ever wanted to do was help people, to make a difference the way her mamá, father, and tío had. When diagnosed with cancer, Trisha thought that wouldn't be possible, but now to hear she had, even if it were only for a few, meant a lot.

"Thank you for that. There is something else I need to discuss with you. I'm assuming you are aware of everything that is happening here." Because nothing ever stayed secret, even at a top-secret facility.

"If you are referring to the fact we now know for sure there is life on other planets, then yes."

"Do you know why the Tornians and Kaliszians are here?"

"To prevent our people from being taken and to negotiate treaties."

"Yes, but there are some that chose not to return."

"Yes, some of the returnees told me that. That several women had decided to stay with the Kaliszians."

'So, they didn't know about the ones with the Tornians,' she thought, so she wasn't going to open that can of worms. "Yes, but what they didn't tell you, because they most likely didn't know, is that those two women, Jennifer and Mackenzie, are both pregnant."

"Really." Monroe leaned back in his chair, giving her a considering look.

"Yes, and one of the things needing negotiated is Earth OB/GYNs to go and assist their Healers with the pregnancies and births."

"I wasn't aware of that."

"You wouldn't be since, as of yet, it hasn't been brought up. The Kaliszians' priority is securing a trade agreement so they can feed their people, but it is going to come up, and I'd like to be ahead of the game when it is."

"How?"

"You're a doctor, and while I realize you're not an OB/GYN, I was hoping you might still be able to come up with a list of doctors that would be interested in the groundbreaking opportunity. The first Earthian-Kaliszian babies." She wasn't going to tell him that an Earthian-Tornian baby had already been born.

"It would be an amazing opportunity," Monroe agreed. "I do know a few OB/GYNs. I'll reach out discreetly, of course, and see if I can do that for you."

"Thank you. Now..." She rose from her seat. "I'd better go take these." She gestured to the bottles in her hand. "Then go meet up with Minister Ruskin."

"Don't overdue," Monroe warned. "Your system needs to get used to this medication."

Chapter Seventeen

Ull had never had a problem with the monotony of space travel before. He liked to use the time to hone his fighting skills, which is what he'd done traveling to Earth. But now, sparring held no appeal. Wray had recalled the Searcher, and he needed to get close enough to Luda to find out why so he could return to Trisha.

Reaching into his vest, he touched the bottle he'd found. Over the last few days, he'd been carrying it, to have something of hers with him at all times. Primarily as Trisha's scent from the pillow, he now rested with, was fading.

Now, a week and a half from Earth, they were finally close enough to contact Luda directly. The only reason he hadn't was because Veron hadn't arrived yet, and if he didn't soon, Ull would start without him.

"I should have known you'd already be here."

"You're late," Ull growled.

"No, I'm not. The scheduled transmission isn't for another," Veron looked at the time, "Two minutes."

Ull had no answer for that because Luda had sent them a comm earlier to arrange the time. Instead, Ull turned to the comm station and began entering the transmission code.

Veron said nothing, just took in Ull's overall demeanor. He'd been a very different male since they'd left Earth. More solemn, withdrawn and reserved as if there was something that weighed heavily on his mind. It made sense as they'd left the negotiations so suddenly, but for some reason, Veron felt it was more than that, but couldn't figure out what.

"You're early." King Grim's face appeared on the comm screen after several moments.

"We didn't want to keep you waiting, my King," Ull said, speaking for both of them.

"I see," but Grim's tone said he didn't believe Ull. "The Emperor will be here in a few moments." With that, Grim moved out of the view of the comm. Less than a minute later, the Emperor's face appeared.

"Veron. Warrior Ull."

"Emperor," they both immediately responded, crossing an arm over their chest and bowing to him.

"Sit," Wray ordered." Once they had complied, he continued. "I'm sure you want to know why I recalled you so suddenly."

The question didn't require either of them to answer, so they remained silent. "There isn't anything dire…"

"Then why did you recall us!" Everyone was shocked by Ull's outburst, including Ull. He knew better than to question his Emperor. Not because Wray refused to allow it, or ended anyone who did, but because it needed to be respectful, which he wasn't. Bowing his head, Ull said, "My apologies, Sire."

"Was there something important going on in the negotiations that I am unaware of?" Wray asked.

Ull lifted his head. "No, Sire. I have reported everything discussed. I feel it is in everyone's best interests that the planet not be left unprotected. Another Ganglian ship could arrive to investigate why the one we destroyed did not return." The possibility of another Ganglian ship arriving and the chance of them kidnapping Trisha had caused him sleepless resting periods since they'd left.

"There is little chance of that," Wray dismissed. "The Ganglians can't communicate as great a distance as we can, even within the Known Universes. So, they wouldn't be expecting a comm from that ship yet."

"That doesn't mean they couldn't have sent more than one ship." Ull felt the need to argue the point.

"You sound like you care what happens to Earth, Warrior Ull."

"Of course, I do!" Ull immediately exclaimed. "They are the key to the survival of our race."

Wray was surprised by this. While he knew Ull would do whatever his Emperor asked of him, he hadn't exhibited this passion in doing so before. Wray responded, "Their females are. Females, I believe you were in favor of just taking. What has changed your position?"

The Emperor couldn't believe the shame that crossed Ull's usually reserved face.

"That was unfit and unworthy of me, Sire. I should have realized that my Emperor, my King, and even my own Lord are wiser than a lowly Warrior with no female."

"You are now against invasion even though it would bring immediate relief to your brothers-in-arms?"

"Yes."

"Explain."

"Sire, before I traveled to Earth, I had no respect for Earth's males. After all, if they were fit and worthy, they wouldn't allow their females to be unprotected. But after interacting not only with their males but several of their females who are powerful world leaders, I have come to believe they respect their females far more than we do. They show that respect by giving their females the freedom to choose how they wish to live, even if it puts them at risk."

Ull wasn't sure he was expressing this well. He was a warrior after all, not an ambassador, but it was what he felt and now believed.

"You support this? Females being at risk?"

"No, Sire, but I now understand it. They believe in giving their females a choice, just as we once did. Many of their females choose to live independently, and if they find a male they wish to *share* their lives with, they do. As equals."

"This is something my Kim has expressed to me many times. She wishes to be a more active Empress, doing more than just giving me offspring."

"As does my Lisa here on Luda," King Grim said, speaking up.

"I believe Lady Abby has also expressed that desire to my brother," Ull told them.

"While honorable," Veron chimed in, "that may be a problem for some of our warriors."

"Then they should be barred from having an Earth female," Ull declared again, shocking everyone. "For it is only these females exerting their right to choose, and them choosing to Join with a Tornian male, that will save us."

"And do you believe they will?" Wray asked.

"If our males just take and force them as we have already done," Ull's gaze went to Grim, who was standing behind his brother. " No. But if they give the females the time to get to know them, and show them the respect they deserve, then yes."

"I see."

"Sire, was this the reason you recalled us?" Veron asked. "To discuss face-to-face with Warrior Ull his opinion on how things are proceeding?"

"No, but I find his change in attitude very interesting."

"I believe Representative Burke had a great deal to do with that."

"The female Queen Lisa insisted you needed to contact?"

"Yes, she and Warrior Ull spent an extensive amount of time together, on and off the Searcher."

Wray ran an assessing eye over Ull, a thought beginning to take root. Wray had been a much different male before he'd met his Kim, just as Grim, and Lord Ynyr had been. Now it seemed Warrior Ull was affected too. Earth females appeared to have the ability to bring out the best in a Tornian male even when they weren't Joining with one. "Earth females do have a powerful influence on our males."

"Truth," Ull agreed quietly.

"So why have we returned?" Veron asked.

"You feel negotiations are going well for us, Warrior Ull?"

"Yes, Majesty. While it will take some time to organize the matchings between our males and Earth females, the Earth Council is going to be agreeable."

"It will take more than one ship to protect Earth, which is why I recalled you."

"I don't understand, Sire."

"Three ships full of Tornian Warriors and the repair units the Earth leaders requested, are orbiting Luda and will return to Earth with you."

"You recalled us so we could escort them?" Ull had a hard time keeping the anger out of his voice and off his face.

"You, Warrior Ull, will transfer to the Protector. Warrior Taup is its Captain, and together you will lead the Watcher and the Sword back to Earth."

"Sire?" Veron asked.

"I need you at my side, Captain, and the Searcher. Captain Taup is a fit and worthy male who understands his duty as do all the warriors selected."

"Are they expecting to be allowed access to females?" Ull demanded. It would destroy everything they'd been working for if a group of rogue warriors descended on Earth and kidnapped unwilling females.

"No, they've been expressly told they will not be allowed on Earth's surface. They are there only to protect the planet from the Ganglians. They will do their duty."

"And who has final authority if one forgets that duty?" Ull growled.

Wray's eyes narrowed, and he tilted his head slightly to stare at Ull. "As I have not yet decided who should become the Tornian Lord of Earth, I grant you the power to deal with any Tornian issues that arise."

"Taup and the other Captains will be made aware of this?"

"They will."

Ull nodded his acceptance. He would make sure that *every* warrior knew that if they disobeyed him or if they caused any friction with Earth, he would end them.

"But I do expect them to be among the first to try out whatever matching system Representative Burke initiates."

"I do not believe she will have a problem with that."

"Is Captain Veron correct?" Wray demanded then watched Ull bristle when he asked. "Have you and Representative Burke become close?"

"She is an amazing female that I have the greatest respect for, Sire. I have done my best in all our exchanges to treat her as such," Ull replied stiffly.

"Done your best?" Grim growled. Trisha was his Lisa's friend. If this warrior had insulted her, in any way, Grim would end him.

Ull looked to Grim. "As I'm sure you are aware, King Grim, Earth females speak their minds and are willing to tell a warrior when they believe he is wrong. It takes some time to adjust. Representative Burke and I got off to a less than perfect start," Ull refused to look at Veron when he snorted softly, "but we resolved those issues and now have no problem working together."

"Is this your belief, Veron," Grim demanded.

Veron glanced at Ull before addressing King Grim. If he revealed how Trisha had initially come to be on the Searcher, Wray would recall Ull for disobeying the Queen's direct order. That wasn't in the best interest of the Empire, especially as Ull spoke truth. He and Trisha had been able to resolve that.

"Captain!" Grim snapped, impatient for his answer.

"It is, Sire. Queen Lisa chose exceptionally well. Representative Burke is an extraordinary female who has succeeded in working not only with us but with Minister Ruskin."

"My Queen will be pleased to know that Trisha hasn't been harmed."

"She was fine when we left Earth, Sire. We haven't been in contact since we left."

"Why?" Wray asked.

"Sire, I inferred from your transmission the need for direct communication, that we were to maintain comm silence."

"That was a mistake on my part for not being clearer. I was in a rush. Destiny was fussy, and I wanted to get back to her."

"Is the princess alright?" Veron demanded immediately concerned. The little princess had captured the heart of every warrior in the Palace.

"She is fine, Veron," Wray quickly reassured him. "Just teething. Kim says I need to stop overreacting."

"There is no such thing as overreacting when it comes to the princess, Sire."

Ull barely stopped himself from growling at Veron's reaction. If the Emperor hadn't been so distracted, Ull could have at least sent a comm to Trisha, and heard her voice.

"My Empress would disagree, but that is for another time." Wray's gaze switched to Ull. "I have carefully considered what you included in your last comm. The Earthian leaders' concerns about the females under King Grim's protection if they never choose a Tornian male. I have discussed it with the Empress, as well as King Grim and Queen Lisa, and have reached a decision. Once matches have begun between Earth females and our males, if any females remain on Luda, who haven't chosen a male, they will be allowed to return to Earth if that is their wish."

"The females on Luda know this?" Veron asked.

"No. I will not interfere with a male's chance to keep his bloodline from ending until he has another option available," Wray told him.

"Earth's leaders are also requesting more educators so they will be able to communicate directly with us and eventually with you," Ull told the Emperor.

Wray looked over his shoulder at Grim. "We have a sufficient number on Luda to send, Majesty. I will make sure they are properly programmed and have them sent to the Protector."

"Will that suffice?" Wray looked back to Ull.

"Yes, Majesty."

"Then we'll see you in two days. Captain Veron, load the navigation to Earth onto a secure chip. Warrior Ull, upon arrival in orbit, you will immediately transfer to the Protector, upload the information into that ship's navigation, and proceed back to Earth at maximum speed."

"Yes, Sire."

"Captain Veron, you will make sure the Searcher is properly cleaned and restocked for the Empress and Princess."

"Understood, Majesty."

The Emperor looked away from the comm and nodded slightly. "Now I need to go. A Joining Ceremony is commencing soon in Luanda's garden."

"One of the females has chosen a warrior?" Veron's eye's widened in surprise.

"Two," Wray smiled. "One from House Jamison and one from House Nizar."

"Lord Callen now has a Lady?" Veron asked.

"No, it was one of his warriors. Lord Callen feels he needs to concentrate on repairing the damage Reeve caused before he can give his Lady the time she deserves."

"The other is a warrior from House Jamison?" Ull asked.

"Yes, Warrior Korin was chosen."

"Korin?!" Ull didn't try to hide his disbelief. "Truth? After everything he did?"

"The female is aware, and it's her choice."

"Every time I think I'm beginning to understand these females, they go and do something like this," Veron muttered.

"They are unique and complicated creatures," Wray replied. "I doubt any male, Earthian or Tornian, ever completely understands one."

∞ ∞ ∞ ∞ ∞

The coolness soothed the heat and clamminess of Trisha's forehead as she rested it on the rim of the toilet. She'd barely made it there before her stomach ejected the meal she'd just shared with Jakob. At first, her stomach had been able to tolerate the new meds Dr. Monroe had given her, but now, two weeks later, it was getting more and more difficult.

Carefully lifting her head, she swallowed hard several times to keep from vomiting again. God, she hated this. She'd hated it when her mamá had been sick, and she hated it now, especially when there was still so much for her to do.

Jakob had heard from his Emperor, and Liron was more than willing to include energy crystals and the technology to use them in the agreement and was preparing a ship to bring them to Earth. Jakob was now negotiating with individual leaders for what they could supply. They were traveling to and from their own countries to prevent questions about their absence.

All returnees were reunited with some, if not all, of their family but remained confined to the base. The majority were handling it well, content to have their loved one back, but a few were beginning to get restless, and she couldn't blame them. They just wanted to get on with their lives.

Her tío had an encrypted computer brought to her quarters so she could begin working on the criteria for matching Tornians with Earth females. She'd been browsing dating websites to see the different types of questions they asked. She'd also been in touch with someone she trusted to help her start designing theirs.

There also hadn't been any reports of attacks with large groups of women going missing. Which meant the Ganglians hadn't returned. At least that's what everyone hoped.

Overall, they had accomplished a lot. The only dark spot was that she hadn't had any comms from Ull. Not that she really expected Ull to contact her, not after the way he'd left, but he hadn't reached out to Jakob or even her tío.

Had something happened?

Was something wrong?

Rising, she rinsed out her mouth, and without looking in the mirror, because she already knew how pale she was, she went into the bedroom and put on her sleepwear. Climbing into bed, she ordered. "Lights off."

As the room plunged into darkness, the ringing of a comm filled the room. Sighing, Trisha began to sit up then realized it was the comm Ull had given her. "Lights on!" Seeing the comm on the nightstand, she lunged for it.

"Trisha?" The faintness of his voice told Trisha just how far away from her Ull was.

"I'm here, Ull," she quickly replied, then frowned when he continued to speak as if he hadn't heard her.

"This is Ull. I wanted to contact you to let you know we are on our way back with three ships to protect the Earth. I will, of course, be contacting the President to let him know this, but I wanted to let you know first. Also, I found something you forgot on the Searcher and will return it to you once we arrive, which should be in approximately two weeks. Ull out."

Trisha fell back on to the bed. In the excitement of hearing Ull's voice, she'd forgotten that they couldn't communicate directly. At least now she knew he was alright and *would* be returning. Two weeks. God, that seemed like a lifetime. *Three* ships of Tornians looking for females? She had a lot to do before they arrived. Getting up, she went into the outer room and fired up her computer.

∞ ∞ ∞ ∞ ∞

Ull stared out the viewport watching Earth growing larger and larger. Goddess, he wanted to get there, wanted to get to Trisha. Something was tugging at him, telling him he needed to get to her.

They'd been exchanging comms as he traveled back, and while he knew the distance could distort a voice, Trisha's seemed to be getting weaker instead of stronger the closer he got to Earth. Fingering the bottle in his hand, he wondered if it had something to do with it.

"We're two hours out," Taup said from the control panel. "I can't believe this planet has been here all this time, and the Great Infection never touched it."

"They weren't part of what caused it," Ull told him, sliding the bottle into his vest before turning to face Taup.

"Truth, but neither were the Zaludians or Jerboaians, and they have both been affected in one way or another."

"Maybe the Goddess took pity on them."

"Do they even worship the Goddess?"

Ull frowned at that. It was something he'd never thought to ask. Every species in the Known Universes knew about and worshipped the Goddess. "I don't know. I never asked."

"How could you not?"

"I was involved with more important things like securing a treaty for the survival of our race." That stopped Taup's questions. "I'll be in the communications room, contacting Earth that we will be arriving soon. Contact the other ships and make sure they have their shielding up. Earth leaders aren't ready to reveal our existence to them."

"Yes, Warrior Ull."

∞ ∞ ∞ ∞ ∞

"So, you'll be arriving shortly?" Aaron waved his niece to a chair as he responded to Ull.

"Yes, Mr. President. Once we have established an orbit, I will shuttle down."

"Will any other Tornians be accompanying you?"

"I had planned on coming alone, but if you wish to meet other Tornians, I can arrange it."

The President was silent for a moment. "No, I think we should wait until all the world leaders are available."

"Do you know when that will be?"

"Now that you are back, I will get it arranged. It will take a few days."

"I will make Warriors available. I'll contact you again when I'm on my way down. Ull out."

"How are you, Trisha?" Aaron asked, running a critical eye over her. He'd been at the White House for the last few days, taking care of the routine business of running the country while taking the first steps to prepare for announcing the arrival of the Tornians and Kaliszians. "You look pale."

"I've just been spending all my time inside working on the application site and app," she deflected. Her tío had given her complete authority to design the project as she saw fit. After spending hours browsing websites where photos and physical descriptions seemed to be the most important thing, she'd decided on a different approach.

The website would give the history of the Tornian Empire, what had brought them to Earth, and the Ganglian threat. It then explained what would be expected of them if they agreed to Join with a Tornian. If, after reading all that, they still wished to apply, they needed to fill out an in-depth application; with no photo. Applications would not be offered to Tornian males or Earth females for consideration until carefully screened. She wasn't going to allow harm to any woman in this. She was under no illusions about the fallout when the leaders made the announcements. It would cause significant controversy. Life on Earth would be forever changed, and not everyone was going to like that. If something happened to even one of the women, especially in the beginning, everything would collapse.

"It's going well. Hopefully, I can show it to you and the rest of the Council next week and get your input."

"You've gotten that far already?" Aaron sat back in his chair. He'd always known his niece was smart and driven but to get so much done so quickly.

Trisha had known that would distract her tío. "It's just the first draft and doesn't have any graphics yet. Hopefully, Ull can help remedy that."

"Ull?"

"Yes, I would think they have to have some photos of their planets in the databases on their ships. One of the Emperor with Kim and Destiny would go a long way."

"I agree, but that wasn't what I was asking about."

"I hadn't realized you'd asked a question."

"You referred to Warrior Ull as Ull."

"That is his name."

"I know, I just hadn't realized you had gotten that close to him, personally."

"He is the representative sent by the Tornian Empire. Shouldn't I have gotten to know him personally?"

"You know what I'm saying, Trisha," Aaron growled, doing an impressive imitation of a Tornian.

"I do, and I'm saying this with all due respect to my tío and my President. My personal life is none of your business. I've done everything asked of me. By Lisa and by you. Did Ull and I get close? Yes. Do we both know it can't go anywhere? Yes. We'll both do our duty to our people, that's all you need concern yourself with."

"Trisha..." He hadn't meant to upset his niece like this. He loved her deeply. He only wanted the best for her, and Ull wasn't it. He needed to explain that, but before he could, his Tornian comm rang again. "What?!"

"I am en route," Ull's voice filled the room. "Fifteen minutes."

Aaron didn't get the chance to respond as Ull ended the comm. "That Tornian needs to learn his place."

"He knows his place," Trisha snapped back, rising from her chair. "He's the first male of Lord Oryon of Betelgeuse. One day he will rule the *planet*. Maybe it's *you* who needs to learn *your* place." Leaving her tío stunned, she spun on her heel and went to greet Ull.

Chapter Eighteen

Ull wasn't sure why the President had been so short with him, but he shouldn't have reacted the way he had. His Empire needed the cooperation of this male, and irritating him wouldn't help them get it.

Taking a deep breath, he forced himself to calm. Soon he'd be back on Earth, and he'd be able to see Trisha again. And hopefully, he'd be able to touch her again. Just touch. Not Join, because he knew if he Joined with her again, he'd never let her go.

Maneuvering over the base, he lowered the shuttle's shielding and descended onto the landing area. The shuttle had barely settled before he was up and moving toward the hatch. He'd just caught a glimpse of Trisha before the dust stirred up from the landing obscured his view.

As the ramp lowered, Ull walked down it coming to an abrupt halt as he took in his Trisha's appearance.

∞ ∞ ∞ ∞ ∞

Trisha was having a hard time catching her breath as she hurried down the corridor that led to the landing pad, ashamed of herself. She shouldn't have talked to her tío like that. Not because he was the President of the United States but because she knew he was only trying to protect her like he'd done her entire life.

But she didn't need to be protected from Ull. He'd never hurt her, and if her heart was breaking at the thought of his Joining with someone else, of him making her his Lady, that was her problem.

She was dying. She'd finally come to terms with that over the last few weeks, especially with the way her symptoms were progressing even after Dr. Monroe was able to supply her with her original prescription.

She knew the signs, having watched her mamá suffer through them, and knew there wasn't going to be much more her oncologist would be able to do. He'd given her a prescription to begin to slow the cancer down, but he'd warned her the cancer was advanced, that she'd need immediate surgery to extend her life any significant length. It's what had had her so distracted the night Lisa and the girls were taken. She'd been trying to figure out how to tell her tío.

Now it didn't matter.

Sweating, she reached the landing pad just as Ull dropped the shuttle's shielding and began to land, kicking up a curtain of swirling dust as it did. Coughing, she turned away until it cleared enough for her to move toward the lowering ramp. She just wanted to see him again but the instant he saw her he stopped.

Should she not have come?

Did he not want to see her?

"What, in the name of the Goddess, is wrong with you?!" he growled, taking in how drastically her appearance had changed since he'd last seen her. Her skin, usually so much darker than his, now had a pallor to it that sharply contrasted with the bruising under her eyes, while her beautiful multicolored hair appeared lifeless and dull. Her lush, full lips had a pinched look to them, and her cheekbones stood out sharper than a Tornian blade.

The angry allegation had Trisha stumbling back. Her heart, already rapidly beating from the rush to get to him, seemed to stop before resuming at a breathless pace.

God, she shouldn't have come. She should have let him decide if he wanted to see her. She'd just thought after all the transmissions they'd exchanged that he'd want to see her.

"I…" Suddenly her whole body began to tremble, and everything went black.

"Trisha!" Ull reached her before she hit the ground, sweeping her up in his arms. "Trisha!"

"What the hell did you do to her?" the President demanded, entering the landing area.

"Nothing!" Ull growled, carrying Trisha passed him. "She just collapsed. I'm taking her to your medical area."

Everyone moved out of the way of the growling Tornian as he charged through the corridors toward medical, the President of the United States close behind. The door to medical banged against the wall as Ull shouldered his way through growling, "Where's the Healer?!!"

"Monroe!" The President shouted in English, knowing that while the doctor had used the educator, the rest of his staff hadn't, and they would have no clue what Ull was saying.

"What's wrong?" Monroe demanded, rushing out of his office. Taking one look at Trisha in Ull's arms, he swore and gestured toward a bed. "Shit! Lay her down over here. What happened?"

"She collapsed at the landing pad," Ull growled, not even noticing that the Earth Healer was speaking Tornian. "Heal her!"

"I warned her she couldn't keep pushing like this," Monroe muttered as he hooked her up to several machines and began taking her vitals.

"What are you talking about?" Aaron demanded coming up to stand beside the doctor. "Why would you need to warn her?"

Monroe glanced at the President. "She hasn't told you yet?"

"Told me what?!"

Monroe finished checking Trisha then wrote down the results before answering. Technically he wasn't allowed to discuss this without his patient's permission, but the President was her next of kin, and Trisha's condition was worsening.

"Mr. President, your niece has stage four cancer that has metastasized throughout her body."

"No!" Aaron denied and would have gone down if Monroe hadn't gripped his arm.

"What are you saying?!" Ull growled not understanding as the Earth Healer had shifted back to English, but from the President's reaction, he knew it wasn't good.

"Trisha has cancer," Monroe told him. "I'm not sure you know what that is..."

"It's what ended Trisha's mother." His gaze shot back to his Trisha.

"Yes, it's in its final stages."

"What does that mean?" His gaze pierced the Healer.

"It means she doesn't have much time," Monroe explained as kindly as he could.

"She told me she'd been getting her annual checkups," Aaron whispered, moving to grip his niece's hand.

"I don't know anything about that. I only know because when the Tornian ship left, Trisha realized she'd forgotten her prescription on it. " He glanced at Ull and saw that while he was listening, he mirrored the President, holding Trisha's hand. He hadn't realized the Warrior cared that much about Trisha. "I used what I had available until I could get the proper drug here."

"And when was that?" Aaron knew from previous experience with his sister just how quickly cancer could advance without the proper treatment.

"With the supplies a week and a half ago."

Aaron cursed.

"None of that matters," Ull growled. "Heal her. Now!"

"Warrior Ull," Monroe waited until Ull lifted his gaze to him. "I don't think you understand. There is nothing I can do for her now except to make her as comfortable as possible."

"No!" Ull denied. His beautiful Trisha couldn't be dying. Not from a sickness. The Goddess would never allow something so cruel. But looking down at her, he could see how hard she was struggling to breathe, and while she'd never been heavy, she'd been noticeably lighter when he'd carried her to medical.

Without a word, Ull scooped her up, ignoring the protests of both the Earth Healer and the President. Ull refused to give up on the female he was confident the Goddess had created just for him. His mission to Earth had to be so he could find her and save her.

"What do you think you're doing?" the President demanded running to try and keep up with Ull. "Guards!

"If you won't help her, then I will!"

"You can?" Aaron held up a hand to stop the guards that had responded to his call, weapons drawn.

"I don't know, but I refuse to let her life end without trying." By this time, they had reached the shuttle with its ramp still down.

Aaron put a hand on Ull's arm, stopping him. God, he wanted to get on that shuttle with Ull. Aaron didn't want the last words ever said between him and his niece to be angry ones, but he wasn't just her tío. Never before had he hated his life choices as much as he did right now. If there was even the slightest chance that Ull could help her, then he had to let him try. "Then go, but please... I'm begging you. Let me know as soon as possible."

Ull looked down at the male he knew Trisha loved like a manno. He suffered at the thought of being separated from her. Not being the one to help her, but he was putting her needs before his own. A truly fit and worthy thing to do.

"I will. The instant I know."

With that, Ull ran up the ramp, started the engines, and holding Trisha in his lap took off as fast as he dared. He didn't want to harm her in her weakened condition accidentally.

∞ ∞ ∞ ∞ ∞

Taup's eyes widened as Ull came storming down the shuttle ramp carrying an unconscious female. Ull's comm had stated he needed an emergency landing, a path cleared to medical, and a deep repair unit ready for him. It had sent Taup rushing to the landing bay, multiple scenarios running through his head for how Ull was injured. He'd never expected this.

"What in the name of the Goddess is going on?!"

But Ull just ignored him, and Taup found himself running full out to try and keep up with the first male, and still, by the time he reached medical, Ull was already placing the female in the deep repair unit.

"Run the unit," Ull ordered the Healer.

"What are her injuries?" Healer Zo asked even as he had the deep repair unit closed to scan the seemingly uninjured female.

"She isn't injured."

"Then why…"

"She has cancer," Ull growled rounding on the Healer.

"Cancer?" Zo stared at Ull in confusion, the Earth word not translating. But as he opened his mouth to ask the Warrior to explain further, the deep repair unit reported its diagnoses and immediately filled with dense white, blue, and red vapors, signifying just how dire the female's situation was.

"What does the unit say?" Ull demanded.

Zo looked at the readout and couldn't believe what he was seeing. A parasite, driven out of the Known Universes over a millennium ago and thought to be extinct, was consuming the female's entire body.

"Zo!"

"She's infected with the Karkata parasite."

"Karkata..." Ull searched his mind for any clue to figure out what that was.

"I doubt you've heard of it. There hasn't been a case of it in the Known Universes in several millennia."

"Can you heal her?"

"The deep repair unit is attempting to, but given the extent of the parasite's infiltration..." Zo raised concern-filled eyes to Ull. "I'd pray to the Goddess for her blessing if I were you."

∞ ∞ ∞ ∞ ∞

"You have endured great suffering in assisting your people along with the Tornians and Kaliszians, haven't you, Trisha Burke?"

Trisha frowned at the melodic voice. She knew she'd never heard it before, but for some reason, it comforted and soothed her and made her want to know who was speaking. Opening her eyes, Trisha was shocked to find the most stunningly beautiful woman she had ever seen standing before her. She was statuesque like the ancient Greek sculptures that always seemed to be of the Goddesses they'd worshiped, draped in one of their flowing gowns that left one shoulder bare. It enhanced her already perfect figure while offsetting her dark eyes and hair that seemed to change color in the shifting light. Was she dreaming?

"You are not dreaming, and you are also an amazingly beautiful female."

Trisha jerked as the woman responded without saying a word and discovered she was sitting in a chair. She quickly looked around the room and realized she wasn't at the NACB any longer. "Who are you? Where the hell am I?"

"I am the Goddess, and you are with me among the stars."

"The stars?"

"Yes."

"Why?"

"Because I wished to speak with you."

"You know," Trisha glared at the other woman. She didn't care if she was a 'Goddess' or not, "I'm really getting tired of people kidnapping me."

As the eyebrows of the Goddess drew together, Trisha realized those were real stars behind the Goddess, and they had begun to dim at the Goddess's displeasure. But Trisha didn't care. She was dying, so she wasn't going to take shit from anyone.

"And if you weren't?"

"If I weren't what?"

"Dying. Would you still take my shit as you call it?"

"If I weren't dying, I would probably be more diplomatic about it, but I would still make sure you knew I was pissed. Kidnapping is not a conducive way to start a conversation with someone."

"It seems to have worked for your Tornian Warrior."

"That was an entirely different situation, and Ull knows he was wrong." Trisha frowned at the Goddess then sighed. They weren't going to get anywhere, and she wasn't going to be able to return home if they continued to argue. "So why did you kidnap me?"

"I didn't." The Goddess made a sweeping gesture with her arm causing Trisha to gasp when the solid black floor disappeared, revealing they were floating above a ship orbiting the Earth. As they moved closer, a room within the ship appeared. "Your physical body is still there, fighting to stay alive."

Trisha didn't understand what she saw in the room. There was a large, coffin-like tube filled with vapor. A Tornian she didn't know stood on one side of it, with Ull, on his knees and an anguished look on his face, on the other.

"I don't see my body."

"That's because the deep repair unit is attempting to heal you."

"I'm inside it?"

"That is necessary for the unit to work. It repairs the injuries of those placed inside while cleansing the body of impurities and parasites that prevent it from functioning at its optimal level."

Trisha suddenly remembered something Vanessa had said. The older female was in the first group of abductees returning because everyone was concerned about her blood pressure and diabetes. But Vanessa said Dr. Monroe hadn't been able to find evidence of either. Everyone had assumed it was because of the difference in the nutrients they'd been receiving from the Kaliszian food. She knew Dr. Monroe had talked to Jakob at great length about it, but Jakob could tell him nothing.

"They have used deep repair units for over a millennia," the Goddess continued. "It is something they have forgotten. "

"You're saying that the Kaliszians and Tornians don't suffer from disease? Any disease?"

"Nor do any species that use the units."

Trisha tried to wrap her mind around that and what it would mean to the people of Earth. Health care was a primary concern for every being on the planet, eating up a significant portion of every country's budget. For them to be able to allocate those funds elsewhere would forever change the world, not to mention the suffering it would ease. She looked back to the unit the Goddess claimed her body was inside.

"You said it is *attempting* to heal me. Does that mean it can't?" God, she hoped that wasn't true, not because it would save her, although she didn't want to die, but because of how many people on Earth it would help.

Trisha's thoughts surprised the Goddess, which was something that rarely occurred anymore. This small human would put the welfare of her people before her own.

"She truly is a fit and worthy female."

Trisha jolted again when the largest male she'd ever seen, in both height and width, suddenly appeared next to the Goddess. He wore only a short piece of material that covered him from waist to mid-thigh and had a sword strapped to his side. But it was his skin that shocked her. It changed colors like a chameleon, and while he had long, dark hair covering his entire head like a Tornian, his eyes glowed like a Kaliszian.

"So it would seem," the Goddess replied, looking to the male.

"I am Raiden, True Mate of the Goddess," he told Trisha with the slightest of nods then looked back to the Goddess to continue his conversation with her. "You doubted it?"

"With the way Ull has allowed Daco to influence him? Yes."

"Wait. What? Who? Daco? Isn't he the God that supposedly stole you from your mate?" Trisha looked from Raiden to the Goddess, that's what Ull had told her.

"He *did* steal her," Raiden growled, causing the transparent walls around them to tremble until the Goddess put a gentle hand on his massive arm, calming him.

"How is that even possible?" Looking at Raiden, Trisha couldn't believe anyone, God or not, could be that daring or that stupid.

"Daco is the first, but never for a minute, believe he is the second. He is conniving and deceitful. He preys on people when they are at their weakest and brings darkness to their thoughts and deeds."

"What does that have to do with Ull?" Trisha demanded.

"He has allowed Daco to influence him," the Goddess said in disgust.

"That's a lie!" Trisha surged to her feet, and when she took a step toward the Goddess, Raiden quickly moved between them.

"Do not threaten my Goddess," he growled menacingly.

"Then tell her to stop slandering *my* Ull," Trisha growled just as menacingly, not backing down. "Ull is a fit and worthy male."

"You have not heard his thoughts as I have." The Goddess moved from behind her mate.

"Maybe you should stay out of other people's heads if you don't like what you find," Trisha fired back at her. "It's no different than what Daco does, using people's private thoughts and desires against them."

The Goddess jerked as if shocked by the comparison. "I... I am nothing like Daco."

"Then stop judging people because of their *thoughts*! Their actions should speak louder."

"She is right, my Goddess," Raiden gently said as he pulled her into his arms. He, better than anyone, knew how finding Daco's thoughts in the minds of those descended from her sister affected the Goddess, especially since Berto. "Warrior Ull has never acted on any of Daco's attempts to influence him. He knows they were unworthy of a Tornian Warrior and resists."

"That is truth." The Goddess snuggled deeper into his arms.

"Then perhaps we shouldn't judge Ull so harshly just because others weren't strong enough to withstand the darkness."

Trisha watched the couple, knowing they were so absorbed with one another that they had forgotten about her. It was beautiful to see two people so in love and in-tune to one another, even knowing it was something she would never have.

"Why won't you?" the Goddess asked, looking from her mate to Trisha.

"I thought you just agreed it was wrong to listen to other people's thoughts."

"No, I agreed that judging someone on their thoughts was wrong, not that I wouldn't listen. So again, why won't you ever have someone who loves you as my Raiden loves me?"

"Because I'm dying, and your deep repair unit can't prevent it."

"This is truth."

Taking a step back, Trisha sunk into her chair, her chin hitting her chest as the air rushed out of her lungs. While she'd known she was going to die, somewhere deep in her heart, after hearing about what the deep repair unit could do, a kernel of hope had started to take root. Now it had been ruthlessly ripped out of her chest.

"For only immortals never die, but the deep repair unit can make sure you live the long life you were supposed to."

"What?" Trisha slowly lifted her head to stare at the Goddess.

"The deep repair unit can eradicate the Karkata parasite attacking your system. It's just going to take some time because of the extent of the damage."

"You..." Trisha had to swallow hard to continue. "You're saying I'm going to survive?"

"That would be truth."

"It will work on all humans?"

"Of course, because your people were once Raiden's too."

"Wait? What?"

Two chairs appeared behind the Goddess and Raiden, and taking his mate's hand, Raiden assisted her in sitting before doing so himself. "To explain, we need to start at the beginning. Many, many millennia ago, the universes were very different. There was one race. A race that had no name because it didn't need one, they were one. They came to be ruled by the greatest Emperor in their history, Raiden Nacy." The Goddess squeezed her mate's hand that still held hers. "Gods and Goddesses are curious creatures, Trisha. We love to see how new life is evolving and sometimes involve ourselves."

"That's how ancient myths of Gods and Goddesses coming down from the heavens came to be."

"Yes, but that happened eons after. What you need to know is that Emperor Raiden brought peace to all the Known Worlds, worlds that included more than just the Tornian, Kaliszian, and Ganglian Empires. They included Earth along with many others." She saw the question in Trisha's mind. "Yes, Trisha, while the people were one, they did not always agree. Petty things caused great wars." She looked with pride to her mate. "Raiden changed that when he became Emperor. Whispers of his feats of bravery and acts of kindness traveled among the stars. So, what was a young Goddess to do when the stars continually whispered about him?" She looked back to Trisha. "I went to see for myself and found my True Mate. So, you can understand why when it came time for me to return, I refused to leave him behind. It caused a bit of a stir in the heavens as few unmated Goddesses were remaining, and the Gods weren't going to lose one to a mere mortal, no matter how fit and worthy he was. They declared I must wait to make him immortal until every God and Goddess could assemble and decide his worthiness, even though they knew it would take more than Raiden's lifespan to do so."

"So, you went ahead and did it yourself." Trisha didn't make it a question, for she would have done the same.

"I believe you would, and I did, but not without first discussing it with my True Mate. After all, he would be the one leaving his people, the Empire he'd spent his life creating. He would be the one doing all the sacrificing, not me."

"There was no sacrifice, my love." He kissed the hand he still held. "Ruling an Empire until the day I died or living forever at your side. The decision was easy."

"Still, it caused great discord amongst the Gods, who immediately insisted on challenging Raiden."

"Challenge as the way the Kaliszians once did before you blessed them with their True Mate beads?"

"Yes." Raiden smiled at how quickly the little female had made the connection.

"And because I made him an immortal without the consensus of the other immortals, Raiden had to accept the challenges or be cast into darkness, as Daco was, after taking me. But before that happened, while Raiden was distracted with the challenges from the other Gods, Daco began attacking everything Raiden had left behind. He spread his hatred for my mate like a malignant disease over Raiden's people. It caused them to attack and destroy one another until very few were left. Because of that, they lost all knowledge of what came before, lost their ability to travel to other planets, and began evolving differently."

For once, Trisha was glad the Goddess could hear the questions flying through her mind as she gave her a small smile and explained.

"Time flows differently for immortals. When something captures our attention, or we physically materialize on a planet, then our time syncs with the beings there. But once we leave or lose interest, that changes. What might be a day for us could be a century for those left behind. A single challenge between Gods can take days before one is victorious, which my Raiden always was. By the time of the last challenge right before Daco was cast into darkness, several millennia had passed for Raiden's people."

Trisha tried to absorb everything she learned as she leaned back in her chair. None of this had been in the educator.

"Because as my Goddess has said, it was wiped out and forgotten," Raiden told her.

"By Daco."

"Yes, as soon as we realized what had happened, we began to intervene where we could."

"What do you mean where you could?"

"What my Goddess means is that most Gods or Goddesses interject themselves into a world so mortals will worship them."

"But aren't you worshipped by both the Tornians and Kaliszians?" Trisha looked to the Goddess.

"I am, but that is not the reason I respond."

"You blessed the Tornians because they assisted you when Daco stole you," Trisha told her what she knew.

"I did, but it wasn't only because of that. My sister found her True Mate with the Tornian that helped save me from Daco, King Varick. Rawnie was much like you, Trisha Burke. She was always concerned and cared about the welfare of others. When she discovered her True Mate was mortal, she didn't react the way I did. She chose to join her life force with Varick's, and in doing so, she became more than mortal but less than a Goddess. Because of that, when Varick died, so did Rawnie. I vowed to her that I would always watch over her offspring and the offspring of their offspring."

"And the Kaliszians?" Trisha got to voice this question.

"They are the descendants from my blood brother, Jadi," Raiden told her.

"Which is why their eyes glow as yours do."

"Yes, it is something from the past that has survived despite Daco's best efforts."

"As your multiple colors survived in the Tornians, just individually."

"That is truth."

"So, what of you survived here on Earth?"

"Very little," Raiden told her regretfully. "Daco seems to have concentrated a great deal of his wrath here for some reason. While your people believe they come in many different colors, they are just shades of one."

"I don't agree," the Goddess chimed in. "While externally humans don't resemble your people from the past, internally they do. They are resilient, strong, creative beings who, despite everything Daco has done to them, can care about other beings. That was the heart of your people's strength, Raiden."

"Truth."

"Which is perhaps why Daco struck here so hard. When you destroy the heart of a being, the body soon follows."

"They do seem to be the heart of so many, don't they?" Raiden gave Trisha a considering look.

"Which is why they are so vital in helping to stop what I created."

"You're referring to the Great Infection."

"Yes. The end has begun thanks to the influence of Earth females like Kim, Lisa, Mackenzie, Jennifer, and Abby. But unless all recover their honor, it will not continue."

"I will do what I can, but not *all* Earth females are going to want to Join with a Tornian Warrior."

"Of course not, for you have many males who are also fit and worthy. The heart will decide that. I was referring to the Ganglians."

"You're telling me the well-being of the Known Universes and the end of the Great Infection relies on the Ganglians becoming honorable?"

"Yes."

"Shit!"

"You take care of your Tornian and your people and leave the Ganglians to us." Trisha stood as the Goddess walked over, placing a kiss on her forehead. "It is time for you to return."

With that, Trisha's world went black.

Chapter Nineteen

"Are you ever going to answer your comm?" Zo carefully asked when it began ringing again. He'd lost track of the number of times it had rung since Ull had placed the female in the deep repair unit.

"Until I know what to tell him, there is no need to respond."

"Her manno will not appreciate that."

"He's not Trisha's manno. He's her mother's brother. He also happens to be the President of the United States of America. A great area on Earth comparable to the Etruria Region on Tornian."

With each revealing sentence, Zo's eyebrows rose higher and higher, his gaze going to the vapor filled unit. This female belonged to a powerful male. A male, the Tornian Empire needed for its survival. What would happen if she didn't survive?

"All the more reason for you to answer him."

"I already vowed to him that I would. As soon as I knew anything." Ull lifted his gaze to Zo. "Do we?"

"No."

"Then there is no reason to respond to his call."

Zo disagreed, but Ull had been given complete authority on everything concerning Earth, by the Emperor himself. So, after giving Ull a small bow, he left the room.

Ull didn't know how long he kneeled beside Trisha, trying to see through the vapor for the slightest glimpse of her. Goddess, he'd thought being far away from her and not seeing her was torture, but to be this close and still not be able to… Being cast into the darkness couldn't be any worse.

'Join me and find out.' Ull jerked, finally realizing the strange thoughts he'd been having, that he'd believed to be his own, weren't. They were from Daco.

"No!" Ull roared. "I am a fit and worthy warrior. I will not succumb to your lies."

'Even if it meant your female would live?'

Ull stilled at that. Females were the most precious thing in all the Known Universes, especially his Trisha. She deserved the chance to find a male worthy of her love. If he had to fall into darkness for that to happen, it would be a fair exchange.

'Then pledge yourself to me!'

∞ ∞ ∞ ∞ ∞

Trisha's eyes flew open to see a white vapor swirling around her as she lay on her back. She must still be in the deep repair unit the Goddess had told her about. As the fog began to thin, she saw Ull, his arms propped up against the dome, his eyes closed, and his lips were moving as if he were praying. What she heard him praying stunned her.

"If I give you my pledge, you vow Trisha will live?"

She suddenly realized he wasn't praying. He was negotiating. With Daco. "Ull, no!" she cried out, thumping a fist against the glass, trying to get it open. "Ull!"

Ull's eyes flew open at the muffled exclamation to see Trisha's fists pounding against the dome, her eyes pleading with his through the thinning white vapor.

"Trisha!" Pressing his hands against hers on the glass, he hollered over his shoulder. "Zo! Get in here! Now!"

Zo rushed back into the room, shocked to see that the female was awake. As extensively infected with the parasite as she was, he hadn't thought she ever would.

"Open it!" Ull ordered. That snapped Zo out of his shock, and the Healer rushed to the control panel. As the vapor dissipated, the cover retreated, and Ull scooped Trisha up into his arms, holding her close. "Goddess, Trisha."

"Don't you dare give that bastard your pledge!" she ordered as her arms wrapped around him.

"What?" Ull lifted his head, taking in her now glowing skin and bright pain-free eyes.

"Don't you pledge yourself to Daco. Ever. Especially not because of me. Daco lies. You know this because *you* are a fit and worthy warrior." Stretching up, she kissed him. She'd nearly died. If Ull hadn't returned when he had, if he hadn't had a deep repair unit, she would have. She knew it in her soul. So, she wasn't going to hold back her thoughts and feelings from Ull any longer. If they couldn't work it out, she'd have to deal with it during the long life the Goddess had said she would have, but Trisha was going to do everything she could for that long life to include Ull. Breaking off the kiss, she told him what was in her heart. "I love you, Ull, with all my heart, even though you are abrupt, arrogant, and aggressive sometimes. Which by the way I happen to like when we're alone."

Ull's eyes searched hers and found only truth in them. Trisha loved him. Even with all his failings, she loved and accepted him. Never had a lowly Tornian warrior been so blessed by the Goddess.

'You have been, Warrior Ull. Don't squander what I have gifted you.' The loving, melodic voice of the Goddess made Ull realize just how insidious and dark Daco's had been. He'd never mistake it for his own again. *'Make sure you don't. You have found the one created just for you. Love her. Cherish her. Sacrifice for her, for when you do, you will find you sacrificed nothing that truly mattered.'*

"I am yours, my Trisha. I will love you every day to the best of my ability. And when the day comes that the Goddess calls me to enter the Promised Land, I will fight to remain at your side." With that vow, Ull recaptured her lips to show her just how much.

Trisha started to sink into the kiss when the clearing of a throat jerked her lips away from Ull's. Standing a short distance away from them was a blue Tornian, who was avidly watching them.

Ull growled his displeasure at the interruption. "What do you want, Healer Zo?"

"Warrior Ull, I understand wanting to be alone with your female, but first, I need to verify the eradication of the Karkata parasite."

"You believe she could still be infected?" Ull's arms tightened around her.

"The readout says she isn't, but since I opened the repair unit before it had completely shut down, I'd like to verify it."

"What does that entail?" Trish asked, looking back and forth between the Healer and Ull.

"You would need to be placed on the diagnosis bed." He gestured to the room behind him. "It will scan you and tell me if you need more time in the deep repair unit."

"It is similar to the beds Dr. Monroe used to assess your people after using the educator," Ull told her quietly.

"And you think I should use it?"

"Yes," Ull said as he carried her out of the room. "Because I never want you to become that ill again, and we need to verify that deep repair units can cure cancer that has consumed so many of your people."

"Oh, my God!" Trisha's mind raced as Ull laid her down. She hadn't had time to process her being 'cured' beyond how it affected her and Ull. Her conversation with the Goddess of how those who used deep repair units suffered from no diseases floated threw her mind. "Do you know what that would mean to the people of Earth?"

"It would ease a great deal of suffering." Ull ran a gentle knuckle along her cheek. "For those infected and those that love them."

"Yes." Her eyes filled at Ull's understanding of how much she still missed her mamá and how watching her die had affected her.

Zo had been silently moving around the couple as they spoke, checking the readings from the bed while avidly listening to them. He'd never heard a male and female converse before. Yes, he'd seen the recordings of the Joining Ceremony that had forever altered their Empire, but that wasn't this. Here were a single male and female speaking to each other intimately and with great respect. The way warriors did.

"The unit has repaired all the damage caused by the Karkata parasite, and her readings are normal. The parasite is gone." He suddenly found his gaze captured by a pair of stunning blue eyes.

"You're sure?" Trisha asked.

"Zo," Ull growled, not liking the way the other male stared at his Trisha.

"What?" Zo ripped his gaze from Trisha's to find an angry warrior glaring at him. "Oh. Right. Yes," his gaze returned to Trisha then quickly looked away, "I'm sure. You are completely healthy, although it will take some time for you to return to your optimal weight."

"Then, I can take her to my quarters?" Ull demanded.

"I see no reason why you couldn't, but she needs rest and to eat." But Zo was already talking to Ull's back as he was already carrying Trisha out of the room.

∞ ∞ ∞ ∞ ∞

Warriors quickly moved out of Ull's way while openly staring at the female he carried. Who was she, and why was Warrior Ull so protective of her? Could he have claimed a female when they'd been told that wasn't allowed?

Ull pulled Trisha closer ignoring the looks they were receiving. He could almost hear their thoughts and allegations, but now wasn't the time to address them. His Trisha had been through a harrowing ordeal. She needed rest, and he was going to see she got it.

Entering his quarters that were very different than the ones she'd had on the Searcher, he carefully placed her in the center of his bed along the wall but didn't join her.

"I'm fine, Ull." She slid over on the bed, patting the space she'd made.

"Now," Ull growled, reaching into his vest to pull out and shake the bottle she'd forgotten. "But you weren't. You were taking these, and you didn't tell me. You didn't tell your tío!"

"Because neither of you could have done anything about it!" she yelled, rising on her knees. "So why should I tell anyone when all it would cause is hurt and despair?"

"And you think your tío isn't despairing now? That he isn't blaming himself?"

That had her sinking onto her heels to whisper, "He knows?"

"Of course, he knows. He was there when you collapsed."

"I collapsed?" She frowned, trying to remember, but it was all a blur.

"On the landing pad." His voice gentled as he saw she didn't remember.

"And he let you bring me here?" She couldn't believe her tío would have allowed that.

"I didn't give him any choice once your Healer said there was nothing he could do except ease your pain."

"Tío Aaron must have been devastated." She remembered how deeply it had affected him when her mamá had chosen not to continue treatment.

"He was, which is the only reason he agreed to let you go on the chance that our deep repair unit could help you." Ull's chin dropped for a moment before he lifted it to meet her gaze again. "He is a better male than I, for I know I couldn't have done that."

Trisha crawled her way to the edge of the bed, then reaching up, cupped his cheeks, pulling his forehead down until it met hers. "Yes, you would have. You would have put my needs first, no matter what it cost you because you love me. Just as I love you."

"Goddess, Trisha!" Ull dropped to his knees, burying his face in her neck, his arms wrapping around her as he finally gave in to all the emotion he'd been ruthlessly holding in check as he'd waited to see if she would survive.

Trisha's arms wrapped around his shaking shoulders. "It's alright, Ull," she soothed. "I'm here, and I'm fine. Thanks to you."

It took several minutes before Ull lifted his wet face. "Never leave me, Trisha, vow it. I couldn't survive it."

"I won't, Ull." Taking a deep breath, she reached a decision that she knew would affect more than just her, but after nearly dying, Trisha realized nothing was more important than what she was gifted. Ull's love. "My vow. Where you go, I will go."

"What?" Ull looked at her in shock. "What are you saying?"

"I'm saying that you are the first male of a Lord. Your place isn't on Earth, so then neither is mine."

"You would do that? Leave your people and all you can do for them to go to Betelgeuse with me?"

"That is your place, so it is mine." Before Ull could respond, his comm began to ring.

"What?" he demanded, ripping it from his belt.

"She's gone?" The grief-stricken voice on the other end had Trisha grabbing the comm from Ull.

"No! I'm here, Tío! I'm fine!"

"Trishy?"

"Yes, it's me. The Tornian healer just finished scanning me. We didn't want to contact you until it was confirmed." She looked to Ull, and he nodded he would agree to that story.

Neither wanted to admit they'd gotten so involved in each other that they'd forgotten to contact her tío.

"And?"

"Cured," she told him, smiling at Ull.

"So, you're in remission?"

"No, you don't understand, Tío, I'm cured. According to the Tornian healer, I was infected with what they know as the Karkata parasite. It's something they've been able to eliminate from the Known Universes with their deep repair units."

"Is that the same as the unit Ull used on our injured soldiers?"

"No." Ull took over the conversation. "Those are only for physical injuries. Deep repair units are larger, more powerful units, that clear a body of any impurities and parasites that keep it from operating at its optimal level. And yes, now that we know how drastically they can help the people of Earth, I will be immediately contacting the Emperor to get more sent here."

"Could the portable units possibly help people until the larger units get here?" Trisha asked, looking to Ull.

"I don't know. We'd have to discuss it with Healer Zo."

"Whatever you can do, Ull, would be greatly appreciated. People are suffering all over the world."

"Trisha has expressed this to me before." Ull looked to Trisha, and while he wanted to keep her to himself, he also knew that while her tío wasn't saying it, he was desperate to see his niece. "We will be returning to Earth shortly. I know your Dr. Monroe will want to examine Trisha to confirm this for your people, but she needs to eat and rest first."

"I'll inform Dr. Monroe and have a meal sent to her rooms. I'll meet you at the landing pad."

"I'll see you in a little while, Tío. I love you."

"I love you too, Trishy." With that, Ull took the comm from her and disconnected the call.

Stretching up, she gently kissed Ull's lips. "Thank you for this. I know you would prefer I stayed here."

"He is your family, which makes him my family. We don't allow family to suffer when we can prevent it."

∞ ∞ ∞ ∞ ∞

"What?" Monroe looked at the President in disbelief. When the man had entered the room, he'd thought it had been to inform him Trisha had passed on. It was the only outcome he could imagine after how ravaged her body had been.

"Trisha is cured. The Tornians deep repair unit was able to eradicate the parasite."

"Wait. What parasite?"

"According to Trisha, what we call cancer, the Tornians know as some parasite. I can't remember the name. They will be returning shortly. I know you are going to want to examine her, but Ull says she needs to eat and rest first. I just came here to let you know."

"I need blood," Monroe demanded.

"What?"

"I want to come with you and at least draw some blood. Trisha can eat and rest while I analyze it to confirm the diagnosis and compare it to her medical history."

"That will be up to Trisha. If she says wait, you will wait."

"Understood."

With that, both men headed for the landing pad.

∞ ∞ ∞ ∞ ∞

"Tío Aaron," Trisha rushed down the ramp into his waiting arms.

"Oh, Trisha," Aaron murmured into the top of her head as he continued to hold her tightly. "I'm so sorry."

Leaning back, Trisha frowned up at him. "For what?"

"For being so absorbed with the needs of others that I didn't see how ill you were becoming. That I kept pushing more and more responsibility on you."

"You didn't do any of that, Tío Aaron," she denied. "I knew I was sick before any of this began."

"So why didn't you tell me? Why did you lie?"

Trisha sighed. She'd known she'd have to explain her actions to her tío. She just hadn't thought it would be so soon. Looking around, she saw that they were alone except for Ull, who had come to stand beside her and Dr. Monroe, who was behind her tío. "I didn't lie to you."

"You said you were getting your annual screenings."

"And I was. I only missed the one right after Mamá died. I couldn't bring myself to see a doctor again so soon. I went to the next one and got the results the day Lisa and the girls went missing."

"That isn't any reason for you not to tell me."

"Yes, it was. If you had known I was sick, Lisa and the girls wouldn't have been such a high priority to you."

Aaron knew he couldn't argue with that. After losing his sister, he would have concentrated all his energy and power on trying to help her.

"You still should have told me."

"Would you have made me Earth's Representative if you'd known?" she challenged. She already knew the answer but saw it in his eyes. "This is where I needed to be, Tío, what I needed to do. I knew what it was going to cost me personally and that you would be upset, but the future of our people…" She looked behind stretching out a hand to Ull, "of the Known Universes, was more important than a single life."

"That is not truth," Ull growled, taking her hand. "Not when it's your life."

Aaron took in the joined hands before looking to Ull. "I will never be able to thank you enough for what you did, Warrior Ull."

"No thanks are needed, Mr. President. Trisha is the most important thing in the Known Universes to me."

That had Aaron's eyebrows shooting up.

"Can we discuss this somewhere else?" Trisha asked, this was private, family business and while she trusted Dr. Monroe not to repeat what he heard, she still wanted to be alone with her tío when he found out she would be leaving with Ull.

"It will be discussed later," Ull growled, pulling Trisha closer to his side. "You need to eat and rest. If that can't be done here, we will return to the Protector."

"That won't be necessary," Aaron quickly said. He wasn't willing to let his niece out of his sight again yet. "A meal is on its way to Trisha's quarters, and as soon as she eats, she can rest."

"I would like to draw some blood before all that," Dr. Monroe finally spoke.

"Trisha will not endure any of your tests until after she rests," Ull growled.

"It's just a blood draw," Monroe argued back. "It will take little to no time, and I can do it in her quarters. Then while she's resting, it can be analyzed and compared to Trisha's past medical history."

Trisha put a hand on Ull's arm. "That would be fine, Dr. Monroe. I know you need to confirm Healer Zo's findings because it's going to change how our world deals with disease, all disease."

∞ ∞ ∞ ∞ ∞

Trisha groaned, rubbing her stomach as she leaned back in her chair. Her tío hadn't just ordered her a meal; he'd ordered her a feast complete with soup, salad, rolls, and dessert. It had all tasted amazing, and while it felt good to have her appetite back, her stomach needed time to adjust to full meals again.

"Are you alright?" Ull had been watching her closely as she'd eaten. He hadn't liked it that Dr. Monroe had come with them into Trisha's quarters, but the Healer had told truth. It only took him a few minutes to draw the vials he wanted, and he'd left. Now his Trisha needed to finish her meal so he could get her into bed to rest.

"I'm fine. It's just too much food." She looked at her tío. "I would never have ordered this much for myself, and you know it."

"You've lost too much weight."

"Well, I can't gain it all back with one meal." She looked at Ull. "You need to eat too."

"I am fine."

"It's just going to go to waste if you don't eat some. Here," Trisha picked up a piece of bread and drizzled it with some honey. "Try this and tell me if it tastes like the hunaja found on Betelgeuse."

Ull gazed suspiciously at Trisha's offering. Trisha knew how much he liked hunaja, and he doubted anything could compete with the delicacy from his homeworld. Still, he opened his mouth and let her feed him. A delicious sweetness immediately filled his mouth, and he fought back a groan, but Trisha gave him a knowing smile.

"I told you we had something similar."

Ull swallowed then licked the remaining sweetness from his lips before answering. "It is delicious."

"It also comes in a variety of flavors depending on the pollen the bees collect."

"Truth?"

"Truth. I'll see if we can get some for you to try."

"That can be arranged," the President spoke, making them remember he was there. "Now, I want to know what's going on between the two of you."

"What's going on is that I'm in love with Ull," Trisha responded, reaching over to cover one of Ull's hands with hers.

"And I am in love with your niece."

"Trisha, I know you're grateful for Warrior Ull saving your life, but don't misinterpret those feelings for love."

Ull stiffened at Aaron's criticism, but it was Trisha that responded. "I am a grown woman, Tío. I know the difference between gratitude and love. I know this comes as a shock to you, but growing up, I saw how devastating losing the love of your life can be, and I've seen you refuse to love anyone because of your career. While there's no guarantee that I won't end up like Mamá, I won't live my life as you have chosen to, Tío. I love Ull, and now that I have a life to live, I choose to live it with Ull, wherever he is."

Aaron paled at that. "What are you saying, Trisha?"

"I'm saying that when Ull returns to his homeworld, I'll be going with him."

"But..."

"No, my Trisha."

Ull knew she loved him. It was in every touch and look she gave him. He also knew she loved her tío. The male had played an important role in her becoming the female she was. He knew how painful it had to be for her to choose between the two of them. As her male, it was his responsibility to protect her from this type of pain. But how could he? His place and future were as the Lord of Betelgeuse. It's what he was born to be, trained for, but where did that leave Trisha? Would she be satisfied being the Lady of a Lord? While things were changing in the Tornian Empire, Trisha would still never be able to do what she could on Earth. Could he do that to her?

The Goddess had blessed him with a female. She'd told him to love her, cherish her, and to sacrifice for her, promising that if he did, he'd discover he'd sacrificed nothing that mattered. He'd do as she advised.

"You will not go to Betelgeuse with me, my Trisha."

"What?" Trisha's gaze shot to Ull. "Ull? What are you saying?"

"I'm saying that I will not let you sacrifice everything you are, everything you can do for your people for me."

"That's my choice."

"It's the wrong choice. For no one else can do what you can here. Not just for your people, but mine as well as the Kaliszians."

"So, where does that leave us?" she whispered.

Ull frowned at that. "Together, of course."

"But you just said…"

"That you will not be going with me because I will be staying on Earth with you."

"What? But Ull, you're the first male."

"And I always will be, but my brother Vali is more than capable of being the next Lord of Betelgeuse. He has a better temperament for the position than I do."

"What you mean is he isn't abrupt and arrogant?" Trisha teased to stop the tears that had filled her eyes from falling.

"No, he is more like my mother. Calm and slow to anger, important traits for a Lord."

"But what will your manno think? Your family?"

"They will understand, especially my mother."

"And Emperor Wray?" the President asked, pulling Ull's gaze to him.

"Will do what he believes best for our people, just as you do," Ull gave him a nod of respect. "But he won't force me to abandon the female created just for me. Especially when she is the one Queen Lisa sent me to find in the first place."

Aaron looked from Ull to his niece, and what he saw was the same strong bond that had existed between his sister and Martin. He hadn't stood in the way of their happiness then, and he wouldn't stand in the way of his niece's and Ull's now.

"Welcome to the family, Ull."

Epilogue

Three months later

"Lisa? Lisa, can you hear me?" Trisha sat before the newly installed comm in her and Ull's quarters, trying to connect with Lisa on Luda. She and Lisa had been sending voice messages back and forth over the last few months, but the advanced relay stations were now finally operational so they could see and talk to each other with minimal delay. The black screen in front of Trisha began to lighten until Lisa's image appeared, causing Trisha to all but squeal. "Lisa!"

"Trisha!" Lisa's excited response quickly followed.

"Oh, my God, you look so good." Trisha took in her friend's fuller face. it was a look Trisha remembered from the late stages of Lisa's pregnancy with Miki. "How are you feeling?"

"I look pregnant," Lisa laughed, "Feel like a beached whale, but otherwise, I'm fine."

"You're sure?" Trisha ran a more critical eye over her friend. Trisha was no doctor, but Lisa's color seemed a little high to her.

"Yes. Hader and Rebecca do daily scans. They'd do them hourly if Grim had his way, but there's no reason to."

"You're carrying a Tornian baby, Lisa. From what I've learned, they tend to be a bit larger than human ones."

"They average between ten and twelve corzites, pounds on Earth, so yes a bit larger, and this little girl," Lisa rubbed her belly, "is at about eleven right now. But she's perfectly healthy, and while my readings are elevated, they're no higher than during my last trimester with Miki."

"The deep repair unit hasn't been able to help with that?"

"I haven't been able to use it yet."

"What?" Trisha looked at her in disbelief. "Why not? I can't believe the difference it's made for me and everyone else that's used it. Not only does it eradicate the Karkata parasite that's caused all the cancers on Earth. It eliminates the 'impurities' that cause high blood pressure, high cholesterol, diabetes, and scores of other diseases. It's also been able to reverse the effects of Parkinson's and Alzheimer's. Chancellor Khatri's father, who was once a brilliant physicist, suffered from late-stage Alzheimer's. After using the deep repair unit, he was back to being who he'd always been."

"That's wonderful, and I bet it's gone a long way in calming down the fanatics." Lisa read the reports on how protests and panic erupted when the World Leaders announced the arrival of the Tornians and Kaliszians along with what the Ganglians had been doing.

"It has, along with Wray and Liron, each sending a ship full of the units. There are still a few claiming we were all under alien mind control and that our females are going to be sold into slavery, but the majority have calmed down after hearing the stories from the returnees and now see it as a good thing. Now stop trying to distract me. Why haven't you used the deep repair unit?"

"I never could get anything passed you, could I," Lisa sighed.

"No, so talk."

"I haven't used the deep repair unit because we're not sure if the unit would consider the baby a parasite and try to eliminate it."

"What?" Trisha's eyes widened in shock.

"Until you were treated, Tornians had forgotten that the unit clears out parasites and impurities as it repairs extreme injuries. They have no records of their females using the units once they've conceived. Not even Isis used it, and she's never heard of any female who did. So I'm not willing to take the chance, especially when I'm feeling fine. Although Grim insists that after I present, I'll use it."

"Good. My guess is it will help in your recovery." Trisha could still remember how gingerly Lisa had moved after delivering Miki.

"That would be nice. And just so you don't worry, I did have Carly and Miki use it. Even though we now know it was a parasite that caused Mark to be sick, I didn't want to take the chance."

"And..."

"They're absolutely fine."

"That's a relief."

"It is."

"Has Dr. Adams arrived yet?"

Dr. Monroe had compiled a list of OB/GYN's he'd thought might be interested in the groundbreaking experience of assisting in the delivery of interspecies offspring. Dr. Adams had been at the top of that list. After being contacted and expressing an interest in the opportunity, the OB/GYN had been extensively interviewed then sent on the next ship, which happened to be heading to Luda.

"No, they're still two days out."

"Well, hopefully between Dr. Adams, Dr. Mines, and Healer Hadar, we'll get some answers and make sure every pregnant female, whether they're human, Tornian, or Kaliszian, is taken care of."

"Rebecca and Hadar have been doing their best, but with there being pregnant females on four different planets..."

"That's a lot of areas to cover. Have the guidelines Rebecca sent out to the other Healers helped?"

"Yes, but every male, including Grim, wants a Healer specifically trained for Earth females on hand at all times, and Rebecca can't be everywhere at once."

"Well, that's going to take some time, so hopefully, Dr. Adams can help bridge the gap until more physicians are cleared."

"Hopefully, not too much time." Lisa's hand absently ran over her belly again. "Now that's enough about me. I want to know about you and Ull."

"Ull and me?" Trisha frowned at her friend, "I already told you all about that in my earlier transmissions."

"You did, but I know you left a lot out, so spill."

Trisha found herself laughing. This was one of the reasons she and Lisa had become such friends. After all they'd been through together, they knew when the other one wasn't being candid.

"I'm not exactly sure what else to tell you."

"Tell me you really love Ull. That it's not just because he saved your life?"

Trisha felt her mouth drop open at Lisa's accusation. It wasn't fair or true, especially after what Grim did to her. "Tell me you really love Grim, and it's not just because he came back for the girls?"

"That's entirely different."

"Is it? He kidnapped you then forced you to agree to Join with him and only him in exchange for getting the girls."

"Truth," Lisa quietly agreed, refusing to lie to her friend, "But once I got to know Grim, I couldn't help but fall in love with him."

"And you don't think I could have that same experience?"

"I know you could, just as I'm hoping other Earth females do. It's because of Ull that I'm asking."

"Why?"

"Because Ull isn't the male I would have chosen for you. Hell, he wasn't even the male I wanted to go to Earth. Wray chose him."

"Why? What have you got against Ull?"

"Nothing really, it's just the dark, angry vibe I got off him. Even after he helped Ynyr with the problems within House Jamison, he still seemed so angry at not being chosen during the Joining Ceremony. Even Miki noticed."

"Ull harmed Miki?" Trisha refused to believe that.

"No!" Lisa immediately denied, "Miki's just gotten more... sensitive to certain things lately."

"And Ull was one of those things?"

"Before I left, Princess Miki warned me to beware of the dark when it speaks to me." Ull startled both females when he spoke. They'd been so wrapped up in their conversation, they hadn't heard him come in after his comm with Emperor Wray. Leaning down, Ull gave his Trisha a quick kiss then looked to the Queen. "You may rest assured, Queen Lisa, that darkness no longer whispers to me. My Trisha has seen to that."

Lisa watched the two share a look that revealed their deep and intimate connection and realized it was just as strong and just as real as the one between her and Grim. All the fears she'd had since Trisha had told her they were in love faded away.

"I'm relieved to hear that, Warrior Ull. Trisha is precious to me and mine."

"As she is to me, Majesty," Ull's gaze was unwavering when it met hers.

"Then, we understand one another."

"We do."

Lisa shifted uncomfortably in her seat, her gaze going off-screen for a moment before looking back to Trisha. "I need to go. We'll talk soon, Trisha?"

"We will. Give the girls a hug from me."

"I will." With that, Lisa ended the transmission.

Spinning in her chair, Trisha stood, stepping into his waiting arms. "Your comm with the Emperor didn't last very long. Is everything alright?"

"That depends on how you look at it." Ull knew she'd been concerned about the Emperor's reaction to his remaining on Earth. They'd sent transmissions to his family, informing them that Vali would be taking over his duties, feeling they had the right to be the first to know. He knew Trisha was worried about how they would react, and while shocked at first, they eagerly welcomed Trisha into the family. Ull knew he had his mother to thank for that, and he would, as soon as possible.

"What do you mean?"

"How do you feel about being a Lord's Lady?"

"What? Wray is forcing you to go back to Betelgeuse?" She couldn't believe it and would have pulled out of Ull's arms if he hadn't stopped her. "I'm getting Lisa back on the comm. This isn't right, and if your Emperor can't see that…"

"No, Trisha, stop. Wray's not forcing me to go anywhere."

"But you just said…"

"He wants me to become Lord… of Earth."

"What?" Ull couldn't have shocked her more if he'd tried. Had Wray decided to invade? "But we have leaders."

"And you still will. I wouldn't be the Lord over the people of Earth, only the Lord over the Tornians that come to Earth."

"Oh." All of Trisha's concerns released on that breath. "So, you'd be more like an Ambassador who works with our world leaders?"

"Yes. It's my understanding the Kaliszians will also be selecting someone to oversee their interests here."

"That makes sense. I know Jakob is anxious to return to his family."

"So, you would be agreeable to me accepting the position?" Ull returned to his original question.

"You haven't already?"

"I told the Emperor I needed to discuss it with you first as it also affects you."

Trisha couldn't believe how Ull had changed since they'd first met. Yes, he could still be arrogant and abrupt, but never with her and never concerning things that affected them both. And this definitely affected them both. Ull was born to be a Lord, but he'd given that up for her. Now, the Emperor was not only naming a new Lord, but he was also creating a new House. One that Ull was ideally suited for.

Ull wasn't sure what his Trisha was thinking as she stepped out of his arms and began walking away from him. While her tío had chosen to be involved in Earth politics, she hadn't. She'd been forced into it by him and the needs of his Empire. Because of that, this had to be her choice.

"I think that Lord Ull of Earth should take his Lady to bed so he can *convince* me." With that, she stripped off her shirt and threw it, hitting Ull directly in the face.

Slowly Ull reached up, pulling the shirt away. Growling, he crossed the room, had her up and over his shoulder and carrying her into their resting chamber before she could do anything more than laugh.

∞ ∞ ∞ ∞ ∞

Michelle has always loved to read and writing is just a natural extension of this for her. Growing up, she always loved to extend the stories of books she'd read just to see where the characters went. Happily married for over twenty five years she is the proud mother of two grown children and with the house empty has found time to write again. You can reach her at m.k.eidem@live.com or her website at http://www.mkeidem.com she'd love to hear your comments.

∞ ∞ ∞ ∞ ∞

Printed by Amazon Italia Logistica S.r.l.
Torrazza Piemonte (TO), Italy